RACHEL
A FOOTMAN F(

C000177126

RACHEL ETHELREDA FERGUSON (1892-1957) was born in Hampton Wick, the youngest of three children. She was educated at home and then sent to a finishing school in Florence, Italy. By the age of 16 she was a fierce campaigner for women's rights and considered herself a suffragette. She went on to become a leading member of the Women's Social and Political Union.

In 1911 she became a student at the Royal Academy of Dramatic Art. She began a career on the stage, which was cut short by the advent of World War 1, whereupon Ferguson joined the Women's Volunteer Reserve. She wrote for *Punch*, and was the drama critic for the *Sunday Chronicle,* writing under the name 'Columbine'. In 1923 she published her first novel, *False Goddesses*, which was followed by eleven further novels including *A Harp in Lowndes Square* (1936), *A Footman for the Peacock* (1940) and *Evenfield* (1942), all three of which are now available as Furrowed Middlebrow books.

Rachel Ferguson died in Kensington, where she had lived most of her life.

BY RACHEL FERGUSON

RACHEL FERGUSON

A FOOTMAN FOR
THE PEACOCK

With an introduction by
Elizabeth Crawford

DEAN STREET PRESS
A Furrowed Middlebrow Book

A Furrowed Middlebrow Book
FM1

Published by Dean Street Press 2016

Cover by DSP

First published in 1940 by Jonathan Cape

ISBN 978 1 911413 71 4

www.deanstreetpress.co.uk

INTRODUCTION

A FAMILY – a House – and – Time. These are the ingredients whipped by Rachel Ferguson (1892-1957) into three confections – *A Harp in Lowndes Square* (1936), *A Footman for the Peacock* (1940), and *Evenfield* (1942) – now all republished as Furrowed Middlebrow books. Her casts of individuals, many outrageous, and families, some wildly dysfunctional, dance the reader through the pages, revealing worlds now vanished and ones that even in their own time were the product of a very particular imagination. Equally important in each novel is the character of the House – the oppressive family home of Lady Vallant in *A Harp in Lowndes Square*, comfortable, suburban Evenfield, and Delaye, the seat of the Roundelays, a stately home but 'not officially a show place' (*A Footman for the Peacock*). Rachel Ferguson then mixes in Time – past, present, and future – to deliver three socially observant, nostalgic, mordant, yet deliciously amusing novels.

In an aside, the *Punch* reviewer (1 April 1936) of *A Harp in Lowndes Square* remarked that 'Miss Ferguson has evidently read her Dunne', an assumption confirmed by the author in a throwaway line in *We Were Amused* (1958), her posthumously-published autobiography. J.W. Dunne's *Experiment with Time* (1927) helped shape the imaginative climate in the inter-war years, influencing Rachel Ferguson no less than J.B. Priestley (*An Inspector Calls*), John Buchan (*The Gap in the Curtain*), C.S. Lewis, and J.R.R. Tolkien. In *A Harp in Lowndes Square* the heroine's mother ('half-educated herself by quarter-educated and impoverished gentlewomen') explains the theory to her children: '... all time is one, past, present and future. It's simultaneous ... There's a star I've heard of whose light takes so many thousands of years to reach our earth that it's still only got as far along history as shining over the Legions of Julius Caesar. Yet that star which is seeing chariot races is outside our window now. You say Caesar is dead. The star says No, because the star's seen him. It's your word against his! Which of you is right? Both of you. It's only a question of how long you take to see things.' The concept of 'simultaneous time' explains why the young first-person narrator, Vere Buchan, and her twin brother James, possessing as they do 'the sight', are able to feel the evil that haunts their grandmother's Lowndes Square house and uncover the full enormity of her wickedness. In *A Footman for the Peacock* a reincarnation, one of Time's tricks, permits a story of past cruelty to be told (and expiated), while *Evenfield*'s heroine, Barbara Morant, grieving for her mother, takes matters into her own hands and moves back to the home of her childhood, the only place, she feels, 'where she [her mother] was likely to be recovered.'

For 21st-century readers another layer of Time is superimposed on the text of the novels, now that nearly 80 years separates us from the words as they flowed from the author's pen. However, thanks to *We Were Amused*, we know far more about Rachel Ferguson, her family, and her preoccupations than did her readers in the 1930s and early 1940s and can recognise that what seem whimsical drolleries in the novels are in fact real-life characters, places, and incidents transformed by the author's eye for the comic or satirical.

Like Barbara Morant, Rachel Ferguson was the youngest of three children. Her mother, Rose Cumberbatch (probably a distant relation to 'Benedict', the name 'Carlton' appearing in both families as a middle name) was 20 years old when she married Robert Ferguson, considerably older and a civil servant. She was warm, rather theatrical, and frivolous; he was not. They had a son, Ronald Torquil [Tor] and a daughter, Roma, and then, in 1892, after a gap of seven years, were surprised by Rachel's arrival. When she was born the family was living in Hampton Wick but soon moved to 10 Cromwell Road, Teddington, a house renamed by Mrs Ferguson 'Westover'. There they remained until Rose Ferguson was released from the suburban life she disliked by the sudden death of her husband, who was felled by a stroke or heart attack on Strawberry Hill golf course. Fathers in Rachel Ferguson's novels are dispensable; it is mothers who are the centres of the universe. Rose Ferguson and her daughters escaped first to Italy and on their return settled in Kensington where Rachel spent the rest of her life.

Of this trio of books, *Evenfield*, although the last published, is the novel that recreates Rachel Ferguson's earliest years. Written as the Blitz rained down on London (although set in the inter-war years) the novel plays with the idea of an escape back into the security of childhood, For, after the death of her parents, Barbara, the first-person narrator, hopes that by returning to the Thameside suburb of 'Addison' and the house of her childhood, long since given up, she can regain this land of lost content. The main section of the novel describes the Victorian childhood she had enjoyed while living in 'Evenfield', the idiosyncrasies of family and neighbours lovingly recalled. Incidentally, Barbara is able to finance this rather self-indulgent move because she has made a small fortune from writing lyrics for successful musical comedies, a very Rachel Ferguson touch. What might not have been clear to the novelist's contemporaries but is to us, is that 'Addison' is Rachel Ferguson's Teddington and that 'Evenfield', the Morant family home, is the Fergusons' 'Westover'. In *We Were Amused* Rachel Ferguson commented that since leaving Teddington 'homesickness has nagged me with nostalgia ever since. I've even had wild thoughts of leasing or buying Westover until time showed me what a hideous mistake it would prove'. In writing *Evenfield* Rachel Ferguson laid that ghost to rest.

But what of the ghost in *A Harp in Lowndes Square*? Vere senses the chill on the stairs. What is the family mystery? Once again Rachel Ferguson takes a fragment of her family story and spins from it what the reviewer in *Punch* referred to as 'an intellectual ghost story'. The opening scene, in which a young girl up in the nursery hears happy voices downstairs, is rendered pathetically vivid by the description of her frock, cut down from one of her mother's. 'On her small chest, the overtrimming of jetted beads clashed …' This humiliation, endured not because the family lacked funds, but because the child's mother cared nothing for her, was, Rachel Ferguson casually mentions in *We Were Amused*, the very one that her own grandmother, Annie Cumberbatch, inflicted on her daughter Rose. 'The picture which my Mother drew for me over my most impressionable years of her wretched youth is indelible and will smoulder in me till I die.' Rachel Ferguson raised the bar by allotting Sarah Vallant a wickedness far greater than anything for which her grandmother was responsible, but it is clear that she drew her inspiration from stories heard at her own mother's knee and that many of the fictional old lady's petty nastinesses – and her peculiarly disturbing plangent tones – were ones that Rachel Ferguson had herself experienced when visiting 53 Cadogan Square.

The *Punch* reviewer noted that in *A Harp in Lowndes Square* Rachel Ferguson demonstrated her 'exceptional ability to interpret the humour of families and to make vivid the little intimate reactions of near relations. Children, old people, the personalities of houses, and the past glories of London, particularly of theatrical London, fascinate her.' Rachel Ferguson's delight in theatrical London is very much a feature of *A Harp in Lowndes Square*, in the course of which Vere Buchan finds solace in a chaste love for an elderly actor (and his wife) which proves an antidote to the wickedness lurking in Lowndes Square. As the reviewer mentioned, old people, too, were among Rachel Ferguson's specialities, especially such impecunious gentlewomen as the Roundelay great-aunts in *A Footman for the Peacock*, who, as marriage, their only hope of escape, has passed them by have become marooned in the family home. Each wrapped in her own treasured foible, they live at Delaye, the house inherited by their nephew, Sir Edmund Roundelay. The family has standing, but little money. Now, in the early days of the Second World War, the old order is under attack. Housemaids are thinking of leaving to work in the factories and the Evacuation Officer is making demands. 'You are down for fifteen children accompanied by two teachers, or ten mothers with babies, or twenty boys or girls.' This is not a world for which the Roundelays are prepared. Moreover other forces are at work. Angela, the sensitive daughter of the family, watches as, on the night of a full moon, Delaye's solitary peacock puts on a full display, tail feathers aglow, and has an overpowering feeling he is signalling to the German planes. What is the reason for the peacock's malevolence? What is the meaning of the inscription written on the window of one of the rooms at the top of the house: 'Heryn I dye, Thomas Picocke?' In *We Were Amused* Rachel Ferguson revealed that while staying with friends at Bell Hall outside York 'on the adjoining estate there really was a peacock that came over constantly and spent the day. He wasn't an endearing creature and ... sometimes had to be taken home under the arm of a footman, and to me the combination was irresistible.' That was enough: out of this she conjured the Roundelays, a family whom the *Punch* reviewer (28 August 1940) assures us 'are people to live with and laugh at and love' and whom Margery Allingham, in a rather po-faced review (24 August 1940) in *Time and Tide* (an altogether more serious journal than *Punch*), describes as 'singularly unattractive'. Well, of course, they are; that is the point.

Incidentally Margery Allingham identified Delaye 'in my mind with the Victoria and Albert', whereas the 21st-century reader can look on the internet and see that Bell Hall is a neat 18th-century doll's house, perhaps little changed since Rachel Ferguson stayed there. Teddington, however, is a different matter. The changes in Cromwell Road have been dramatic. But Time, while altering the landscape, has its benefits; thanks to Street View, we can follow Rachel Ferguson as, like Barbara Morant, she pays one of her nostalgic visits to 'Evenfield'/'Westover'. It takes only a click of a mouse and a little imagination to see her coming down the steps of the bridge over the railway line and walking along Cromwell Road, wondering if changes will have been made since her previous visit and remembering when, as a child returning from the London pantomime, she followed this path. As Rachel Ferguson wrote in *We Are Amused*, 'I often wonder what houses think of the chances and changes inflicted on them, since there is life, in some degree, in everything. Does the country-quiet road from the station, with its one lamp-post, still contain [my mother's] hurrying figure as she returned in the dark from London? ... Oh yes, we're all there. I'm certain of it. Nothing is lost.'

Elizabeth Crawford

CHAPTER I

1

THERE ARE country houses and country houses.

There is the type of mansion where the wrong kind of guest tips the staff too much and is regretfully dissected in the servants' hall as his car slides off down the avenue, and there is the mansion where the right kind of guest is hardly able to tip the staff at all, and for whom the butler and footman continue to feel a warm affection.

There are houses, manors, halls, granges and abbeys in which Queen Elizabeth is known to have slept, and a larger number from which sheer lack of time compelled the indefatigable recumbent to abstain. There are country seats that get illustrated in *Country Life*, or pass, via midnight smart set pillow-fights, into *The Police News* and the divorce courts, and others possessing a priest's hole but no ghost: an oubliette and ghost but no hidden treasure: a moat and no muniment room: a plentiful staff but no mention in Domesday Book, or Saxon ruins in the Home field and no butler at all.

There are denes, priories, castles and manors, in the rooms, galleries and grounds of which Catherine Howard still screams and Jane Grey had pricked her finger, Bloody Mary exclaimed 'God's death!' Raleigh had smoked the first pipe of tobacco, Charles the Second hidden in an oak tree, someone else had signed something historic and damaging, Barbara Castlemaine had threatened to throw herself out of the window and Prince Arthur had actually done so: where the Queen of Scots had given away trinkets to faithful retainers and Wolsey had had all his taken from him. And there are English families with fairy banners and 'lucks' famed in ballads, and others of equally ancient lineage and no luck at all. One contingent still entertains the autumnal shooting party and is pictured in the papers filing like portly Sherlock Holmeses across the moors, while the second party emerges from posterns at sunset and hopefully pops away at rabbits for the larder on their own mortgaged acres.

And somewhere in England, in rating between the extremes of screaming queen and the pedigree'd pursuit of pot-luck, stands Delaye, seat of the Roundelays, presently occupied by Sir Edmund Roundelay, his family and various collaterals.

2

Delaye is not officially a show place, mainly because the family recoils from exposing portions of their home for gain, love or charity, to that mythical trio, Tom, Dick or Harry. Inevitably, the polite and the genuine enthusiast alike have made the suggestion, backed by those who see in the arrangement a sensible source of profit to an overtaxed landlord which should also be educative to the bourgeois sightseer and teach his descendants — who knows? — that the fourteenth-century refectory table is not a mere surface for the carving of initials. But Sir Edmund, brushing aside the notion, would merely answer with the unfinished sentence that silenced without convincing '. . . playing darts on the tapestry . . .'

Delaye does not possess any objects which could be actually labelled as priceless, but its furniture and the tapestry alone would make a very fair sum at Christie's, and if the portraits are not a galaxy of old masters, of the type that biographers write in for permission to reproduce in their Lives of Caroleans and Tudors, it possesses a respectable quota among the latest of which is numbered what Musgrave, the butler, alludes to as 'The Hair-Comber', as he cleanses the canvas half-yearly with a raw potato.

The principal rooms are always chilly and can be enjoyed only in a virulent heat-wave. Their windows all face north, as the direct result of that conventional parental gesture which sent its sons, on completing their education, to make the Grand Tour, a journey which commonly took in Italy, with an admiration real or inculcated of its architecture, and that was to be responsible on their return for north lights in two-fifths of the mansions of England, from a universal overlooking of the fact that the climate of the British Isles was not that of southern Europe. Thus, since the eighteenth century, from early spring to the following winter, the drawing-rooms and boudoirs were invaded once a day (and four times in the cold months) by a file of menservants, the firelight twinkling on their crimson plush and smiting flashes from their aiguillettes, bearing logs and brass scuttles of coal.

In the first-floor corridor there still stands in a dark recess a log-boy's stool, relic of the life of some small disregarded member of the staff, whose duty it was to time by an hourglass the exact minute at which the next load must be fetched and carried.

3

It is a tendency of human nature to measure the history of any large house by the yardstick of the family in present occupation. About the atmosphere of Delaye, therefore, the world at large thought nothing in particular, for the current family is never the interesting one to its contemporaries. But, as no house which has stood for four hundred years (and portions of it for five hundred) can have completely evaded the incident, the scandal, whiff of picturesque or skeleton in the cupboard, so Delaye can look back upon a time that was not solely a matter of tweeds, tithes, cold mutton, mutilated conversation, clean living, sobriety and the monotone that is security.

Nothing very spectacular had happened at Delaye, even in a past which offered more scope for assorted violence. There were no eminent bloodstains on the floor, no immured nun, no headless horseman driving oscillating family coach up the avenue at nightfall; there was in the Delaye archives, no absolutely historic parchment, no counterpart of the Luck of Eden Hall, or fairy banner of the Macleods of Dunvegan, no Airlie Drummer or Glamis monster. But every period had produced its contribution the atmosphere of which no humdrum twentieth century can ever quite disperse.

The Lacquer Room, antechamber to the drawing-room, had known the flap of cards and scent of frothing chocolate, the promised elopement with one fearful eye upon the door, the slipped billet and the swoon. The drawing-room air had rustled with acid criticism, behind the fans of painted chickenskin, of that cat, Sarah Churchill and her influence at Kensington Palace with Her Majesty. A mended rent in a dining-room curtain bore witness to the carving-knife a Georgian Roundelay had cast in a fury at the toughness of his venison, as did a broken banister-rod (never replaced) in the servants' quarters to the rage of an eighteenth-century father on discovering that a flunkey had connived at the admittance to his daughter's apartments of a rascally but charming ineligible. In the testers of which, century after century, the family had found itself too inert or unwilling to be rid, and whose valances were so difficult to reach for dusting purposes, had slept and borne and died not only generations of the house's rightful family, but names which would be instantly recognized by the more erudite historian, if not by the world at large, whose memory sticks at outstanding celebrity. In the Tapestry Room had lain for two nights that gentleman who had so mistakenly been funny in Parliament about an entertainment tax upon the playhouses of London and the mistresses of a monarch who could be funnier than anybody when he so chose, while a court poet to a Tudor king had taken his ease in the pleasure grounds, and there, by rumour, committed to his tablets that lyric entitled 'I Attempt From My True Love To Fly'.

In the linen room, now a slipway between bath and secondary staircase, the pious Roger Ascham, much troubled in his mind, had fled the religious turmoil of the city to ponder his Bible and search within its pages for riposte and refutation that he might strengthen a beloved pupil in imminent peril of a nine-days throne — not that the Lady Jane Dudley, God wot, lacked ability to defend herself before the chosen Catholic interrogators and their smooth, crafty verbal traps. . . .

4

Upon the window-pane of a servant's bedroom was spiderishly scratched the words

Heryn I dye
Thomas Picocke. 1792

The pathetic statement excited little comment among the Roundelays. It was left to the visitor to exclaim and conjecture, with wild, leaping surmise which took no account of probability and period, and ranged in speculation from a last message of the Princes in the Tower to a nothing dashed off in an idle moment by Guido Fawkes, gentleman, of Northamptonshire.

It was always Sir Edmund Roundelay who, smiling, would gently pull the rein of his guests' careering fancies.

'I'm afraid we can't lay claim to anything so interesting. These Upper rooms, of course (except for the butler's pantry and bedroom in the basement), were always the servants' quarters.' In that one sentence he indicated clearly that typographic suitability had triumphed, as it doubtless always must, over the romantic.

'But — the diamond! Messages were always scratched with a diamond!'

'Apparently not, in this case. The diamond leaves a clear, incisive cut. This signature and message, or whatever you like to call it, is thickened, blurred —'

'But it must have been somebody important, or interesting, you know —'

'Why? The instinct to achieve a species of visual immortality is still abundantly prevalent in the modern tripper who treats us to the atrocious spectacle of his obscure initials and amatory intentions upon any likely surface.'

'*Oh!*'

'There are vandals in every epoch, and no doubt John Doe of Clapham Junction may, a hundred years hence, also be subject of respectful surmise.' And then, if further pressed, the master of Delaye would gently spring his mine and shatter the pretty fancy and the dramatic dream. Oh yes, there had been a Thomas Peacock; he was an outside servant — that settle by the second kitchen fireplace was no doubt his bed at night. His place in the domestic hierarchy was a low one. He was, in point of fact, a running footman, his duty to footslog over hill, over dale, through bush, through briar, herald and warning to the approaching town or hamlet or to any pedestrian that the coach of his master was imminent, and that a way for it must instantly be cleared. Hardly human, the running footman was more in the nature of a social gesture to the world at large, an earnest of the importance of the family he served, a panting castemark. Without change of linen at the end of a heating run in all weathers, including winter's snows, the running footman must wait for hours in the kitchen, steaming in front of the open hearth, before word was brought him via a chain of house servants, that his family abovestairs had concluded its visit. He then took staff and nerved himself for the return footslogging. Oh yes, these fellows, poor devils, died off like flies of consumption — the local graveyard were known to be peppered with them. Pay? Oh, five pounds a year, livery and all found. And, oh yes, it might interest Sir Edmund's visitors to know that the staff borne by these footmen possessed a metal cap at the tip in which was placed one hard-boiled egg to sustain them during the runs.

And at this point, Sir Edmund was always willing to show the household accounts books. Dating from the reign of Henry the Seventh and housed in the whitewashed cellars: quaint, dream-like entries of a casual day which combined the fantastically lavish with a medieval cheeseparing, seasoning the entries with a spice (spices amany) of the need or ingredient both unexpected, incalculable, or obsolete to the twentieth-century eye.

On the yellowed pages from the years 1790-1792, the name of Thomas Peacock intermittently appeared. Here, indicated the unerring finger of Sir Edmund, who soberly loved every entry and in the summer would sometimes spend an hour in a thick and ancient leather shooting jacket in the cellars, privily enchanting himself with the huge books, were the humble sums expended upon the running footman. A new livery, a shirt, the re-tipping in 'metall' of his stave: businesslike items, the bare-bones essentials of his occupation, with never an alleviating indulgence. . . .

'And even the hardboiled eggs,' Sir Edmund would sometimes add, handsomely mixing his metaphors, 'were only a means towards keeping his nose to the grindstone.'

He would often say, as the visitors dispersed, or were assisted, up the cracked and rather dangerous cellar steps, with an enforced courtesy and arming of the ladies which smacked more of the heyday of Beau Nash than of the heartless present century, 'So you see, there's really no secret mystery about this Peacock follow, and precious little romance.'

Sir Edmund was a Shakespearean browser, but apparently he had not yet awoke to the fact that there are more things in heaven and earth than were dreamed of in the Roundelay philosophy.

5

The Roundelays were of Norman-French descent from that Rohan de l'Oeux who accompanied William the Conqueror to England. As with all subsequent Roundelays, the founder of the family was neither spectacular nor scallywag, but, as far as was publicly possible in the eleventh century, an accommodating law-abider who concurred in the right places with authority. He was, without achieving any fame in the process, inevitably advanced by the Norman William, a patronage and recognition that included land in

Normanshire as recompense for his abandoned estates in France, a tenure which encroached upon the border of Brittany. In the pleasant land of Britain, he had built himself the small fortress dwelling of de l'Oeux, here married suitably and produced his family, here crashed the stillness of primeval forest after the wild boar, with its large, facetious face and calculating eye.

A family tree interests few. Inevitably, Delaye was partly ruined, partly restored and wholly burnt down over the centuries, coming at last to stability, presenting the front that it does to-day at the accession of James the First, whose reign was to leave little mark upon the house save for the apeing of sundry Scottish embellishments of which the Turret Room was a typical example.

The Roundelays themselves tended, in their matrimonial arrangements, towards the clannish. Cousins married cousins. It was very seldom that the name suffered obscurity through entanglements too alien, although there had been a bad period during which, through the death of an heir and the wedding of his sister who produced daughters only, and who, if they bore sons, lost them by battle, flood and field, Delaye had actually been possessed for two reigns by masters whose right to occupation was through that enfeebled and shameful cause, the distaff side. But just as in even the Lancers, partners, on the whole, do find each other at the finale of that confusing dance, so the Roundelays would ultimately sweep together and mate sooner or later via many a narrow squeak, family conclave and scene.

The foreign alliances were, of course, regrettable. The Roundelays all agreed about that, answering, when it was pointed out to them that the original founder of the name was a foreigner himself, that that wasn't the same thing. They did not know very clearly what they meant, but they felt it with fervour. The enquirer, thinking it over, came to the conclusion that the solution lay in the fact that, whereas a Norman-French background, remote enough, was a recognized social asset, a concrete French woman of any considerably later date in your very drawing-room was suspect and eccentric: something you explained carelessly and smiling as brightly as possible, over the tea-table.

The Roundelays, in common with the bulk of England, were unable to think of William the Conqueror as anything but an Eng-

lish king who uttered the language as she is spoke. He was Wil-
liam-the-Conqueror-1066-1087, and the probability that his brother (if he had one) addressed him as Guillaume was too far back to
be taken seriously.

There had been a French Roundelay, a chatelaine culled from
a Grand Tour of the late seventeen-hundreds, but Delaye had been
too much for her, the meals and chitchat too heavy, and, proceeding by stages to the environs of Paris on a visit to her relations, she
had been slain untimely by a misunderstanding in the salon of the
Château at the hands of a renegade gardener in a tricolour cockade,
whose mind, if any, and ironically enough, was confused by her surname which she never could, or would, learn to pronounce in the
English manner.

Delaye itself was large enough to absorb the few traces that the
unhappy lady had left behind her, and which were represented by
a tambour frame and a frivolous bed in a lumber room, a scatter-
ing of gilt chairs which were uncomfortable, and skidded, some
enamel-and-pearl comfit boxes that the occasional tables in the
drawing-room swallowed whole, a marble temple in the Versailles
taste in the grounds which succeeding generations of Roundelays
frequently spoke of doing something about and making something
of, and in which, on wet days, the current peacock sheltered and
looked critical and malevolent through the pillars, and a half-finished sunk and paved garden that you catch your heels in to this
day, and the completion of which is now beyond the pocket of the
present owner, and likely to remain so.

There had also been that deplorable specimen, the dashing
bride, who not only insisted upon a Continental honeymoon (marriage, it was felt, ought to have been fast enough for any virgin)
but who brought her complaisant husband well-nigh to the Jews
through her passion for that fatal association of ideas-jewellery. In
the very nick of time she was curbed of this taste removed from
temptation and installed at Delaye, where, between them, she and
Stacey Roundelay variously expressed their ill-humour and relief
by the production of a series of daughters, who were nostalgically
christened Amethyst, Crystal, Emerald, Jacinth and Sapphire. The
possible names of Diamond and Pearl were mutually abandoned
on the ground that the abbreviation of the former was undignified

and the latter theatrical. Of these, only Crystal and Emerald had succeeded in being found by husbands, and Miss Emmy became lady to Bertram Cloudesley (spoken Clousy) of Cloudesley Hall in the adjoining county, only to lose both husband and status at the end of the Boer War, and to decline, at the age of forty-four, into dowagership through the marriage of her son, Marcus. Miss Chrissy, making a match of considerably less lustre, though still suitable, was translated to London, where she was safely delivered of one child, Maxwell, and where, the initial novelty and excitement passing off, she had ample leisure to pine for country life, air and routine — a psychologic condition which, with wives, it is customary to ignore as a piece of ungrateful rebellion in poor taste. She relapsed, finally, into a belief that we are one of the Lost Tribes. Her argumentative tedium, her friends agreed, was only to be equalled by the Golf Bore, the Card Maniac and the Roman Catholic convert. Hasty agreement with her view was no safeguard whatsoever: incredulity fatal, while indifference brought down upon your head a shower of booklets.

With the remaining daughters, Amethyst, Jacinth and Sapphire, of the once dashing Mrs. Roundelay, the realization of spinsterhood came slowly, taking the assorted form, from their thirtieth year (or just before all hope was extinct) of sport welfare and culture.

Miss Amy became the tennis star of the county, in long piqué skirts, black ribbed stockings and a small sailor hat, which was all very nice and brought her name forward, as Mrs. Roundelay confided to intimates, but which was also heating (men didn't like flushed faces which were not the direct or indirect result of their own words or actions) and which, of course, led nowhere since a girl of her class mustn't become too conspicuous even if it is only on a grass court.

Miss Jessie's furtive dismays at her single state were drowned in charitable soup: as her expectations of marriage and motherhood receded, the old and infirm of the village of Delaye became more drastically visited, read to and cheered with every year that passed, and by the time all hope was abandoned few cottages were safe from her. The plight of Jessie was far more acute and remarkable than it would be to-day, where post-1918 daughters assume in advance that all men are liars, frequently confuse the issues and queer the more paying pitch by week-ends unblessed by any church and conducted on a fifty-fifty basis, and are practically forced into careers, however much, in reversal of the old order, they would prefer to be at home doing the flowers and walking the dog in peace and content. But in Jessie Roundelay's day, to arrange the flowers for too long was an unmistakable sign that you yourself were going to become another bloom of the Wall family. And even if the Jessies of the period liked the pretty employment they got no credit for it. There are spinsters-by-instinct in every epoch, a fact which is consistently denied, and although Jessie was of their number, a circumstance of which she was unaware, public opinion was against her, downing her with its condolence. All girls wanted to be married. Whether they possessed one single qualification for that difficult and manysided relationship: if they were culinarily, temperamentally or even physically fit to undertake the job was a point left, as it is to this day, entirely to chance. Men, on their side, chose their horses and dogs far more carefully than their wives and with greater intelligence. A horse was a serious matter, its wants and ailments known and listed. And yet, with that engrained ability to muddle through to victory which is the feature of the British army and the British marriage alike, and that is arrived at by a combination of procrastination, good nature, good luck, rough humour, fair dealing and more good luck, the Roundelay marriages held. There had been no family divorce for over two centuries, though it was felt that poor Marguerite, had she not been murdered in France, might possibly have been a very near thing. The French, you know ... toojoors femm varry, the male Roundelays would sometimes say over the walnuts and port.

Miss Sapphy's outlet of culture was perhaps the hardest to come by. Tennis was unmistakably 'in', though poor Amy couldn't hope to play it for ever. Good works, on the other hand, though boring, thankless and smelly, went on for ever, but Jessie had long cornered that meagre market. As you couldn't get your body off on men, you tried your mind on them. The job was laborious, and, as with the professional entertainer, precarious. Few people (even women) wanted 'Annie Laurie' and 'The Blue Danube' sung or played to them until at earliest, after tea, and once the men diners had been shown your hand-painted tambourines, poker-worked boxes and water-colours of local views, that ended the current output, and it took at least six weeks more to assemble a new form of artistic detainer, a hiatus in which you read up the news in the morning paper, a process which brought rewards incommensurate with the mental effort.

There were occasional visits to Chrissy, in Kensington, where culture, thanks in a measure to W. S. Gilbert, could raise its head and was at no time dealt such staggering blows as it was in the country, but the advantages of Kensington were, Sapphire Roundelay was to find, largely cancelled out by the Lost Tribes, who kept the drawing-room ominously empty on Sunday afternoons, a time long recognized as being dedicated to the following-up process by ballroom partners, and where intentions could be assumed without committal on either side, the glittering English tea-table of that period serving the dual purpose of charming the male prospector with the sight of dainty hand poised (the sugarbowl), and chaperoning the possible familiarity through barricade (the spirit-kettle). The household was not even relieved by the presence of Sapphire's nephew, Maxwell. Chrissy Dunston as a matrimonial agency was a hopeless proposition, her sister soon discovered. The men might arrive with flowers, but they left with pamphlets, and quite soon they ceased to arrive at all, and there was not a sandbin or even basement area within a two-mile radius, from Campden Hill to Queens Gate, from High Street to Brompton Square, which did not contain at least one Tribal tract, and some of them two. And Sapphire would return in a four-wheeler, making the six-mile journey from the market-town of Norminster which was, at that date, the nearest point to the village of Delaye, and be driven up the avenue, and passed by poor Jessie on her tricycle, bound for the village, and leaving in her wake splotches of soup and nodules of half-set jelly upon the gravel.

6

Two events marked the timeless days at Delaye for the unmarried daughters, when they became aunts, to Marcus and Edmund through the marriage of Emerald Roundelay to Bertram Cloudesley, and to Maxwell Dunston through Crystal's match with Colonel Dunston, and when, at close upon sixty years of age, they became great-aunts through a similar process on the part of their junior nephew, Edmund, the present owner of Delaye, who re-entered the family as a Roundelay through deed-poll, with the approval of the entire family.

It was felt, though never admitted between the ageing sisters, that to be in a superior blood relationship to those whose existence had come about through an intimate action everlastingly debarred to themselves of a brother or sister was the next best thing — though, of course 'removed', like distant cousinship — to matrimony itself.

The present household at Delaye consists, then, of Sir Edmund, his wife Evelyn, his son Stacey, who was seldom at home, being occupied with his studies in estate management at an agricultural college, his elder daughter Margaret, his second daughter Angela, the great-aunts Miss Amethyst, Miss Sapphire and Miss Jessie, his cousin Maxwell Dunston, who, on leaving the army he had always chafed against and refusing the Kensington home of his mother, had made a mutually advantageous offer to Sir Edmund, which gave Maxwell the country life he preferred for the sum of five guineas a week.

The domestic staff at Delaye was headed by Musgrave, the butler, who on the strength of long service, sometimes presumed ever so slightly in alluding to the senior Misses Roundelay as 'the old ladies'. The mutual affection and respect in which servant and family equally participated was only intermittently ruffled by Musgrave's dislike of Miss Sapphire, whom, at these times, he addressed as Miss Sophia, timing his occasion always to coincide with tea-parties and other social occasions. His antagonism was half professional, half private. Miss Sapphire would never come to the table punctually, but after an entire afternoon of doing nothing ascertainable, would wait for the gong to sound, and then begin flurrying round her room putting the finishing touches to her hair and dress, and, once arrived in the dining-room as the soup was removed, and occasionally as the fish came in, would discover for the remainder of the meal forgotten portions of her equipment that she commonly permitted nobody to fetch from her bedroom, and the courses were punctuated by little rushes from the table in search of handkerchief, spectacles and handbag, thus generating a restless and dyspeptic atmosphere which was the equal exasperation of Musgrave and of Major Dunston. The private dislike dated from that evening of 1912 when Miss Sapphire had seen Musgrave in his pyjamas, and about to enter the bathroom for the weekly cleansing that all the servants were permitted in rotation. There was no second bathroom at Delaye. In the Victorian era it was regarded as superfluous, and ever since, no master of the house could afford one. Thus butler and mistress had each other equally in their power, for as surely as a reminiscent gleam came into the eyes of old Miss Sapphire, so surely did she become Miss Sophia at the next tea-party.

Had there been a proper domestic hierarchy at Delaye, the housekeeper would have jointly reigned with Musgrave. The financial situation had outruled that possibility; for two generations, and even if the cook stayed for a period of years, Musgrave, though strictly respecting her professional rating, still regarded her as an inferior with whom the post-luncheon cup of tea could not be drunk. She might prepare the tea-pot, but, his cup once handed, Musgrave would disappear into his pantry to drink.

After the cook, there were an upper and an under housemaid, when they could be obtained, or, alternatively, a stop-gap of village girls who were glad to come to Delaye, and whose services were called in so frequently, these days after the Great War, that they needed no longer to be 'shown' and were house servants in every sense, save that at night they bicycled back to their homes.

Lowest of all came the kitchenmaid, whose name, Sue, on first hearing, seemed incredible for these high-flown days. But the mother of Sue was very properly and thoroughly old-fashioned, and did not believe in annoying her employers by bestowing names above the station of her daughters.

Sue Privett was the latest of a line of Privetts to serve the Roundelays. Sometimes, Sir Edmund, pondering the accounts books in the cellar, would re-tally the Privetts who had been kitchenmaids to former generations.

There were eight, and the first had appeared in 1789.

Polly Privett.

Sometimes he meditated her: flitting the stone-flagged passages. Perky? Saucy? In chintz gown or glazed, beflowered calico, a mob-cap set upon her young, bright hair . . . or unthinkably bedraggled? The kitchen butt? Little slave to everyone?

7

Somewhere between the modest rating of the regular servants and the status of the family itself was Nursie.

Nursie, like Musgrave, had served three generations of Roundelays and now, at a stupendous age and in common with the old retainers of so many other families, she had long been rescued from becoming a social problem and was comfortably installed as family curse. The Roundelays were all devoted to her in a profoundly exasperated way, and the fact that her keep, her pocket-money, washing and whims were a drain on pocket and nerves alike, that was borne without a murmur by all and as a matter of course, did not prevent some of them from occasionally desiring to strangle her.

Nursie ran true to type and was now slightly senile. She constantly asked the family or any passing servant which battle we were fighting now, a query that became progressively easier to answer, but she also believed that Queen Victoria still occupied the throne, and when assured *à haute voix* (Mr. Maxwell did best at this) that the present sovereign was King Edward, George the Fifth, Edward the Eighth, or George the Sixth, would shake her head and answer, 'Ah, they'd never get rid of *Her*'. Nursie also believed, and stated, that she had once seen King William the Fourth, when in service in London. If anyone pointed out to her that, if this were so, she must now be quite one hundred and thirteen years old, she would silence them for ever by announcing 'I'm ninety and I've got my lines to prove it', upon which, and in spite of polite protestations of belief and congratulation, she would toddle to a chest of drawers and soon transform her room, large though it was, into a lamentable jumble sale, at the very bottom of which, and when the floor was ankle-deep in clothes, photographs, albums and various precious knicknacks the very purpose of some of which was baffling, her birth certificate would be discovered and handed round (only it was sometimes a wedding favour, and twice a funeral card).

Nursie, the family sometimes thought, could be really awful, veering from garrulity — her tiger story was the Diamond jubilee — to that rudeness which society allows to old age on the ground that that condition is sacred, although nobody has yet been discovered capable of connecting the two propositions. Visitors, sometimes of courtesy, often of curiosity, would ask to be 'taken up' to Nursie, rather, one supposes, in the way in which the British public will pay sixpence extra to view the Chamber of Horrors, and were to find that almost any way you handled her was fatal. If you were sympathetic, your twitching feet were glued to the floor by reminiscence of weddings you knew nothing about, children you'd never heard of and were never likely to, they, by now, being middle-aged men and women, but set, for Nursie, in an eternal plush frame of youth, and, of course, by memories of the Jubilee, which a large proportion of Nursie's audience would not admit to remembering in any case. If, on the other hand, you were kind, but crisp and firm with her, she was rude at once. (Her favourite gambit was 'I don't remember *you*', which pronouncement, oddly enough in one you pitied and profoundly regretted, had the effect of making you feel at once outside all decent social pales, a parvenu, a bounder in grain. . . .)

So there sat Nursie, talkative, rude and sacred, and apparently everlasting. She had unreliable periods of being pleased with trifles, but on the whole the best of everything was good enough for her. She had the servant's unerring flair for imported meat, however perfectly cooked, and could scent by some devilish extra sense the presence of any substitute matter in fresh butter; imported eggs were, in the Great War, sent down on her tray, via caustic messages to the cook and a subsequent flood of tears that the current Mrs. Roundelay must waste one hour in mopping up. It was price paid for a lifetime of very genuine devotion. And it was Maxwell Dunston, always sarcastic, who dared to put Nursie into a nutshell. 'She reminds me of that song — y'know, "She was poor but she was honest" — though I'm hanged if she was ever the "victim of a rich man's sin". But there's no doubt "she drinks the champagne that we send her though she never can forgive".' But the Major was extra rasped, that morning, on discovering that the book of stamps which somebody had given Nursie for the letters that she still laboriously wrote in a hand wholly illegible to addresses most of which had been razed to the ground twenty years ago, had had every stamp in the book removed by Nursie who had pasted them on to the wall. 'I'm putting by for the future,' Nursie had announced. 'I must look after myself.'

Nursie, when at long last the scheme had been made clear to her, had refused the Old Age Pension which would have slightly relieved the financial strain on the Roundelays on the grounds that she had never taken charity yet and didn't intend to begin, and had worked hard all her life. She had a post office savings book buried full fathom five among her possessions, none of the family knew if she knew where; this nest-egg, it was hoped, would defray her funeral expenses, but, as Major Dunston remarked, by the time the book was unearthed there'd probably be no one left alive at Delaye to bury her.

CHAPTER II

1

IN THE TURRET ROOM of Delaye, Margaret Roundelay bent over a letter to her old schoolfriend, Ortrud Bohm. The good Ortrud had never been a favourite of hers; one respected Ortrud's sterling worth, valued her affectionate loyalty — and, in short, dear old Ortrud. Ortrud, on leaving the English school to which her far-sighted father, Friedrich Bohm, had sent her, was now returned to the family bosom in Berlin, where her English enthusiasms placed her beyond all marriageable pales with the citizens, just as her nationality and accent in England had contrived to create a social vacuum for her at all entertainments to which she secured an invitation. Deprived at one blow of the standing of the Sofaplatz, as of the British silver tea-pot — those badges of married hostess-ship — she was now in full cry of child welfare work.

Margaret Roundelay never gave her a thought between Crises and international ultimata, but the moment the political air became thick with Notes, and, as cousin Max caustically remarked, the government prepared as many White Papers and Blue Papers as would supply Seidlitz powders to the entire population of Scotland, so surely was she impelled to write to Ortrud. It was a real pity that one had never been able to learn German. German was the sort of language that made you comfortably feel that you were, anyway, a sound French scholar. Of her school classes, all that she carried away home to Normanshire were a shrill, peevish 'DOCH! Expletive. Miss. Go on,' from Fräulein, and a resultant quota of bad marks; that, and the fact that declensions were impossible to memorize and that the verb must be stuck well at the end of your sentence as a cockade decorates the coachman's hat. The timeless afternoons at Delaye had brought Margaret a few more gleanings; from the novels of 'Elizabeth' she had acquired perhaps fourteen more words. Among these were numbered *Herr Je!* (useless, because an ejaculation apparently only employed by the lower classes), *Backfisch: Geheimrat: Duselfritz: Kaffee Klatch: Schwerm: Oberleutnant* and *Appetitlich*. The songs of Schumann had also supplied *Warum: Nussbaum* and *Am Kamin*. Impossible to frame a complimentary sentence to a German correspondent which should successfully combine and mainly consist of such conflicting elements as flapper, dunderhead and coffee party, an appetizing crush on an army officer, plus Why?, a nut-tree and the fireside. And, would it be true politeness if one succeeded? Was it not a greater courtesy to waive Ortrud's nationality and assume for her a gratifying Englishness? Ortrud would like that. In common with most foreigners she was a fluent linguist, even if the British idiom would remain eternally beyond her powers. Ortrud's notion of eulogistic English slang was still in the Ripping epoch, though she had of late years added the adjective Grim to her repertoire. (Where did you get that hat? — *Wo hast du dass hut bekomm?* laboriously pondered Miss Roundelay.) And Ortrud never helped out one's own vocabulary by a single German word or catchword. She was too English for that. Yet Ortrud must *know* that you knew she was German, but she always gave you the impression of hoping you'd forgotten she wasn't English. You didn't know, as a result, whether to be sympathetically insulting about Hitler or respectfully hopeful as to his policy.

Margaret had begun her letter upon a high wave of loyalty and Auld Lang Syne, the current Crisis being distinctly more acute than usual. The letter was intended not only to show Ortrud that one wasn't insular and to hint that her nationality wasn't being held against her, but was inspired by a genuine glow of feeling that the Crises of England punctually called into being, and, during which, friends and acquaintances wrote letters that were not of Christmas or birthday, and a feeling of unity and brotherhood was set up. When the Crisis was over, the friends fell back once more into their places of relative importance in each other's regard, and all was normal until the next Ultimatum. But it was, while it lasted, a state of emotion both warming, charming, and a little pathetic.

Margaret sometimes wished it could last, this goodwill towards men that was bred of anything but peace on earth. Though of course it would cost a lot in stamps.

When she read through her half-finished letter, she was astonished and dismayed to find that with the best will in the world it grew progressively more tactless.

September 1938

Dearest Ortrud,

So here we are again, fighting other people's battles for them! But it really does look, this time, as if Chamberlain was going to prevent another frightful war. It's rather wonderful to think that he can go anywhere abroad with just an umbrella and be feted all along the route, while the Dictators daren't show their noses even in their own country without an armed guard and bullet-proof glass, etc. But if things *should* come to a head, there is a general feeling in England that we are far better prepared. Even in 1914, with hardly anything ready and muddle everywhere we contrived to come out on top. As usual, how we did it I can't imagine, except on the principle that 'thrice is he armed who hath his quarrel just', etc., and it must be too *awful* to enter a war feeling that your leaders' aims and motives are all wrong.

My dear, this is just a line to hope you and your mother and Mr. Bohm are all well and reasonably happy. I see in the newspapers that you've been short of butter and stand in queues for ages. We aren't, yet, and don't: You'd never know there *was* a war impending here, any more than you did in the last one, and I can guess how you must be missing fats, because —

Margaret leant back, appalled, and murmured 'Glory!' But there was still Claudine Vernet, who lived at Versailles.

Ever since their brief life together at the Villa Cyclamène, in Lausanne, she and Claudine had come to a working agreement about correspondence: Claudine to write in English but to be free to make her meaning clear in her mother tongue, Margaret to reply in French and similarly explain her remarks in English. At school they had understood each other's spoken remarks almost perfectly, and it was only the answers that went to pieces. Which was very odd, as the fact that they could listen to each other intelligently must indicate that they knew a great deal more French and English than they were aware of. Then, where did the words go to when you came to speak? With Claudine, Margaret had never felt the Crisis-impulse of patronizing protectiveness that she experienced towards Ortrud. Claudine, being French, was able to take care of herself; also, being an Ally of England, she was among the respectable nations for whom you had to feel no pity and no apology. Claudine's country had never been a Menace that dated from long before your own nursery years, whereas about the German friendship, these days, one felt as one did with curates, Jews and nuns: that they were not only not quite human and normal, but needed special treatment as well, of the kind you gave to the invalid, to tradesmen and the servants, and which consisted of extrapoliteness, a form of apology for being a superior being, and a great, grave kindness and humouring. Tact, and a little joke here and there, suited to their capacity. . . .

To write to Claudine was always a pleasure, to write to Ortrud a duty. Claudine was charming, Ortrud had no personal graces. Yet Claudine was a fearful liar in a perfectly nice way, and not too honest about money. There were those expeditions to the Patisserie for Palmiers, chocolate and brioches, and quite often Claudine forgot her purse, and you paid, or Ortrud paid, and that was the last ever heard of the matter; whereas Ortrud would flog a mile or rise up in the night to repay you a forgotten franc. Also, Claudine's lay conversation was apt to be rather prone to references that you felt you oughtn't to understand, whereas Ortrud's talk was as open as the day, and sometimes as long.

Was it a pity that England couldn't have a reshuffle and join up with the Germans, so sterling, so kindly and so tedious? But there it was. The nations had picked sides as in party games and had apparently got struck so for good. But then, of course, there was Hitler, who prevented everyone from thinking clearly or fairly. While Hitler lived and flourished it wasn't safe to value Ortrud in public. . . .

And would there be wars any more if all girls and boys all over the world were sent abroad to finishing schools? Already, one was not mentally at war with one German in the person of poor old Ortrud. Multiply that instance by millions — and the citizens of the future would be at peace. But finishing schools, and therefore understanding, were costly, and so still the perquisite of the middle and upper classes, which virtually left tolerance in the hands of the already educated.

And would it answer? Wouldn't it perhaps tend towards keeping the masses from knowing their place? A British footman who took to shrugging his shoulders and spreading his hands at guests at the front door would be quite awful, so would a Devonshire cook who cried 'Corpo di Bacco!' instead of 'drabbit it!' and dieted one on spaghetti instead of roast beef. And if there were no wars it would throw the Services out of work. . . .

There was one Italian girl at the Villa Cyclamène, a luscious creature with gummy brown eyes, who ate salted melon seeds that were sent her in large envelopes bearing the Florentine postmark. But at seventeen, Cecilia (pronounced Chaychillia) had looked so mature and was so very nearly about to become engaged by her parents to an officer on the staff of the Count of Turin, that as a contemporary pupil it became impossible to believe in her, let alone make friends. Cecilia was lazy, vehement and noisy. She kissed the most improbable people on the mouth when she wasn't lying on sofas in Hogarthian décolletage and abusing them in a loud, manly baritone, and her taste in dress was only to be equalled by Ortrud's, and ran to immense earrings in sky-blue mosaic, while Ortrud had once gone all Scottish on the Villa, and made herself a synthetic tartan skirt, well pleated round the stomach, ending in a flounce, and dipping two inches in front. (That was the term they had been reading Walter Scott.) Impossible to classify Cecilia. As an Italian, she belonged to one of those rather betwixt-and-between nations which were, by rumour, decorative and tourable, and not of quite sufficient importance to give any trouble to anyone. Garibaldi, apparently, had been Italy's full-stop in high endeavour, and the rest was tickets at Cook's. There was Mussolini, of course, but somehow, for at least a year, he had begun to assume the proportions of an understudy, in spite of the way in which he stood in Italian excavations for The Movietone News and made strong-man faces and flap-mouths, and designed himself headgear that reminded one of *The Chocolate Soldier*.

'My dear Lieu—ten—ant Bu—mer—li'

hummed Margaret Roundelay reminiscently.

2

Elbows on table, Margaret gazed out of the window.

Wars and rumours of wars, and as far as the rested eyes could see, green-ness, of lawn and topiary work, of paddock and walled garden, browning leaf, tangle of michaelmas daisy and dewfilled dahlia, and apple trees (which needed spraying and pruning) the life of the place broken like a drowsy sentence by the sudden exclamation of pigeon, gunshot, or mowing-machine, by the screech of a peacock or Hasty's excited bark that meant a sighted squirrel flicking up a tree, or the raucous proclamation of a cock. How one loved every inch of it. But that must not be spoken of. Instead, to interested parties, one drew attention to the house's limitations and inconveniences, gratefully sheltering behind the undeniable.

3

Margaret abandoned for further consideration her letter to Ortrud and began to express herself to Claudine Vernet. She hoped it wasn't going to be too risqué, but you never knew, in French, and found yourself, according to Claudine, becoming quite brilliantly improper over such unpromising material as the news that, yesterday, you had tried in Norminster market to buy a mackerel for your cat — and if one had *wanted* to be that sort of person, thought Margaret laboriously, one couldn't have achieved it in a lifetime. She had been too proud to query the answering scream of laughter with which Mademoiselle Vernet had received this domestic detail, and it would be no good asking anyone at Delaye what Margaret had said because Roundelay French was too straightforward to know the answer, and if it were too awful, and they should know it, they mightn't tell one. Well . . . if Margaret was now rated as an improper wit in Versailles, it was too late to do anything about it. But one could at least keep off the subject of animals. *And* fish.

'On parle,' [wrote Miss Roundelay, for she had been to a first class Swiss finishing-school,] 'encore d'une guerre, et je me doute point que vous avez aussi entendue parler de cette dommage. Si c'est possible, j'espère vous revoir en Angleterre whenever you want to come over. (Faire la traversée?) Mon frère qui est au Lycée Agricultural nous assure que les nouvelles d'une guerre sont un canard, et que nous avons étés fooled (blagués?) trop longue depuis le dernier Crise. (He means that if there'd been going to be a war there would have been one *months* ago and that this is all bluff.) Apart from that, on ne dirait qu'il y a de malheur, chez nous, et la vie passe en paix. Pour moi, je suis maîtresse de Guides au village, et nous rencontrons à l'Institut des Femmes. Le travail est interessant, et j'ai dix-sept enfants et jeunes filles dans mon bataillon. Pour la reste, je m'occupe au jardin, etc:, ou il y en a toujours beaucoup à faire, à cause que nous manquons un (sufficiency) des jardiniers . . .'

A distant, vibratory booming came to the ears of Margaret. Musgrave, sounding the dressing gong. She rose instantly, stacking her papers with system. It was a dull letter, and she knew it; she had been about to tell Claudine that sometimes she and her father went out shooting rabbits, but that suggested the cat and mackerel, and probably meant something you didn't speak about, as well. Claudine said the English had no humour, and that the Englishman's idea of seeing Paris was to buy rude post-cards in the gutter, and the Englishwoman's to buy pink suspenders at the Galleries Lafayette, and eat, whenever possible, at English tearooms, when they had finished getting lost and being rescued by taxis.

As she dressed before a heart-shaped Chippendale mirror, which presented her reflection as a steely blur upon which were super-imposed mysterious brown smears (father would know how to treat that), Margaret wondered what Claudine would have made of her own younger sister.

Angela had missed boarding- and finishing-school life. Too sensitive, they said. Yet she seemed to be physically up to standard. Angela was a Roundelay, with a misleading appearance of fragility, whereas Margaret herself was a Calcott, like the aunts, mother's sisters, tall and stock size, with good figures.

4

The sensitive mechanism of Angela was a cloud upon the unemotional happiness of her mother and father, and against which they had fought for years, admitting at last a partial defeat by sending her on visits to other counties, and to relations, though never, thanks to her great-aunt Sapphire's spirited and still untarnished account of that *ménage*, to Crystal Dunston, in Kensington, a decision in which Maxwell Dunston gloomily but unhesitatingly concurred.

Angela at the moment was at the Cloudesleys, which seemed to be considered suitable for her, possibly because she was not overhandled with solicitude at Cloudesley Hall. Nobody expected grandparents to understand their grandchildren. The older generation had inevitably skipped important points about the younger, and there could be, Margaret quite saw, some restful element in the kindly obtuseness of age. Sending Angela about to stay with relations, whether in London or the next county, was a parental shot in the dark, and quite a successful one. And Angela wasn't missing very much, except Delaye itself. The Roundelays in these days could no longer entertain on a large scale, and though the country tradition of keeping open house remained, the doors were not so much open as perpetually ajar, which just meant stray requests from London friends who'd lost their way or were wanting to be put up or were 'passing through', or near neighbours whose boilers had burst or cooks walked out on them. Even now, at Delaye, luncheon and tea were anybody's meals, and neighbours put their heads in for a cup from four o'clock onwards, if, in the summer, the Roundelays were eating in the lounge hall for its coolness. What with these, and the inevitable motor out of water or petrol, plus ignorant or impertinent trespassers to whom a notice of Private on gate or pale meant anything on earth (including the hope of satisfying every one of their bodily requirements) but its actual significance, the avenue and drive were seldom deserted for long.

... Of course, if there should be a war, Angela would come back for good. And it wasn't, her sister thought, as though there were anything the matter with her. Doctor Elmslie had said himself that, physically, he could find nothing wrong ... it would be interesting to see what a war was really like. Margaret had been one year old in 1914, and even Stacey only three. But she had found that, however accurate 'the survivors', they were no real good, because everybody saw events from their own angle.

5

For two years, while Europe simmered, Margaret Roundelay had set herself, coolly and impartially, and with that efficiency which, combined with her standing in the neighbourhood, had made her a successful District Superintendent of Guides who must be addressed as 'Madam', to discovering what she could about the last war.

She emerged at the end of all her study of war literature, whether horrific (*My home was in Hamburg*), scandalous-revelatory

(*The Guards Want Powder*) or sentimental (*Sergeant Sally*) with the conviction that only the experienced could give an idea of those times. Horrors, tactical blunders, and sentiment were of every epoch . . . and all these books and publications were probably just as unreliable as history books.

She was to find that all the 'survivors' coloured their accounts by the way they themselves had been affected. The great-aunts, for instance: aunt Jessie's version of the Great War was that it had almost caused her to lose her faith, and it was no good asking her if there'd really been food queues at the Norminster shops, because God, so to speak, stood in every one of them. To aunt Sapphy, on the other hand, the 1914-18 affair was centred in the considerable amount of 'attention' that she herself received at regimental dances at the Assembly Rooms. Aunt Kathleen Calcott's impressions had consisted mainly of boredom.

'You see, my dear, aunt Helen and I were still girls, at a pinch, and we weren't the type of young woman who made capital out of the situation, and gold-dug officers on leave and wangled presents, and so on. To heaps of girls the war was the time of their life, but it was usually the wrong type of girl. We just saw fewer men than ever, and wound bandages at depots and went to working parties at friends' houses, just as my mother did in the Boer War. I think we all resented the war and the way it was crabbing our chances. Only, there again, that was a thing we were too decent or too stupid to discuss openly. Then, too, we didn't feel really "of" the war because we had no near relatives at the front. That gave most women some standing and dignity; but all we got was the petty, obstructive, limiting side of it; we just had a rather thin time that wasn't the least ennobling or heroic — things like not having enough sugar, and people bringing their own saccharine to tea-parties. Oh, it was deadly, seeing nothing but brownish stodge in the bakers and not a piece of icing to relieve it! We were never in much danger, though we did get a piece of shrapnel through our little conservatory window in Hereford Square, and we were *never* hungry, only dissatisfied and bored with our vittles — a most ignoble state of being, and even that wasn't a voluntary sacrifice, but rationing, though many of us would have gone without far more, as a gesture. Only it was a gesture that wasn't necessary, and one didn't want to be holier-than-thou.'

Aunt Helen Calcott, always more direct and pungent, wrote to her niece:

'Yes, it *was* boring. I've got to admit that I've forgotten huge quantities of what really *did* happen. Can't even remember any eminent deaths except poor little Prince John, and some actor-managers you never saw, two of whom were a national loss and one a blessed release! (*never* believe his biographers: he was terrible, poor heart!) The theatres havered about opening because of the man-shortage, and then all opened with a bang, got on somehow, and remained open for the duration. Can't remember one single war play, but only several revues, including *Business as Usual* (one of the then catchwords) and *The Bing Boys* series at the Alhambra.

'We were in the upper circle on the day Peace was signed and Violet Loraine made a speech, ending, "This is the most wonderful day since the world began", which struck me as slightly excessive even at the time, though we all cried a bit and everyone was shouting.

'It's extraordinary, but I can't remember one single war *Christmas*; we must have had turkey, and been somewhere, but it's a complete blank. Auntie K. *thinks* Brighton, once, but I do remember running out into Hereford Square in my nightdress to see a Zeppelin at 2 o'clock, a.m. and they *did* look like the descriptions you're wading through. Large aluminium cigars. And we had a houseparlourmaid who always hid under the side-board, in raids.

'My memories of Mafeking Night are far more vivid than they are of Armistice Day, though I was only in my teens, then. But I do remember a lorry going down past South Kensington station full of yelling workmen and girls, and digging out bunting from the boxroom left over from God knows when (Queen Victoria's Jubilee, I should think!) and that, as I unfurled it on the balcony, almost weeping with emotion, a *blizzard* of moth's eggs fell out of it on to a tradesman, and that he looked up and called out, "Oh well . . . they say blessings come from above", as he dusted off his joints, which made me laugh till I cried.

'Yes, I dimly remember there *was* a scandal about the Panjandrum you mention — tendency to sit about longer than time allowed with Mdlle from Armunteers — and of course one can never forget or forgive that the income tax was 6s. in the £. Everyone said the country couldn't stand it, but of course we cursed, paid and did. N.B. Are we the most splendid and adaptable people on earth or just bovine and minus initiative?

'I think the worst features of the war were the jokes, some of the songs (including "Tipperary") and the female hearties in uniform. They were an innovation, and the plague of the newspapers for quite eighteen months or more. They were largely led by elderly horrors and horse godmothers with cropped hair, whose fronts were so flat that at a distance you didn't know if they were coming or going. The Press was all over them: Brave Women, Our Gallant Girls, etc.

'I have a retrospective suspicion that quantities of 'em went that way as an opportunity to express a latent masculinity, and that the fluffy-wuffies jumped at the chance of getting away from Home and Mother. I think they were all perfectly *harmless*, only offensive. I saw three of the typical ones at close quarters, and they made their girls, whom they called 'The Men', address them as 'Sir'. To me, this completely cancelled out the good they were doing (if any), the example they were setting to England (if any) and their public spirit (as before). Most of them weren't gentlewomen — *they* seemed to gravitate more to the Red Cross and the V.A.D.'s.

'About the air-raids: I frankly enjoyed them. I felt that, for once, we were really taking a hand in the game. I don't mind admitting that the first three went to my knees, but after that I was stimulated. They weren't very numerous, as they will be, next time, or very serious, though the Press did what our cook calls "create alarming" at women and children being killed — as though the Germans could *see* what they were aiming at, at that height! But it was a popular bit of anti-German propaganda, of course.

'Don't think, by the way, that I object to women in uniform. I don't. And in the next war you'll find that the old exhibitionists will have been largely weeded out and a fresh crop arisen which takes the service idea more as it should be taken, and not as a maladjusted challenge or an ogle to men.

'Yes, it's perfectly true about women giving white feathers to men (including Staff officers in mufti and commissioned ranks home on leave!). The officious bad taste and worse manners of it

as coming from a sex which by its numbers alone is completely surplus makes me curdle to this hour!'

Lady Roundelay told her daughter: 'Well, you see, I hadn't been
married very long and was too busy having all of you to take much
notice of what went on. There was, I believe, a shortage of potatoes,
but of course we didn't feel it, here.'

Margaret's cousin, Major Dunston, contributed: 'Well, I was all
through it, and the thing I remember most clearly was being unable
to open a tin of veal loaf from Fortnum and Mason's when I hadn't
had a bite for fourteen hours because the field kitchen bogged down
in a turnip field. Hated it all? Of course I did, but I never had wanted to go into the army. I should have joined up in any case, but only
for the duration. I'll kick a fellow in the backside with the best, but
doing him in out of a chemist's shop isn't my idea of a scrap. What
the world needs badly is a return to the good old hand-to-hand
combat: it's cleaner, gives men a chance to prove themselves as individuals, and will make towards a survival of the fittest elements.'

Musgrave, cleaning 'his' silver in the pantry, dusted a chair for
Miss Margaret and told her: 'The war years, for me, chiefly meant
the death of my mother, Miss. We was very attached, very attached
indeed, and when she went, I didn't seem to care much *what* 'ap-
pened, except that I naturally wanted our side to win. I shall never
forget Sir Edmund's goodness in lettin' 'er come to Delaye to be
near me and to end 'er days in comfort, nor the constant kindness
of 'er ladyship . . . you see, I wasn't by no means a young man. I was
forty-three, in 'fourteen, and under the Derby Scheme they didn't
call up the older men not for some years later and as a last resort. I
went to the recruitin' office, with Sir Edmund's permission, before
actually called up, being wishful to do my bit, as the saying went,
and they rejected me for active service, but drafted me to an officers'
mess. I did put in for transfer to the Major's regiment — I should've
liked to have looked after the Major, 'e was only a Captain at the
time — but that fell through. Well, I was with the —th for the duration, and never 'eard a shot, as you might say. The young officers
was a very pleasant, affable lot, high-spirited and full of their jokes
and what not, but I thought it a mistake to be so free with commissions as what the War Office was. 'Temporary Gentlemen' we called

them, and it didn't answer. They was uncomfortable, the N.C.O.s and privates didn't like it, being very quick to note the difference, an' averse to being ordered by one of themselves, and we upper servants don't like it. They 'avn't the manner, or the 'abit of authority: too stiff one minute, too free an' easy the next. . . .

'I should very much appreciate it, Miss, if, one day, you could spare the time to let me show you some of my mother's letters and photos . . . I think I 'ave every one she ever wrote me.'

Nursie's version of the war was: 'That'd be the time I dropped my specs into the pond, and they're there to this day.' Pressed by Margaret for her more stirring impressions, the old woman stated that Master Stacey was a regular One for catching colds, that Lady Roundelay made a shocking slow recovery from the birth of Angela, and that Margaret herself had always been the sturdy one of the three and practically no trouble at all.

When her nursling at this point showed an impatience that was also of healthy growth, Nursie said Hush Lovie, and added that it must have been in one of those wars that the family had been so unaccountably unkind to Nursie herself in the way of sweet-stuffs and butcher's meat: that she couldn't abide mashed swedes, but that all had come right, the family had apologized to her, that she was never one to harbour ill-feelings, but that it did seem curious, she being known to be partial to butcher's meat and sweet-stuffs.

Dickon the gardener, tackled by Miss Margaret in the potting-shed where he was enjoying a mid-morning mug of tea, retained his chair, dumped his mug upon a bench, told her to make herself at home and them seedling trays weren't too mucky to sit upon, and proceeded to indicate the political and international situation of 1914-1918.

There had been a bumper crop of apples, followed by a plague of caterpillars. The price of seeds rose. The present potato bed was under cauliflowers at the time, but was not, of course rotated by cabbages, they bein' of the same family, like, and them beds went to runners. The tomatoes was a picture and had won a First at the Show of /17 when the committee 'ad decided to 'old it agen. Bin out in France? Nah . . . he was wanted at Delaye. He wuz a *gardener*. Yes, he and Mother 'ad lost their eldest and it seemed as though it 'ad to be. But they'd allowed 'im to go. Cowpons for food? He and Mother'd taken no notice o' them. Always get what we want in village. Culling (grocer) and Wagstaffe (coal merchant) were 'is sons-in-law weren't they? Delaye made no odds about *cowpons*, no more than Roon did. Land Girls? There was two over at Brouncker's fornicatin' about in britches, poor things, and he hadn't heard of any particular harm they'd done to the crops. . . .

His daughter questioned Sir Edmund Roundelay. Here, she met a verbal explosion as her father, eyes gleaming and moustaches twitching with retrospective indignation, expounded the struggle of the nations twenty-four years ago.

'Red tape, that's the curse of the country — sending a parcel of young jacks-in-office from the Ministry of Agriculture to teach me my business, making me plough up four acres of good grazing land so that all the cattle had to be shoo'd off somewhere else, and it wasn't even good ploughland, as I told 'em. So there we were — agricultural implements were almost impossible to get, at one period — all metal wanted for munitions, so those fields simply lay fallow for about fifteen months, no good to man or beast. Then they ringed about eighty of my trees for timber, and it wasn't any use my telling 'em they were earmarked already to a local firm. Down they came. And they suggested my replanting with conifers — *conifers*! I nearly had a lawsuit over that. Why, they even commandeered half-grown trees though you'd have thought any fool could have seen that the timber would be worth double in bulk and cash if they'd wait a bit. But not they! They'd been sent to get wood. The government looks on the land as a bran pie, to draw what it wants out of: it doesn't realize, not being a specialist, that land is a live thing and resents unintelligent upheavals, and goes back on you in a dozen ways by improper treatment. Like invalids.'

CHAPTER III

1

THE GONG sounded again, and Margaret caught up handkerchief, tidied her dressing-table and ran down the turret stairs. The passage was dark, but two doors at its nearest and farthest end opened simultaneously, throwing oblongs of light upon the carpeting, and her great-aunts Sapphire and Amethyst were disgorged.

Perceiving this, aunt Amy closed her own door and retired again within her room. This was a more or less nightly programme. For the old ladies weren't on speaking terms.

'Ah, my chee-ild, there you be! Dear! It seems as though one was always eating!' Aunt Sapphy didn't mean that in the least, her niece knew: she would have hated unpunctuality for any meal, was a hearty trencherwoman always, but she was also of the epoch which had been trained to fill in any conversational gap by some bright nothing, and to work at men if they were silent in her company, a habit which, with years, had become sexless. Therefore a descent of three flights of stairs must be accompanied by vocal sounds. Silence might be golden, but in her youth it was also social failure.

Aunt Sapphy was wearing her purple, that evening. She moved, as far as personal contrivance and her private means allowed, with the current fashions from the shoulders down, but her head remained inexorably nineteenth century; the thought of shingles and bobs withered in her presence, and the head of Miss Sapphire Roundelay raised a monument to the memory of Alexandra, both as Princess and Queen.

In face of almost unsurmountable obstacles, of which a waning custom was not the least, Miss Sapphire still paid the afternoon call: it involved a telephone message to the firm in Norminster which, unmoved by the advent of taxis, still hired out its string of four-wheelers and victorias, a changing of the luncheon hour, another (anxiety) call when, booted and gloved and florally toqued, aunt Sapphy stood hovering in the hall of Delaye, mother o' pearl card-case in hand, and a grating cross-country progress to the big houses, into whose drawing-rooms she entered diffusing a smell of stale straw and oiled harness while the cab drooped outside in the drive. Miss Sapphy never hired taxis, saying that they would seem discourteous and too informal to her hostess and looked flurried' when waiting, also, they ticked up pennies quite impossibly, while Jamieson charged by the hour.

Quite often, the hostesses were most unfairly in another county, made accessible by possession of a car: oftener still, they were supplementing staff in the garden, and would arrive, pulling off wash-leather gloves, casting raffia hats on to settles, and apologizing for overalls, and once, an extra-harried lady, her thoughts reaching out lustfully to a half-finished border, had even stirred her tea with a small trowel.

But any tea is better than none, and it was an unhappy fact that, owing to the eye that Miss Sapphy must keep on the clock with regard both to the cost of her conveyance and the distances to be covered, she often spent an entire afternoon without any sustenance at all; she called too early, too late, or if her arrival coincided with a normal tea hour, the family was from home. It was seldom indeed that the time, the place and the tea-pot altogether were to be enjoyed. A thermos in the carriage and a packet of cake to be consumed on the road would, she said, soil her kids. And so, at six-thirty or seven o'clock, the cab would crunch up the avenue of Delaye and from it Miss Sapphy would step, famished, irritable, but triumphant.

Cards had been left. She had kept in touch.

2

On the landing below, Margaret and her aunt were joined by Miss Jacinth, also emerging from her room. At this stage of the general mobilization to the dining-room there was invariably a slight delay, for the old sisters paired off and concluded the progress downstairs, while Margaret paid a hasty good-night visit to Nursie, a custom which might or might not run smoothly, according to Nursie's mood and occupation, but that was apt to be infinitesimally delayed by the cautious advance of aunt Amy, as ever hoping to make the dining-room in Jessie's company while avoiding Sapphy, and, as ever, failing.

To-night, she arrived, failed, and as usual said to her niece 'Going to see Nursie? The gong has sounded', and as ever Margaret replied that she knew, upon which aunt Amy moved; off, murmuring 'These stairs!' as though she had not, for well over half a century, negotiated them, as plaid-frocked child with snooded hair, as girl, in basques and Serpolette frocks, as woman, in collars of boned net, and circular skirts.

To-night, Nursie was peacefully poddling about her room, occupying her time in the unguessable ways of age; her windows overlooked that part of the garden nearest the kitchens, and the identification of menus by the arising savours was a keen interest to her.

'Roast mutton to-night, so you'll do well, lovie. There was a time you was always the tiresome one about meat, but — '

'Nursie dear, I *must* go.' The old Nurse's reminiscences once started were apt to take turns as dismayingly embarrassing as those of Juliet's, and the most respectable memoir to end in byways of intestinal stress and adolescence that made the hearer hot. For once, Nursie was placid before the implied rebuke. 'Well, come here and let me fasten you up behind, you was always a terror for tangling your hair in the buttons.'

'There *aren't* any buttons. It's a zip fastener I can manage perfectly well — '

'You look very nice, dearie, very nice. *And* neat, though it's time you asked y'mother for a new dress.'

'Oh gracious, Nursie, I'm *twenty-five.* I've got an *allowance.*'

'. . . very neat, though I never could abide that Guards uniform.'

'*Guides.* Girl Guides.'

'It makes you look like the postman. What you put it on for I'm sure I don't know.'

'It helps discipline with the girls. And now — '

'I never needed aught but a cap and apron to keep *you* all in order. Yes. Roast mutton. Leg, by the smell. Tell your father to cut me some of the knuckly bits near the bone. They eat a bit stringy, but tasty, and I can grind and swallow the goodness and then spew the waste.'

Margaret kissed the old woman and ran downstairs. Her life was so inextricably bound up with Nursie, her loss would be so irreparable, her presence as one of the family was so right, that Miss Roundelay was free to indulge in a strong desire to slap Nursie's face until it rang.

3

The Roundelays were at dinner.

In the lingering daylight, the large framed portraits gleamed oilily. In the initial silence, Miss Jessie was heard to express a wish that this blest food that she was about to take might do her good for Jesus' sake. Catching it by a long experience in timing, Musgrave ceased to extract a bottle of burgundy from the lead-lined cupboard of the sideboard and looked respectable and attentive. The aspiration concluded, and indeed nobody at table paid tribute to it but he, Musgrave duly clock-clock-clocked his portion of wine into Major Dunston's glass.

'If that dog — ', began Sir Edmund.

'How's this lasting out, Musgrave?'

'Two bottles left, sir.'

'Don't want to run out, with all the manoeuvring it takes to get Stone to deliver here.'

There was, at Delaye, no time-wasting gallantry of offering wine to the women: the family all perfectly understood each other's financial state, and what each individual could afford was served to him or her exclusively without any ill-feeling whatsoever. Delaye, in common with a thousand other houses of similar standing all over England, was in a transition state between the rich security of the cellar and a willy-nilly recourse to the pump and, while Major Dunston would give his last drop of stimulant to any necessitous member of the family if he were dying of thirst himself, and as a matter of course, he did not, until that condition arose, see any need to offer one sip to anybody.

'And what have *you* been doing with yourself all day?' aunt Sapphy enquired of her niece, with bright civility, as though she had seen her for the first time that moment.

'I got up the worst of that bindweed — '

'Leg of mutton,' mused Sir Edmund, '"a joint upon their barbarous spits they put on".' He carved, gently chuckling.

'We had a spit in the kitchen, once,' supplied Miss Amy. 'I often wonder where it is now.'

'Cart-house,' answered her nephew. 'These old contraptions — and he entered into a dissertation upon spits, their antiquity evolution and causes of disuse. To this only aunt Amy listened and commented with the maximum of anxious unintelligence.

'Edmund, *do* go on carving, we're all starving at this end,' Evelyn Roundelay exclaimed, between exasperation and affection. 'I'm sorry, aunt Amy, I didn't hear what you said.'

Miss Sapphy began to fidget, hunt, and discover that she had left her glasses upstairs, and hurried from the room. Miss Jessie looked resigned.

'Had a letter from the Mater this morning,' grumbled Major Dunston.

Sir Edmund accepted potatoes from Musgrave. 'Ah . . . keeping well?'

'She seems to be a bit on edge about things.'

Lady Roundelay said, 'She'd better come here for a bit.'

'Very kind of you, Evelyn, but I'd leave her alone.'

'Well . . . hadn't you — oh I do wish aunt Sapphy wouldn't *always* leave the door open, Musgrave *please*! — hadn't you better run up to town and see her?'

'Good God, no!'

'You could catch the 11.5 and we'll ring up the station after dinner for a car — '

'That house of hers is a horrible place . . . came to choose it . . . beyond me.'

Lady Roundelay abandoned the idea, but Miss Amy was faithful unto death. 'And if you caught the 11.5 there might be somebody who'd be glad of a lift in the car to Delaye.'

Maxwell Dunston drank burgundy.

Miss Sapphy hurried back into the dining-room hoping, as usual, that nobody had waited for her and asking how far we had got now, before resuming her mutton.

Miss Amy turned to Margaret. 'Will you ask my sister to pass me the salt?'

'We shall want about a hundred and twenty yards more barbed wire for that fence, Evelyn.'

'Oh, my dear! and it is such a price!'

'Ring the bell, will you, Margaret?'

'Aunt Sapphy hasn't quite finished, father.'

'Only a little bit left, Edmund. I can be finishing it while — '

'No, no, no. Take your time. No need to choke — '

'Your aunt has dropped her table napkin.'

'Aunt Amy, aunt Sapphy says your napkin's on the floor.'

'It's these slippery silks. They always slip off.'

'Let me.'

'Thanks, dear.'

'That dog's got a touch of eczema, Evelyn. Better tell Dickon to treat him.'

'Eczema,' confirmed aunt Amy. 'I thought he seemed scratching. Dickon will treat him.'

'College pudding or fritters, aunt Amy?'

'The pudding, I think.'

'Aunt Jessie?'

'Well — I — they both look — '

'Then have some of each.'

'That looks very greedy!'

'Oh, have the courage of your convictions.'

'Then, perhaps — '

'Is anyone going in to Norminster to-morrow?' asked Sir Edmund. 'I want some tobacco and two gallons of whitewash and six dozen duchesses and half a — no, a quarter — of a gross of ladies.'

'You *are* funny,' said aunt Sapphy.

'Duchesses,' said aunt Amy.

'Nails,' gloomily elucidated the master of the house, 'use 'em for slating according to size. Even the nail world knows its laws of precedence.'

'The duchesses go in first, I presume,' capped Miss Sapphy, smartly.

'That's the idea.' He was off on one of his hobby-horses. 'It's curious how the caste idea permeates nearly everything: first, you get your nails, then it crops up in card games — take Canfield, for example — where a Queen may not be played in her own right, as it were, but only with reference to the priority placing of your King. Same with the Knave — the noble — who must follow the Queen . . . it's a perfect feudal system in small, with wealth following on behind the Royal Family — '

'Demon is beyond me!' cried Miss Sapphy, scenting a fullstop.

' — and then you have the king-pin, the king-pole, the prop that keeps the whole structure together — '

Lady Roundelay rose.

4

The Roundelays filed into the drawing-room.

As each member of the family had its chair or occupation, the effect was always as of a smoothly produced comedy, with the unimportant differences that the décor and properties, of rose brocade causeuse, gilt chairs, water colours, and objets d'art happened to be genuine, and that nobody present had an illicit lover, a dominant grandmother, or, at the other end of the scale, threw cocktail shakers and gramophone records at each other's heads while the family drug-taker played the 'Rhapsody in Blue' upon a grand piano. There was a Brinsmead in the long room, but evasion was its portion: it had remained with the family from the cultural girlhood of Miss Sapphire, and now, through questions of cash, unprofitableness and inertia, its life was one of guaranteed security and neglect, though the maids quite often ran an unintelligent duster down its keys and so sifted the superficial deposit to the vital parts and attracted moth to the felt upon the hammers.

Evelyn Roundelay moved to the shell-shaped armchair in the summer and to a sofa in the winter: reading and sewing, whether the latter were domestic or personal, she was content. There was no wireless or gramophone at Delaye to fret the scene with their outside reminders. The question of installing a wireless set had often been touched upon, but never with real feeling, more as two cronies might impersonally agree that the rhododendrons at Kew were exceptionally fine this year. A battery set, it was rumoured, was always in dock for costly repairs, and an electric model to be plugged into the wall would be dangerous to the old panelling in a thunderstorm, should anyone forget to disconnect it (the Squire's pantry had once been discovered to be smouldering and they had had to dig up half the drive with which to extinguish the contrivance). Besides, the electric lights were all earmarked for family eyesight.

By 8.45, everyone was settled down for the evening.

Major Dunston read *The New Statesman* with every appearance of dislike: it was his bread and butter before the cake of Dorothy Sayers and Sydney Horler. Edmund Roundelay examined *The Times* from end to end as conscience-money for the frivolous ten-hour day of toil that he put in on the estate: Margaret, at a table of brass and inlay, worked over the Guides accounts and addressed postcards giving details of coming fixtures to members in outlying villages; the drumming of her fingers as she computed could sometimes be heard. Miss Sapphy at another table nearer the Lacquer Room into which the drawing-room led played solitaire, with a cool clicking of marbles, and supplied remark when the silence became too unsociably prolonged. Miss Amethyst read anything left over by somebody else; Miss Jacinth, too resigned to the will of Providence to interfere with the news, sewed and knitted for the poor of the parish, occasionally twitching at the soft mass in her lap and causing the ball of wool to bound towards some relative, upon which the latter tossed it back without comment or aim, as one might play tennis in hell.

When Angela was at home, she ostensibly read, as well, but actually sat in her place by the window, her feet upon a little footstool of gros point, and thought about the occupants in the room.

She would never lose her capacity for conscious gratitude at the graciousness with which fate had treated her in allotting to her this home and this family, and her discontents were all vicarious. Of the entire roomful, it was Angela alone, watchful, dark-eyed and pale, who sensed that aunt Sapphy was still longing for someone to ask her to play the piano to them all, longing for as much as she dreaded the ordeal of parading a rusted talent. It was that consideration which kept the girl from making the request herself. To hear her great-aunt falter and fail, to listen to the patter of reassurance and thanks, to guess at the bed-room laughter, kindly as it would be, was unthinkable. . . .

Sometimes, even now, her friends would ask Angela Roundelay 'Aren't you frightfully bored having all the old ladies about all the time, and your nurse. Four!' but that was a question which never yet had led by stages of laughing derision to disparaging anecdote and open complaint, and the cool, clear gaze and voice with which the answer was given ('They're my *family*, you see') was final deterrent to further pressure or condolence. Nursie, of course, except that her age was pathetic in itself, needed no sheltering from Angela. She was strong in her weakness, would always fight for her own hand. Even Lady Roundelay had once said of Nursie that she reminded her of that hymn whose final line was 'I hope to die shouting the Lord will provide' (Nursie, one felt, might rely on the Lord in the last resort but would put the family through its paces first, and shouting, at that.)

It was her mother's sister, Helen Calcott, who had once said to Angela, 'I always thought it was hopelessly out of date for daughters at home to have no grievances', and then, 'You know, my dear, you ought to have been called Ruth. It's a warm, *dark* name, and you have such a singular capacity for pity'.

The family once settled, and not until they were, for his timing by now was instinctive, Musgrave brought in coffee. Lady Roundelay had for years refused to make it herself: she felt that, as with salads, she ought to have theories and phobes about its concoction in which eggshells and attar of roses figured, or the alternative alarmed and unintelligent watching of a glass container to rise up, call her blessed, and explode, but after considerable pondering she had come to the remorseful conclusion that she wasn't that sort of woman. If the coffee was good that was all she asked of it, if it was not she said so, and another possible combination of quantities, brands and containers was tried out.

From ten o'clock to ten-thirty, and seldom later, these days, the exodus from the drawing-room began.

Aunt Jessie went first to bed, whether of choice or as a general act of mortification nobody knew; gathering up her work she would pause in the doorway as a visitor might leave the lounge of an hotel with the bulk of whose inmates she was as yet imperfectly acquainted, and say 'Well — good-night, everybody'. The response was a little like that of the piano, in that some of its notes were muffled and others completely dumb. The next departures were Miss Sapphy and Miss Amy. As they would not proceed upstairs together an indefinite period of mutual, covert watchfulness set in, punctuated, if the pause became too prolonged, by sotto voce messages to their niece, who passed them to each aunt. It was aunt Amy who commonly gave way first, leaving the field to aunt Sapphy, who, pouring her marbles back into a lacquer bowl, would jauntily announce 'I think I'm for my downy'.

Sometimes Margaret accompanied her, sometimes, having stacked her notebooks and postcards into a satchel, she left with her mother. The men followed on, the time of their exit contingent upon the state of their lit pipes.

When the room was deserted, and not until then, Musgrave would come in, remove the coffee tray, plucking cups and saucers from their customary nooks and crannies, and in the summer months drawing the curtains, of which there were four pairs to be dealt with, counting the Lacquer Room window (in winter he dealt with them between courses at dinner). He would then extinguish every bracket light, standard and table lamp, run his eye computingly over the result, mentally seeking with a meditative cough (augh) for the never yet discovered forgotten duty, and tray in hands disappear to his own quarters.

In the upper storeys, the serried rows of golden windows were flicked into darkness until the moon took charge, flinging over the house its small change of silver.

Delaye slept.

CHAPTER IV

1

As WITH ALL large households, the occupations and idleness of each member of the family tend to weave themselves into a pattern as unchanging as the movements of the cast in any play. So, at Delaye, it was usually possible to forecast at any given hour the whereabouts of anyone, which, though useful when the telephone rang, was not helpful in any other respect, as the rooms being many and large and the outbuildings and grounds innumerable and larger, by the time Musgrave had located the person called up, the telephone sometimes went dead before that person's arrival. It was a great distress to Musgrave's orderly and conscientious mind, and, having summoned his family, he would sometimes stand, receiver at ear, emitting a deferent version of 'She is coming, my own, my sweet' into the instrument, reassurances which, on occasion, had to be supplemented by a shout from the flight of steps that led down to the drive, cries which were too respectful to carry far enough. His subservient yelps, punctuated by coughs of distress, made sorry hearing.

'Miss Margaret! Miss Margaret! (augh!).' Or
'The telephone, m' lady (oh dear . . . augh!).'

The occupational pattern was only blurred at times of temperamental upset or national emergency. Family illness, on the whole, left it unchanged, owing in part to a staff that was still adequate by the breadth of a hair and to the fact that it was not seriously out of the ordinary for the old ladies to take their meals in their own room. It put more work on the servants but was a breather that Evelyn Roundelay welcomed, what with Sapphy's exits from the dining-room, the resigned almost-speechlessness of Jessie, which convicted one of bad hostess-ship, and the apparent brainlessness of Amy. Sapphy, Evelyn had had explained to her in the early days of her life as mistress of Delaye, was once the clever one and the agreeable rattle of the family, and she, one must suppose, had rattled ever since out of sheer reflex action.

But Evelyn Roundelay had escaped that antagonism with which in-law relationship is almost invariably a sine qua non through the sheer age of her aunts by marriage. You can't quarrel seriously with three women all over seventy, and their adverse criticisms could be lumped in with the querulousness of their years, leaving your personal withers unwrung. Also, in houses like Delaye, escape was easy. Nor had Lady Roundel to suffer the guerrilla warfare which is the attempt at divided authority; the Roundelay women were too well drilled for that, and in the last resort, too well-bred. They had for so long now rendered unto Caesar the things that were Caesar's, which some-times, as in the present instance, created a situation on the face of it difficult enough, and which not only involved acqui-escence in the arrangements of a bride over a quarter of a century younger than themselves, but more or less dependent deference to the wishes of the master of Delaye who, as in the present case, was not even a father, but merely a nephew, the younger child of a sister. Evelyn Roundelay often wondered with real sympathy what the old ladies thought about it themselves, but the Roundelays were a reserved lot, except, perhaps, her cousin-in-law, Maxwell, whose forthright explosions were doubtless more traceable to the army than to heredity. One never enquired however indirectly or adroitly; the Roundelay atmosphere was too strong for one in that respect. Besides, two of the aunts weren't on speaking terms, a con-dition as far as Evelyn could gather, which had already endured for about fifty years, and which was accepted by the family as a matter of course, before which the cries of 'Why?' beat themselves in vain. If Evelyn's husband ever did know the reason he had forgotten it long since. 'Oh . . . some old woman's nonsense . . . you know what the aunts are.' Wherein Sir Edmund erred, for when your pres-ence is taken for granted, kindly and unjoyfully, nobody wastes time upon analysis of your psyche. The tangible result of this social whim of Miss Sapphire and Miss Amethyst was that, unwilling to speak to each other, they were also unable to let each other alone, and contact was established by the conveyance via a daughter of the house or Lady Roundelay herself of postcards to their bedrooms, a fatigue never entrusted to the servants who were officially intended to be unaware of the breach. The whole situation was evidently too late to do anything about, if, indeed, it had ever been in time. Evelyn had once tackled Maxwell upon the subject.

'Hey? Oh, those old packets. We're a rum lot, Evelyn. Too much intermarriage. It's a standing wonder to me we aren't all dotty, or born with pigs' heads.'

2

Evelyn Roundelay was nobody's fool. She had come to Delaye well primed in theory through a vast quantity of assorted reading with the life she might be called upon to lead, the tastes she might have to forego, the tediums and bores she might have to suffer, the human adjustments that she might have to make and the position she must win to through means other than the purely nominal change of surname. A young woman of spirit, she had at the same time determined not to succumb too slavishly, or be overhandled by anybody, and if she intelligently and dutifully memorized the family portraits, she, of good family herself, was neither overawed by them (not even by The Hair-Comber) nor prepared to identify herself too eagerly with their originals. To be too easily pleased was as contemptible as being too difficult.

What she had actually expected of Delaye she now, on looking back, perceived to be a blend of Pinero's *His House In Order*, in which the entire family snubbed the bride as they sat round on sofas lamenting a dear departed and crushing the governess when that obviously amoral fribble played Chopin upon the piano, with perhaps a dash of *Kenilworth*, plus a soupçon of *Cranford* and a faithful maid who cooked a gingerbread Hon for you when you lost all your money, like Ralph Nickleby, 'in one great crash'.

And Delaye was none of these things. It was, unbelievably, and in a period of time so brief that Evelyn marvelled at it still, a home. It was no doubt the space that made for content and well-being. And it was the leisure, if that was what you needed, humming as your nervous system was with the impacts of London. The country, hitherto, had been a place to which, once a year, you migrated en masse, thus missing its guises of winter and spring entirely: or a place to which various lines ran cheap day excursions for which you saved up and made an early start that turned your inside upside down for the rest of the day, and you walked about villages, mutu-

ally estranged, and your shoes felt towny and your eyes sandy, and
always at the back of your mind was the train that must be caught.

And suddenly, one day, you became a countrywoman yourself,
and were able to do the thing properly. It took months for the various implications of this to soak in. The things that space alone
could give you! For the first time, all the pet animals you wanted,
with appropriate accommodation for each: the fact that you could
have a fête on the lawn (or even a full-sized charitable circus in
a field!): that the attractive garden luxuries, the rubber swimming
pools, the swing-seats, the bulbs could all find a place if you could
find the money: the incredible fact that you could confidently give
a garden party to a number of guests that ran into three figures
instead of having to draw the line at ten and running into all of
them! The blessedness of Musgrave handing tea and of the maids
dispensing cake! Food and drink were the ruin of small parties in
rather small houses, and one had had to be a wearing mixture of
Hebe and Madame de Stael for too long . . . no wonder the art of
conversation was dead! ('What I always feel about Churchill is —
you did say two lumps?')

Evelyn had, after her first introductory party to the county, run
to her husband and gloated 'There wasn't one single contretemps!'
and he had been gloriously unimpressed. 'Why should there have
been?' And the sun had shone and the grass had smelt delicious and
Evelyn saw with a reminiscent glow of almost affectionate pleasure that what she had ordered at some unremembered period, of
cake, iced coffee and fruit drink, had quite miraculously appeared
and was being handed by anybody on earth but herself. And for the
first time in her life, save on rare country house visits, she could
do that which a certain type of novel, portraying a similar func-
tion, describes as 'drifting about the lawns', while it was now even
possible to give your tongue the run of its teeth to people without
your mind's eye on hitch or domestic betrayal. Country servants, it
seemed, didn't let you down in public: they saved up their tiresome
nothings for the proper indoor occasion, and as for Musgrave, he
shielded you at every turn, and it took a major mishap to evoke
from him a murmur, and that a low one, as, for instance, when the
Archbishop's apron came untied and hung like a portière from his
left hip as he talked to Mrs. Brouncker. That had called for a con-

spiratorial importation of Major Dunston to the scene of the wreck and a dégagé suggestion that his Grace might be interested in a quiet and closer view of The Hair-Comber, his visits to Delaye being (most unhappily) so few.

In those early years, Evelyn Roundelay, distinctly tipsy with enjoyment, had even dared the unconventionality of an autumnal garden party. Why should those with no gardens to speak of (though she hoped she didn't speak too much of hers, and if betrayed into admiration, jesuitically told herself that the garden, strictly speaking, wasn't *hers*, but only an in-law) be deprived of the heaven that was burnt umber and yellow ochre and old rose and mauve? Or of the sight of the apple-spangled trees? There were, of course, in September, no strawberries, and one couldn't exactly put bowls of nuts about on tables and have people cracking them all over the paths, with Musgrave handing individual screws of salt (what fun if one could!). But she did arrange grapes in baskets and dishes, lying on their leaves, and the weather had been perfect, with a sun warmly smouldering through the trees.

Since then, she had given several autumn parties, but, although they had obviously enjoyed themselves in a distrait kind of way at the latest party in 1938, the guests had left at five o'clock to listen in to the symptoms of the Crisis on their wireless, and or of them, who had motored from town and was absent from her party, had later rung up Delaye to tell her, rather unkindly, that we were practically on the verge of war and that the situation was a great deal more grave than the country areas had any idea of. And then, to Parliamentary cheers, Mr. Chamberlain had flown to Munich and had brought back with him not only his suddenly beloved life and his umbrella, but a pact with Germany that should bring peace for ever. And Britannia, always the perfect lady against heavy odds, believed it, and somebody sent the Chamberlain's pet cat a fish all to himself, in Downing street, and Evelyn Roundelay took it out in another party (fireworks, sandwiches and hot soup).

What the bulk of England, blinded with relief, failed to see was an instructive and momentary incident in the ensuing topical newsreels in the cinemas. And that was the brand of smile exchanged by Herr Hitler and the representative of another European Power behind the back of the signing English Prime Minister as he bent to the Treaty of Munich.

And so that blew over until the next time. But there were distinct symptoms that Britannia, though still your perfect lady, was also becoming an exasperated woman.

3

There was, of course, even now and after all these years, a slight kick in remembering that one was Lady Roundelay, a state which, in spite of family prophecy, Evelyn had not found to have added appreciably to the summer holiday bills. Knights' ladies were six a penny. She had once asked her husband, when she knew him a little better, to what cause the country was indebted to him to account for this title, and he had told her simply and seriously that he believed it was a mistake, and had probably been a misreading of the list by a secretary (such things were more common than was suspected) or that the honour was possibly meant for old Edmund Rulley who had made a fortune in 1914 by supplying army huts at retail prices to the Government and then buying them all back after the war at wholesale rates for cricket pavilions for his own staffs.

Evelyn Roundelay had married into an epoch of financial calm. It did not last very long, but even the ensuing depressions could not take from her the things that Delaye had and was and looked, though a certain erosion of security was observable about the grounds, where, owing to the reduction of gardening staff from three men to one and a boy, the large lawns never seemed to be completely mown at one blow, but were always in a semi-shaven state, for by the time Dickon had barbered one tract and been called away to even greater urgencies, the other half was three inches high, and when he'd dealt with that, the mown half wanted attention again. Economy, as usual, was no economy except on paper, and a rusted cog, as any experienced landowner could have told her, can paralyse a whole machine. When the Government wanted more cash, it was to the country it turned, draining and depleting it, oblivious, as it triumphantly hauled in the swollen net of death and succession Duties, of tithe and land-tax, that the ready money was the equivalent of living on capital, and that, historic and sentimental associations apart, the break-up of an estate is an investment sold out and gone for ever: a boomerang smiting the workless cities with rural unemployed who knew but one craft, the earth and the creatures thereof, who came in due season, via the dole, upon the urban rates, problems helpless and unhelpable.

Lady Roundelay had lived to see tears on the furrowed face of a dismissed groom when the horses had been sold to the Cloudesleys . . . she had come to realize that Delaye was a microcosm of the politics upon which she was unable to concentrate in newspapers. Disputes of The Farmers' Union, the arguments of Pig and Milk Marketing Boards, might confuse and even bore you in print, but — impossible not to understand the workings of the agricultural problem if you looked out of your own windows. And in time, she saw as well, that England was in very actual danger of the collapse of a semi-feudal system which should be a final one, the full-stop of social history. Her husband had once said that the passing of the great house and the great name all down history had in point of fact signified little: an earl Surrey fancied the home of an earl Sussex and bought it; other castles and estates had been wrested by or bestowed upon ambitious Seymour or Howard. But is a Seymour better than a Surrey? The point was that these estates passed intact, whether by arrangement or confiscation, into hands of an equal social rating, whereas to-day they were pulled down, converted into centres of so-called education, acquired by wealthy nobodies or put under the hammer, their ground sold in parcels for the horror that is the bungalow and the allotment — gone for ever, untraceable in some cases to their original ownership. It was the beginning of the end. And Sir Edmund would gaze out of the window and murmur 'Just for a handful of silver we lost him' . . . and go about his business.

But even statements of that sort cannot perpetually darken a profound content, although they lurk at the back of your mind, and Evelyn continued to enjoy her life: to revel in snow thick upon lawn and steps that the public foot could not despoil, even to build snowmen, a childish necessity never satisfied by London's exiguous and unreliable deposits of her girlhood, though she did square her conscience by making the children of neighbours, and later her own son and daughters, an excuse for the exercise of a private desire.

And when she found that holly grew plentifully in an unexplored shrubbery, her cup was full, that, and the sight of daffodils and narcissi in the avenue, fresh, brittle, rustling, and of remembering their cost in florists' shops. And there was the preposterous business of being able to have picnics on your own land, outings that involved a genuine walk and saying 'It's time we packed up and went home', and remembering that they all *were* home, in a sense. And the fun that was finding neatly-concealed debris left over from the previous picnic.

And then there was the fact that she could invite people to stay, three at once, if she wanted them, and no qualms about their getting on your nerves and sitting on your bones where escape was so easy, so unremarkable, as it never could be in small houses. At home, if anybody said that they were 'going to their room for a bit' it simply meant that they were in a temper, or that nervous endurance of the guest was becoming seriously frayed. But at Delaye you simply invited, and nothing remained but to glance at the spare rooms at the eleventh hour and go and do what pleased you best, until such time as Musgrave came to tell you that the station taxi had arrived. The chauffeur and a housemaid, or even little Sue Privett, took the luggage up the wide, shallow flights, and you came, welcoming and unheated, into the drawing-room.

The hours for the use of the bathroom were the nearest approach to any domestic upset. Otherwise, you merely said to the staff let there be light, and there was light. Even now, guests really cost little in a house already committed by sheer numbers to a certain standard of expenditure. Delaye, in Evelyn's time at any rate, had never been a Daimler and caviare place; they grew their own fruit and vegetables, though the orchard crops were deteriorating through Sir Edmund's inability to attend to the trees, and the outstanding expenses were groceries and meat. And wine. The cellars ran rather to cobwebbed bottles still laid down in their tan, and dated from the eighteenth century, and which nobody dared to broach on the grounds that their contents had probably turned to vinegar in the days of George the First, or would by now be of a priceless potency that might put the tableful of guests spectacularly under it. It was only Maxwell Dunston who went on hoping. There was a certain Frontenac . . .

CHAPTER V

1

EVELYN CALCOTT had first met Edmund Roundelay at a hunt ball in the Assembly Rooms at Norminster, an unexpected invitation, for her, to which her family, with extra cash and a little lending, dyeing and altering, had generously risen. They didn't want to lose her but they felt she ought to go. . . .

Edmund Roundelay, immensely attracted from his first sight and dance, had taken it for granted that she was of some neighbouring family, only to find that Miss Calcott was one of a devoted family, mother and two sisters, who lived in Hereford Square, S.W.7. That fact accounted, perhaps, for her finished appearance and ready repartee — she made quantities of the county family daughters look a little crumpled and sound hoydenish, their humour three seasons old at least, unassailable though he knew their pedigree to be. Her open, preliminary announcement of a total lack of ability to distinguish between a pastern and a hock should have placed her outside all reasonable pales, but contrived to please Sir Edmund. He valued honesty and moral courage. Also, he wanted an heir, regretting as much as anybody his own indirect succession, even if his conscience was satisfied that no actual son of the house could better have filled the bill than he. And Evelyn had achieved a son and two daughters (he would have preferred a rather larger margin of security), and they all loved each other as a matter of course, and liked each other, which is a higher compliment, and a rarer. They even contrived not to feel inimical about each other's endless in-laws, and the Calcott girls came quite frequently to stay at Delaye and though extremely modern in outlook (which seemed in the last resort to fine down to the question of how far it was safe for young women to go in the amorous department, and having gone there, whether it was not hopelessly outdated to regret the consequences — State Aid — more of Our Class needed — frustration — surplus women — asylums — how long? — and what about it? —) he was always willing and even pleased to house them. One really only saw them at table and in the drawing-room after dinner. . . .

Evelyn's first letters home as a young married woman were typical.

'Come soon, and whenever. There's a butler for Kathleen to adore and a rather shattering old nurse straight out of a problem play for Helen to walk round and explore. The important thing is *not to mind her*. Treat her like someone she once nursed and if she says she did don't contradict her, just drift on her stream. Saves times. You'll be all sorts of people to her including small boys in plush knickers, but never mind that. I *think* she's tumbled to my position here, though you never know, and I *may* be Princess Helena Victoria for all *I* do. But old nurses have an extra sense where "the family" is concerned and usually recognize a household acquisition! The aunts-in-law are quite maddening and disheartening when one's tired, but pathetic social tragedies of unwantedness when one's bought a new dog, or the chrysanthemums have come up to their advertisements. I'm all *over* moss, and I don't know whether I want it scraped off me and to rush to London and see plays and go to sherry parties and talk nonsense and pretend I'm enlarging my outlook when I'm only spending money and getting heartburn on cocktails, or let the moss grow thicker. Thicker, I *think*. Inertia is very catching and comforting. There's as much to do here as you want to, or as little. I may feel frustrated and thrown away and misunderstood later, but haven't begun to yet.

'Tell Kathleen she needn't be in the *least* alarmed about anything here. We aren't one scrap dressy except at garden parties and local dinners, etc., but at home we're strictly semi-demi in the evenings and there's *no* personal maid to look tossy about your outfit, and Musgrave doesn't wait in the room between courses. The house is large enough to have a quiet fit in or feel bilious if you want to without being noticed and the old ladies melt away after meals a lot and so does "cousin Max", whom I like. He's rather fun and simply hates most things and people (except Edmund and me) and says so.

'By the way, mother seems to be in a bit of a mix-up about the family tree, but if you tie a damp towel round your head and suck pieces of ice, it's quite easy. Tell her:

(1) That Mrs. (Frances) Roundelay had no son, but five daughters that she named after jewels.

(2) That of these, only two married: Emerald, who's now Mrs. Bertram Cloudesley, and Crystal (Mrs. Dunston, mother of Maxwell. A bore who lives in Kensington and who you ought to call on, I'm afraid).

(3) That Mrs. Cloudesley had two sons: the elder is Marcus and the younger Edmund who is

(4) My husband.

That Frances Roundelay's unmarried daughters are now "the old ladies" and my aunts by marriage.

'Have you got that? It's all done by mirrors.

'Oh, P.S., and by the way: we actually run to a peacock, here, but only one, and I don't think he'd stay if he knew how much less well off Edmund is than the house suggests! We're one of "the big people" round here, but Edmund isn't the Squire, though a local J.P., which I find impressive, even if I ask myself what *can* private men know about the law? I'll tell you lashings about the village, next time. I'm approaching it with a mixture of excitement and apprehension.'

CHAPTER VI

1

ON LOOKING BACK, as she frequently did, to her anticipations of life as mistress of a large house, Evelyn Roundelay had not omitted to visualize the family breakfast.

There were many possibilities. The first one composed itself of negligée, chocolate, French maid and petulance, while her husband, booted and breezy, soothed the charming tantrum and Marie tossed her head in a corner. The second derived more from Pinero and Chekhov, and was a morose gathering in which to the accompaniment of gallons of freshly-made tea, the Roundelays gave long-winded vent to their assorted aspirations and neuroses, while somebody else strode out of the room and their lives for ever and was later discovered hanged in an outhouse, upon which, general regret was expressed on the ground that he was a Roundelay of Delaye (the senior branch) and not to be confused with the Roundelays of Hereford, a scion of whom had married a woman *who was once on the stage*, a player, damned, curst, exposing herself, oh God! to the shillings of the mob. In this picture there was always a daughter who burst into wild weeping at table, until Evelyn remembered with a jerk that that daughter would be her own, and that she herself being still only engaged, quite nineteen years must elapse before the girl could begin to weep for any really dramatic cause.

A third picture was inextricably bound up with the Christmas calendar and supplement; here there were also tears, but of domestic sentiment and joy, and however hard Evelyn wrenched her tableau about with proper reference to the unsuitable months, a meet on the lawn, and burly Master and Whips quaffing in pink, and stir, and jingle, and hikes, and huntsmen having extra places laid for them at the table, and a huge, unholy consumption of mutton chops.

Or there was the Victorian picture in which one sate in an atmosphere of cap and shawl, always smiling and alert to greet the incoming breakfasters, and very attentive before the remarks of one's husband, even if his speech were an interruption: one would sit, agreeing, at the foot of the table while he dispensed large sausages from a silver entrée dish, one's eye the first to note the lowering brow, one's ear to check the ebullience of the children: one would raise a very mountain of tact and pour barrels of oil upon troubled waters: one would shield the children and (unexpectedly) lie on their behalf, and develop into a Good Woman without one abstract idea in her head, or vice or temptation to her back, and the wreaths at the cemetery would be numerous and costly, and one's identity lost for ever upon the headstone as Dearly Beloved Wife of Edmund Roundelay, Knight.

That breakfast table was of the backbone of the nation type supported by the moral corsets of Tory newspapers. These would never be offered to the women, because politics was men's province: if, however, indignation and indulgence took hands and paced towards the ladies of Delaye, the current Prime Minister would be dismissed as fool, the Chancellor of the Exchequer as that Knave, the Home Secretary as a Jack-in-Office, and the private members of Parliament A Pack of Sheep.

There would, of course, be family prayers at which her husband surlily ordered the Almighty to bless that house with His everlasting peace, before he hastily rang the bell and gave the servant hades for forgetting the marmalade; and having made a hearty breakfast, the master of the house would take his firstborn into the study and thrash him for kissing the gamekeeper's daughter, ostensibly because it was an immoral act, but actually because the *droits de seigneur* were now outdated and dangerous.

And the breakfasts at Delaye were none of these things. To begin with, there were no morning prayers. Sir Edmund found God embarrassing to speak to in public, the cook didn't like him, perversely preferring Abraham whose bosom, for her, was inferentially in a permanent state of décolletage, and Major Dunston wanted a walk before breakfast. The only desirous suppliant, Miss Jessie, was apparently never consulted upon the matter of public worship and made, presumably, her own arrangements in her bedroom. As for the newspapers, they never arrived until eleven o'clock, a.m., at which hour they were skilfully tossed over the entrance gates of the avenue by the carrier's cart from Delaye village, strict punctuality of delivery depending upon the state of the horse's knees and hoofs, which, on giving out, were replaced by the bicycles of any passing errand boys whose employers also supplied the village of l'Oex (spoken Lex) two miles on the other side of Delaye itself. Thus the news of world affairs first penetrated the house by rumour, through the man who brought the milk from a farm, by the gardener and his boy who arrived an hour later for the day's work, and by the postman who shot up and down the avenue twice a day on a motor cycle and retailed such journalistic headlines as his eye had caught to the staff, by whom they were passed up, sifted, refined and sub-edited by Musgrave, who, if questioned, would impart them to the family (Musgrave on the subject of outraged nuns in Spain was, Major Dunston often reminisced, well worth the cost of Civil war). Therefore, the absence of news threw the Roundelays upon their own resources, and except for the vagaries of the great-aunts, the breakfast table, Evelyn thought, was singularly like that of everyone else save for the inevitable rural motif running through the conversation and from which she became mistress of many and assorted bits of knowledge, interesting, tedious, odd. Nobody wept tears of sentiment or frustration, and so far no Roundelay had strode out of their lives for ever: their silences were ruminative and not the devil's brew of some psychologic ill. At eight-thirty a.m. nobody even called the Prime Minister a fool. The essential mischief of Westminster's hired bravos could wait until after dinner, indeed, it had to, where all the family were so occupied, and the more usually pressing and predominant question was apt to be 'Is anyone going into Norminster to-day?'

2

Housekeeping without a car, with a village two miles away whose shops were wholly inadequate, and on means just not sufficient to run a well-stocked store cupboard of emergency meats and delicacies, partook, Lady Roundelay was to discover, more of the nature of a game of chess than an exercise in domesticity. In a household of that size it took a long apprenticeship to compute quantities of anything where goods were, alarmingly, reckoned by the stone and feed by the peck and hundredweight.

Over this the aunts had been unhelpful. The size of a joint for twelve to fourteen people? They really couldn't say, my dear. A good, large one, no doubt. Large joints were more flavoursome, too. Mamma had always kept, of course, a very good table.

Evelyn, damning her dashing but defunct predecessor, made at first many mistakes. From a relatively small home herself, she possessed a little housekeeperly knowledge where complete ignorance would have served her better; a feature of this was a perfect comprehension of the wastefulness and greed of the average domestic and an overlooking of the fact that when you were faced with such a kitchenful as now confronted her, few joints can be made over and used up, because, so to speak, the servants had cut in first, and that which you had earmarked for cottage pie and hash was now one shocking bone and very little else.

You telephoned the Norminster butcher and the line was engaged, and that meant more expense: having got on to him, you found that he did not deliver as far out as Delaye but only to the village of that name. Two alternatives then presented themselves: one, to free the gardener's boy to go to the village and rescue the meat from the public house, or to telephone the Norminster wine-merchant to call at the butcher before he brought along Major Dunston's burgundy.

The tradesmen of the market town were immensely obliging both to Delaye and each other, and by a little dovetailing and manoeuvres it was possible to establish a sort of endless chain — respectable dope traffic — by which a commodity passed through as many as three hands before being finally delivered by fourth. As on the morning when Lady Roundelay, telephoning for a pair of ducks, was promised by the fishmonger that they should be sent to the baker who would take them to the grocer with the Delaye order of loaves and by the grocer be put into the butcher's van with the ordered joint and the stone of flour. Truly, the townsman does not know how the countryman lives. Nor would he believe it if told, and small blame to him, thought the mistress of Delaye: or, as the manager of the long-established grocery at Norminster remarked with respectful facetiousness, 'Delaye by name and delay by nature'.

Having run her daily bread to earth with as much worrying as hounds put in over their fox, Evelyn Roundelay believed for several months that she would then be free to enjoy the sight of the old city in peace. Wherein she erred, for no sooner did the rumour spread that she was spending the afternoon or the day in Norminster, than requests for the execution of small commissions came to her from all over the house. Even aunt Jessie was apt to want more wool at that tiresome little shop down a pernicketty little turning that led to the bridge under which flowed the river Lex, or to have the newsagent (who was poked away near an alley by the Guild Hall) complained to because of a forgotten delivery of the Parish Magazine, while even the Major was apt to shout a request from the ground to Evelyn as she was descending the flight of steps into the drive that he'd run right out of cobalt or rose madder and if she didn't mind very much — and he'd settle with her in the evening, and that meant a detour of the cathedral and a turning into Hogsflitch Lane where, for over a year, Evelyn had lost herself completely and handsomely, and from which she had been twice rescued by the Church of England, in the persons of a small choir-boy and the Archbishop himself, gracefully stepping the cobblestones on the way to his car that waited in Morionyard at the end of the lane to convey him back to the Palace of Normansmead two miles out of the city.

That short walk had been awful. To begin with, the Archbishop's name had escaped her entirely, and she was uncertain as to whether, having remembered it, it was customary to address him as Archbishop or as Doctor Mimms-Welwyn. Servants here had a most unfair advantage in being compelled to call him Your Grace. The ecclesiastic brick, of all others, was probably the most damning to drop; also, the Archbishop evidently didn't remember if he remembered her or not, and that ruled out any secular exchange about his flowers and his wife — if he had one. The only churchly question that Evelyn really wanted to know (What *is* The Feast Of The Assumption?) was no doubt an unfortunate choice, for once you became involved with the Virgin Mary (if it were her) it was always a nice question to determine whether the conversation was seemly or not in mixed company. And if of his kindness and benevolence he parted from Lady Roundelay with a blessing, and said *Pax Vobiscum* or something of that sort, what was the correct answer? 'Thank you very much' or 'The same to you'? She had muttered to herself, 'High cockalorum to you, sir,' and then, quite insanely, she thought, 'and it would be very High cockalorum indeed. With incense.' But the Archbishop had let her down lightly (one really must get in to the cathedral services somehow, and oftener), and raising his hat had even offered her a lift, and she had lost her head and asked him to Delaye, and, respectability having been established, his face humanized, and he had begun what promised to develop into a chat, until his secretary leant out of the car and reminded him that he was expected at the Palace at four-thirty. Lady Roundelay tumbled into the artists' requisites shop, resolved that very night, as she put it, to mug up the Archbishop with the help of her husband.

3

She was to discover, gradually, contentedly, that Morionyard actually led out of The Portcullis where the famous antique shop stood: that Keep way faced the taxi-rank and that Vintnerstave Street led in, and was a short-cut to, Stone's, the wine merchant. And it was fun finding out that Regent Street was a shameful but picturesque slum whose windows almost met and kissed and whose every beam and board had been aspired to and haggled for by wealthy touring Americans for some half a century.

Sometimes, pausing on the narrow pavements to stare like a tripper at some antick goblin carved in wood grey'd by the weather and winds of six centuries and keeping still its blurred, derisive grin above the windows of a wireless shop, Evelyn Roundelay would think 'I am on holiday, and soon there will be trunks and the train to think of, and a present to the landlady! and I shall never see all this in the winter or spring', and then is would sweep over her that Norminster was now her county town, these her shops, her tradesmen — even the Archbishop of whom one read in the newspapers was hers in the sight of God!

She was never entirely to lose the incredulous mood, would always remember its potency even after that day upon which she became an accredited daughter of the city through being greeted by the real residents, those tall, flat, neat women from surrounding estates and houses who had also 'come in' for their weekly paying of housebooks, catering and diversion. As with the residents of any other town and particularly of cathedral cities, these women were unmistakable twelve yards off; their clothes were well made and of excellent material and never looked smart, the stockings on their long, slender ankles were never silk but of good wool mixtures, their shoes useful and strapped, their hats basonic, their ages fair to middling. When lingering in pairs to talk they spoke in clear voices as of those having authority: they made Lady Roundelay feel sartorially and mentally flippant: they knew, she sensed, the difference between a Dean and a Canon (to say nothing of the Feast Of The Assumption): they could drive cars and breed dogs and shout the right noises in the hunting field. Above all, they knew and told you where to lunch and tea in Norminster.

Coverley's, for instance, had been 'going off' for some time now, and 'we always go to Silver's, in Norman Street, they do all our fêtes and wedding breakfasts and the hunt ball, and so on. It's rather expensive downstairs, but they've a very decent two-and-six luncheon *up*stairs — as a matter of fact I spoke to Silver about starting that two years ago. We've put quite a lot of work in his way at one time and another.'

This was reassuring, kindly and massive, but Evelyn insubordinately wanted to make her own discoveries, one of which was that perfect agreement with the conclusions of Lady Shelter in regard to the catering of Silver was not universally felt by the neighbours. 'Yes, oh they're quite good, but too ornate for me, and I can't *bear* that downstairs room of theirs. Gets too full from one o'clock on and then they keep you waiting for your food and you miss the two-thirty bus.' Mrs. Holland, personally, always lunched at the tea-rooms over Greensleave, the Fortnum and Mason of Norminster. 'All the girls know one', generously intimating that, this oblique advice taken, the waitresses would extend their protection to Lady Roundelay in time. 'And their cream scones are delicious.' Mrs. Galbraith, on the other hand, patronized Tatfield and Winter, the principal drapers in Norman Street, because of the view over the river from the restaurant upstairs. Evelyn mentally blackballed Tatfield and Winter for permanent use, though as a good Norminsterite she would go there once. Meanwhile, with smiles and thanks, she walked the highways and byways, eating now at The Cathedral Café, which, though terribly Ye Olde also happened to be three hundred years of age, and to possess a tiny lavatory which had been constructed out of a powder closet, and now at some raftered Inn, drawing no attention to itself as its faded sign creaked in the breeze, and where the service was entirely twentieth century in its unsociable badness, and the roast beef of the nineteenth in its luscious cuts.

In those beamed and panelled parlours Lady Roundelay sat, interested, unaccompanied, revelling in her midday dinner (which is so infinitely removed from that attenuated refinement, a luncheon), worrying a little as to what social solecism she was committing in the eyes of the county. She was, and knew it, no pioneer, no trail-blazer, and to shock the community was an undesired feat.

Back at home she would do penance, sleuthing her husband to have her latest discovery in public hospitality dispassionately translated.

'The Armourers' Inn? I didn't think any of us went to that, oh it's perfectly respectable, but I wouldn't make a *habit* of it, it mightn't be understood. It's more a man's place. The farmers feed there, and the wholesalers on market day, and so on. Yes, the ordinary is excellent. I remember the present landlord's father well when I was a boy, remember the Pater driving me in in the trap and my first taste of ale — '. He was off. 'The winter was so hard there was snow right up to the sills of the smoking-room, they had to dig a way in.'

Tenaciously she brought him back from the purlieus of reminiscence.

'And then I found the most heavenly little black place made of boards right down on the water, Edmund. I came on it quite by accident when I was more lost than usual, and it's *witchlike* with eld, and they gave me a huge plate of wonderfully fried fish — and nobody in the world's found it but me.'

'Down Linklighter Lane,' said Sir Edmund, unerringly, 'you can't go *there*, you know. It's no place for your likes. That's a favourite haunt of the bargemasters and waterside folk.'

'Have I almost been murdered?'

'Lord, no. But it's not fair on the usual customers. You'd either hear a lot of language you never dreamed existed, or these fellows be so stunned by the sight of a lady in their midst they'd go off their food. As a matter of fact that little place — no, it's got no official name, it's known as Punshions — did have a shocking bad reputation in the eighteenth and early nineteenth century when the women of the town used it. If you'd looked on the wall by the ingle you'd have seen a bit of a sailor's skin nailed there.'

'How *lovely.*'

'Looks like a thin piece of black wood, by now. Yes . . . many a good fellow has lost his all, at Punshions . . . *and* woken up to find himself in the next world. You stick to Silver's and Greens-leave.' And she had, within reason, finding an amusement in herd movement, by which she would pass the Squire's wife paying the check as she herself entered, in catching sight of Mrs. Holland vanishing into Greensleave's, her person hung with parcels, punctually at one o'clock: in finding at Silver's on the table she had chosen a handkerchief with Mrs. Brouncker's initials on it, and inspecting the plates to guess what that lady had had for luncheon, in being told at shops that she had just missed Lady Shelter. . . .

It was, so to speak, the same only more so at Christmas. For then (why was one so prone to enchantment at trifles?) the afternoon callers, braving the dusk in bootees or arriving by private car, would, once in each other's lit and warm drawing-rooms, pass on the rumour of where to get the best cards and which shop specialized in what seasonable luxury, and when and how to order, as though, thought Evelyn happily, we were a fort in a siege or a town in a famine, handing on the essential tip, hint . . . and going into Norminster to confirm information and finding it all true, even down to the Christmas cards (Lady Shelter had admired those hunting-field studies very much, your ladyship), and even discovering a card that Mrs. Brouncker had described, still unsold in the rack . . . and being moved, also, to leave one imprint upon the shop by placing another card slightly crooked and finding it still askew when one next came in. . . .

'It's too much,' thought Evelyn, 'either I'm not quite right in the head for enjoying it all so or it can't last.' That was, perhaps, on the morning she had discovered that Norminster if common with so many other provincial cities possessed its own exclusive delicacy, inimitable (though efforts were made all over the country). Pork and veal sausages that were known as Puddings and which weighed anything you like from four pounds to four ounces; smooth, creamy, of a savour indescribable, they knew not the word gristle, nor were their inn'ards made repellent by cubes of fat. They were the making of any Christmas hamper, but extra care must be taken as to the exact calculation of despatch for when a Norminster Pudding goes bad it does it grandly, imperially, as befits a king among meats.

Or perhaps one might date the childish gusto of Lady Roundelay from that afternoon when she broke down a local tradition and smashed a goddess upon the cobblestones.

Everyone in Norminster knows Dolly's. It is not, as the name suggests, a nineteenth century disorderly house, but a cake shop and confectioner, which sells boxes of toffee with an etching of the cathedral upon the lids, thus combining high living with higher thought. Dolly's cakes are never less than fourpence each, and when you have eaten one you have had breakfast, dinner and tea for they are jammed, marzipaned, whipped-creamy and some times fenced about with thin squares of plain chocolate, the whole fortification held together by a silken ribbon. Should you ask for 'something plainer' you are brought a sullen and opulent slab studded with cherries, chopped almonds, sultanas and angelica. But its top is not iced. Honour is vindicated, and the strict letter of your demand fulfilled.

Before the name of Dolly even the most sensible women buckle; cakes of an equal elaborateness could be bought elsewhere, there was no caterer in the city whose cups of tea cost as much, Greensleave's scones were definitely nicer, Tatfield and Winter's coffee was indisputably finer to any discriminating mind, yet their combined efforts availed them little. They were not Dolly. To buy your children's birthday cake at Dolly's put you and your party into the right category at once; to 'run to' her sweets (Dolly was a wealthy and rotund little man who was a member of the Town Council) was to admit both to extravagance and the best that money could buy. For such a purchase you laughingly apologized by implication to your friends to put them at their financial ease, or if that wasn't the idea even God will never know what was.

Evelyn, bemused in advance, found herself tacitly concurring about Dolly's to the county, also found that she had never yet darkened its pale-green doors. 'I must not', she told herself, 'be disparaging through contrariness, nor will I admire of hypnotism.' She ate the cakes and found them mawkish: she drank the tea and even the coffee (that ultimate test of an equitable mind) and found the one about the same as everybody else's and the other open to a strong suspicion of essence, though the dollop of cream on the top put one slightly off the scent. Finally, she took home those sweets and fondants in their signature sacs of pale green with a Dutch doll depicted upon every one, and found them *fade* and tallowy. She had won in fair fight. Dolly's was a rumour and a delusion. It would endure, possibly as a landmark, certainly as a tradition in the ancient city from one generation to another until some Cromwell of the future sacked it and all its works; bogusly picturesque (it dated from 1910), battening on cash and reputation to the end, it would impose and intimidate.

And even that was fun.

CHAPTER VII

1

THE BUSINESS of making friends had offered another territory for the exploration, the serene inquisitiveness, of Evelyn Roundelay. It was a question, looked back upon in after years, which should have bulked much larger and more formidably to any young married woman than in point of fact it ever had, involving as it did the uprooting from a London to a country home with the sudden bestowal upon herself of the bigger rôle of chatelaine, the translation from carefree ingénue to leading lady.

Here, again, her mixed reading acted at once as help and hindrance, steering her clear on the one hand of those gaffes to which a new environment alone can commit the latest bride, but rendering her too prone, on the other, to postulate types rather than to allow for a normal humanity. By this method, the Vicar even before introductions, was an eternal Vivian Foster who intoned 'Yerse, I think so!': the curate was bespectacled, consumed Bath buns and was the dart-board at which all the local spinsters (frustrated) shot their knitting-needles. She saw him clearly before ever she saw him at all, mincing with mild, foolish benevolence along the road to Delaye, round his attenuated neck a loving muffler, mittens upon his clasped hands, his feet shod to all eternity in the carpet slippers of the faithful, their uppers sprawled with purple heartsease. Alternatively, he was the muscular Christian of the manly damn who clapped choir-boys upon the back (though never chucked them under the chin, Delaye, somehow, wasn't that kind of village), and for them got up boxing-matches in face of much opposition to keep the lads off the village wenches. One clinch against another . . . and both Vicar and curate were, interestingly and insubordinately, none of her inventions.

The Vicar was very seldom seen at all except in the pulpit, and socially was doomed to be the kind of conventional bore that happens to so many of the laity: his sermons were impeccably respectable and contained, no matter upon what promising text he ostensibly hung his discourse, the sole idea of being good and keeping in that condition, like a crate of greengages.

The curate, Basil Winchcombe, on the other hand, had, and looked it, begun his career upon the stage, first as a marked-out member of the O.U.D.S. and later (the right manager being in front at the time of his pleasant reading of Brutus) upon the stages of endless Number One provincial theatres and one or two West-end ones as well. His sermons were sincere and sensible, but among the villagers they were felt to be so like a person talking to you that you didn't feel you'd got your spiritual money's worth since you could get his conversation and advice any day in your own cottage without an offertory bag in sight.

It was true that with all his sincerity, Basil Winchcombe was still unable to keep from bringing the footlights up to the altar rails, and his discourses were invariably prone to sudden turns of theatrical phrasing, as on the occasion when he said that, in doubt, it was always safe to take your cue from God, that every time you resisted a mean temptation you gave Satan the bird, that Christ stood on the Prompt Side of God the Father, and that the policy of Herod was a complete flop. Of these locutionary lapses he was, when chaffed by Evelyn Roundelay who liked him immensely, profoundly ashamed. 'It's awful. But you wouldn't believe how the stage gets into one's bones.'

'You'll be urging them next to queue up for Communion.'

'Well, if you get down to bed-rock, does it matter how one gets 'em in? I'd stage a bottle-party if I could make them get together — '

'Bribery — '

'*No*. What I mean is that they ought to see *beyond* manners and idiosyncrasies.'

Evelyn was sure of her ground. 'That's no use in a village. I know what you mean, but the people here aren't ready for it. The only drama they understand is hell fire and Elmer Gantryism, because it's both pictorial and unreal. That's why the Chapel's much fuller, in most villages, that and the Socials and buns. It isn't experimental, like the Church of England. It hands out an unvarying line of goods that they know where they are with. Take Delaye. Our church havers. Here's the Vicar being perfectly nice and null about Ahab's mother-in-law and at the other end of the scale yourself, telling them that Christ isn't a long-hair'd abstraction in a white bath-robe but a decent idea, the idea of not sanding sugar and seducing servant girls

out of boredom. Of course you're right, and you're between the devil
of that meaningless somnolence that is induced by Ahab's mother-
in-law and the deep sea of beginning to make them think and realize. All you can hope to do with the average villager is to make him
uneasy, restless, like wounds itching when they're healing.'

'And my lot are in the scratching stage? I know . . .'

'If that! You see, Mr. Winchcombe, the poor wretches *are* rather
bedevilled. My husband tells me that the Vicar's predecessor was
fearfully Low church, then came our Vicar, and he's middling, and
next time we may get someone who wants confession and banners.
They're all within the law in being Anglican, but they're unsettling,
and haven't even denunciation and hell fire to fall back on, like the
Nonconformists. The Chapel has stripped itself of all the trimmings
and is down to bedrock, and bedrock is at least something to sit on.'

'Oh yes. But you've forgotten the chief snag, which is that
broadly speaking neither Chapel people nor their ministers are ever
gentlefolk. This gives 'em an enormous advantage at once because,
mentally, both preacher and congregation are *en pays de connais-
sance*: they talk the same language. Whereas in our church broadly
speaking we're all gentlemen, therefore it is taken for granted by
our flock, especially in rural communities, that we shall never understand each other at all, and for what success we have we must
fall back upon personal attributes, or social nous. I can dig a ditch
with anyone, but it would never occur to the Delayeites to hand me
a spade because they'd either assume I'd make a botch of it or that
I was patronizing 'em because my father went to a university. You
know as well as I do that we've been the target of the legitimate and
vaudeville stage for a century, and you may also have noticed that it
is only the Anglican parsons who are held up to ridicule, never the
Chapel minister or even the Roman padre — '

'It's sickening — '

'You don't get my point, which is that for centuries we dogsbod-
ies of curates have probably asked for it and deserved it, and we've
deserved it because of this never-mentioned class question and our
consciousness of the resultant difficulty of approach to our congre-
gations. Of *course* it makes us nervous and fatuous or ultra-brawny
and backslapping. But it's a point that has never been aired because

officially we're all equals, and in any case it's a very difficult subject to talk about. Oh well . . . exit curate L.U.E. through gap in teeth.'

'I hope — we all do — that you're not going to let it get you down, and leave us?'

'Lord, no! I came into the church with my eyes open — it's quite possible to combine having no illusions with enthusiasm, and that's why I hope, one day, to feel I've really done some tangible good, because I shan't be sapped and daunted and driven out by personal grief, and disappointment. And because I came into the business expecting everything I found, I get a lot of interest and fun out of it without at the same time ceasing to know that even the most apparently hopeless cases are in very truth lost sheep, who only need a good dispassionate crack over the rump to put 'em on the right track again. Most clergymen approach their parishioners from the point of view that they're already angels who ought to respect the fact, then the angels go all old Adam on them and the holy man in direct ratio to his inherent holiness is dismayed and confused. Now I take the line that my lot are all devils and acting as such — doing their stuff, true to type, and then I'm free to hunt for reasons that make 'em play up, and to see the good in 'em sticking out in the rummest places. But I tell you, there's one thing that narks me. Our respected Vicar doesn't like it when I have a drink with the men in our pub. You see the idea? It's undesirable because I'm of the ruling class, someone who mayn't touch their beer- and-darts life lest he 'lose influence'. I'm all for caste and class distinc-tions (and even if I weren't, they'll persist), but there's something wrong in that particular snob-barrier. And the devil of it is that I'm so spinelessly fair-minded that I absolutely see his point without being absolutely convinced.'

'Yes, but don't you see, too, that the whole point of the church is that its congregation may have something or someone to whom to look up? Who's valuable because he *doesn't* appear for beer and darts — '

'But they *don't* look up to me, except once a week! From Mon-day to Saturday I'm a sort of hermaphrodite, neither wholly male nor completely clerical . . . what we've got to realize and allow for is that the Church of England to-day is more or less a hangover: exist-ing on its medieval hump, dreaming of the days when it had power and really ruled by force and superstition. But all we can hope to do with it now is to divert its vanished glories into social channels, questions of giving one's worldly experience to the ignorant, of becoming a magnified soup kitchen for the relief of physical suffering, and seeing wherever possible that the community is harmlessly entertained and brought together. And all that could be done by the local Squire, if he were the right man.'

Winchcombe wheeled upon Evelyn. 'All humbugging apart, do *you* feel any nearer God when you're actually in church?'

'No, not particularly, but that isn't to say that other people don't. I find that God is an elusive person and not always on call while we sit in neat rows waiting for him to arrive. Most times when I'm in church I feel nothing at all, and plan out lunches and dinners — *you* know, and then when I get back to Delaye, he's there in the hall, or in the drawing-room, which I adore. It's so full of atmosphere.'

Basil Winchcombe nodded. 'I know. I can see him liking Delaye with its space and mannerly air. Why not, if we do?. . .'

'It's funny you should say that about the drawing-room, because I remember that once, when Sir Edmund showed me the whole house for the first time, I got a very vivid sensation of Christ. It wasn't in the hall, though, or the drawing-room, but it was a very real thing, to me. I remember when your husband opened the door of that room and I stood inside looking about me that I was suddenly *steeped* in the conviction that I was in the presence of some high and hidden beauty. It was horribly sad as well . . . like a remembrance of the crucifixion. But there was some peace there which had come at the eleventh hour — I'm explaining badly, but there it was. Unmistakable.'

'Which room?'

'On one of the top storeys. It's the bedroom that has that inscription on a window-pane. "Heryn I dye. Thomas Picocke".'

2

They had looked at each other without embarrassments. Evelyn said, 'That's strange, your feeling that way about the room. My younger daughter, Angela, can't bear it. Luckily nothing ever takes her there, but she was like that from the very first. I once took her up there when she was only about six; I wanted all the children to know and love the place as I do and not to feel that "the servants' quarters" were something the family never saw or alluded to, and Angela began to whimper at once and ran out of the room. I thought it was just because it was a strange place to her, and I tried her again with the room, later. But it was no good. It wasn't just caprice. She hated it: got a shivering fit and turned cold all over.

'Mothers, you know, are supposed to be a mass of intuitions about their offspring, but they aren't. Perception doesn't automatically follow on maternity, though it makes a pretty story that it does.'

'Then — have you any theory about Angela and the room?'

'Not one in the world. She's a nervous little creature and very highly-strung.'

'And your other daughter, Miss Margaret?'

Evelyn Roundelay smiled as she shook her head. 'Margaret's a great dear, but more, as they say, on the Girl Guide side.'

3

In regard to her friendships with the laity, it was many months before they emerged as personalities; prior to such knowledge, they had stood to Evelyn Roundelay, confused by their numbers, for snatched remembrances and associations. Thus, for weeks, Mrs. Holland was merely a hot lawn, ices that called themselves peche Melba but were frozen custard and tinned apricots, flatfaced parlourmaid whose name was Annie, a lobby full of chipped croquet mallets, and a dinner from which Maxwell Dunston had returned cursing and apostrophizing as Sauce Hollandaise.

Lady Shelter, at first, had been memorable on account of the long drive with private lamp-posts which led to her house, and which for a considerable time caused Evelyn to imagine garlanded festivities and much rich entertainment of the *Hollyleaves* type. Closer acquaintance with the Shelters had, however, revealed each lamp-post as a species of *ignis fatuus* leading to assemblies which, no matter how the hostess strove, everlastingly contrived to be Institutional and to make the guests subconsciously feel like an annual treat to Fallen Women.

Cautiously, Evelyn had early attempted to sound local opinion upon these gatherings, believing, at first, that as one's eye will fail to focus during a liver attack, so the impression that the Shelter hospitality made upon herself could not be the true one, and as with the passing of time the parties remained inexorably public, Evelyn privately called them The Home Away From Home. About them her neighbours were unilluminating. The Shelters were wealthy and kind and their parties were always like that.

It was with her children and Basil Winchcombe that Evelyn found her safety-valve, carefully at first, with many a firm allusion to the Shelters' kindness, and then by giggling stages to delighted exchange, comment, mutual interruptions and the room ringing with supplementary shouts and exhumations of some forgotten frightfulness.

'How does she *do* it?' Evelyn herself would clamour. 'There's every apparent advantage, large house, money, servants, h. and c. laid on, yet it's all stone dead.'

'It is beyond doubt,' contributed Mr. Winchcombe, 'that some hostesses blast everything they touch.'

'That's a hot one,' approved Evelyn's son, 'but it's my turn now. Lady Shelter once gave the men boxes of cigarettes at a New Year party. They helped themselves to their boxes from a salver at the door as they went out. I don't expect you to believe me.'

The curate's eyes glazed. 'Was that before my time?' he asked reverently, and lay back in a coma of pleasure.

'May I tell you a better one than that?' Margaret placidly suggested. 'Once she gave a mixed party — all ages, you know — and I was invited, and while everyone was standing about waiting for the fun not to begin, she came up to me and some of my friends and said "We'll just get you young people amused and then we can make a start".'

'Wonderful . . . wonderful,' murmured Winchcombe, his eyes still closed.

Stacey Roundelay beat the air. 'And that kids' party! Presents for all — d'you remember, Margaret? "Dolls for the girls, soldiers for the boys, dolls for the girls, soldiers for the boys".'

'And yet she has no vice in her: it's all kindly meant, and not a cross word,' regretted Lady Roundelay. It was true. If you were a guest of Lady Shelter it was also a certainty that you would never sit next to the congenial person; it was rumoured that Lady Shelter kept a typewritten list pinned up in an inconspicuous place upon which was catalogued the programme of amusements, gift bestowal and games, together with the estimated time that each item would consume . . . So much for Buckingham . . . When you received your present it was never the thing you wanted; no present was cheap, yet by a stroke of genius it was seldom appropriate and always impersonal. About the Shelter gifts their recipients were left with the eternal conviction that they had been quite expensively bought *en masse* and then labelled at random from the guest-list. "The Shelter luck still holds", the Roundelays would exclaim on returning from one of her parties, as they laid upon the hall table of Delaye a pair of alabaster book-ends, brass door-knockers from Rye and two-foot boxes of sweets with a coloured photograph of a rose-garden upon the lid and a one-layer contents in which distressingly was featured fruit jellies, fondants and coconut squares. If Lady Shelter included an entertainer, she was apt to engage him three years running, a system by which, were he a conjuror, the Roundelays laid bets on the present number of offspring of the bright-eye'd, kicking rabbit gently removed from the performer's top-hat, and were it — oh heavy day! — a magic lantern show, the sequence of slides, including Rochester cathedral both by night and day, could in time be audibly forecast, if you were rude enough.

'You'd think a children's fancy dress party was fool-proof,' almost shouted Evelyn Roundelay, 'but Lady Shelter can over-come even that.' Winchcombe looked imploring and she put him out of his pain, holding up one hand and ticking off with the index finger of the other. 'Always overcrowded, so that the imaginative dresses aren't seen, and a pierrot or a Santa Claus gets the prize because the judges, God mend us all, are quite clear about that; a marshalling of the children for a treasure hunt, with all the presents hidden so obviously that you can see them without moving (children hate that. They like using their intelligence), and at the end, the poor toads are lined up and set to fishing for muslin bags of sweets with a rod and a hook. If they don't circulate quick enough, the butler stoops down and fastens the bag on to the hook. And children hate that, too. Angela once deliberately let her bag fall off three times, but they were ready for her! They merely took the rod out of her hand and gave her the bag.'

And, just in the way that Lady Shelter had materialized from a private lamp-post to the detailed status of family joke, so did the other residents take on personality, and that which had been but a plated stocking, a lean ankle and a basonic hat coalesced for instance into Mrs. Galbraith, who, Lady Roundelay was to discover, was hard up, bred Persian cats with large, disappointed faces and chilling manners, and owned a small house so nearly on the roadside at the Norminster end of Delaye village that when she returned by motor bus hung with parcels of household necessities and condition powders she practically leaped into her own drawing-room window from the conveyance. In summer, by pressing your nose against the omnibus, it was possible to note the progress of Mrs. Galbraith's reading matter from the circulating library in Norminster, and to wonder what had happened to that jumper she was knitting last Friday, it being no longer on the table by the verandah. On encountering Mrs. Galbraith at garden and dinner parties or sales of work and fêtes you pictured her, in time, picking her way to the gatherings over and round a roomful of detentive cats, resentful of her pleasuring. When long evening dresses came in once more the hems of her gowns were apt to appear spattered with faint pansy markings of their paws and the urgencies of her dumb friends' league could be gauged according to the height to which the damage extended: worn places upon the hip usually meant that Galbraith Bluebell had smelt his dinner, or that Champion Milk of Magnesia wanted to be let out very badly indeed. Marks or little unravellings at or below the knee could signify nothing more pressing than affection.

CHAPTER VIII

1

THERE ARE in that part of Normanshire of which the city of Norminster is a landmark, many subsidiary hamlets, some of which are connected as are Bramber and Beeding, in Sussex, with the larger village of Delaye by nothing more than footpaths. Solitary sign-posts bear those names whose original meaning lies back in the mists of time and of which such appellations as Old Maid's Pan, Half-penny Toll, and King Gibbet are not unfair exaggerations.

To village life, Evelyn Roundelay had come, as she had written to her sisters, with a mixture of excitement and apprehension. She had hopefully asked her new cousin, Maxwell Dunston, if there were a village idiot, to which that pessimist responded that in all small communities there was always a village idiot, and that sometimes it was the village idiot and sometimes the Vicar.

Delaye village was in point of fact like many other communities in England at the present time, in being in a rather dreadful period of transition, by which the curtsy at the lodge gates was not wholly eliminated, yet the gaitered gaffer in his cottage could listen in to a terrific and indigestible combination of chamber music and highly subversive speeches from Moscow. Respect to the known families and the big houses which employed their sons and daughters still gappily prevailed, but the charm of rural life was mongrelized, and the future of the village of Delaye probably hung upon the relative density of intelligence of the present population, and fined down to the question of whether the village youth were going to choose to be offended at the lack of tone inherent in forking hay, or whether, unwittingly, they were going to give up all hope of making thirty-five shillings a week by esteeming themselves to be mute inglorious but potential members of The Léner Quartette, or (far better) one of The Six Silver Saxophone Kollege Kids. A little knowledge had as ever, proved quite fatal, and the wireless, with the present generation, had done its work well by at once failing to expand their minds and successfully implanting a general, vague discontent that impaired their efficiency in the work they best understood.

And the B.B.C., tapping a quaint and bumpkin source in its search for novel features, worked havoc the extent of which no man can foresee before putting back all its usual features on the air. Even the Postmistress at Delaye had not been safe from Broadcasting House, and with a prepared sheet of typewritten cues and answers in her shaking hand, revealed in a chirp of refined terror to the citizens of London, and with a solicitous midwife in attendance in the shape of a handsome young announcer: 'Yes, it is true, I am the Postmistress, though you would not think it looks very much like one. Our post-office is housed in a cottage.

('And, do you have much trade, Miss Tybonnet? What about telegrams, now?')

Cue: *Telegrams now.* 'Well . . . we *do* have wires, and a great stir they *make* in our village, but they are always punctually delivered however long the distance.'

('Perhaps you will explain how?')

'Oh, they are sent up on bicycles; we keep one boy for urgent messages, and when he is in school there is usually *some* body willing to oblige.'

('So you have a boy on a bicycle . . . that sounds very exciting. Suppose we ask him to speak to us himself! . . . now, what's *your* name?') *Faint chirrup.* 'Martin Sheppherd.' ('Well, come along, Martin.')

Martin: (*in an obedient and rapid drone*) 'It's my jawb out've schule to take tallygrams hither and thither. Often I haster cycled a matter've tan miles.'

('Ten miles? That's a big distance in all weathers, Martin. How do you get on?')

'Well . . . I haster get off and lift cycle over stiles, sometime, and ar've got perdew come snow lies thick an' the evenings drawin' in.'

('Thanks very much, Martin. That's been very interesting. Now I'm going to ask Miss Tybonnet to come back to the microphone and tell us about that word "perdew"'). And, to the interpolated ministrations of the genial midwife, carefully extra-polite before the preposterous nature of her surname, Miss Tybonnet explained the word perdew, which was, it appeared, a local relic of Norman-French origin for 'lost', upon which, delivered of her contents by the midwife, Miss Tybonnet was thanked, faded out, and the hamlet of Rohan put upon the map.

But the principal public house at Delaye had been the leading attraction. Here, it was felt by the B.B.C., was if not the heart, at least the stomach of rural England: here, if there were any still extant, were Hey Nonnies and Rumbledumdays and those choruses prefixed traditionally by 'With a' and 'Oh, it's' and 'Oi be'. The tendency of townsmen to regard the provinces and Shires of England as exclusively Somerset was, apparently, ineradicable, and knowing but one exception, Lancashire, which had leapt into being with the rise of Gracie Fields.

The broadcast from The Coach and Horses, Delaye, was a peak feature and had involved but one rehearsal, during which, from his improvised enclosure in the jug and bottle department, the controller of sound had unwittingly recorded smacking lips which, had the actual broadcast been started, would have penetrated like thunderclaps to the Hebrides, and that caused his own hasty emergence.

'Oliver! What *are* we doing?'

'These gentlemen,' Oliver with careful respect for the yokels indicated a handful of villagers at once grinning, bashful and mentally vitriolic, 'are all enjoying a pint of the best.'

'Oh. It *sounded* like Niagara.' The young man retired, only to put his head once again round the door. 'Or the Victoria Falls. I've heard they're larger.'

The yokels had been goodnatured but disconcerting, and when asked by Oliver to give him a favourite chorus 'that the towns might hear what they were singing in the country', burst obligingly into a ragged but insuperably recognizable roar of 'Sally' and 'The Miner's Dream of Home', which Oliver, still genial, was unable to pass, Delaye not being a mining district but more, as he put it, on the agricultural side.

2

It was at Rohan, that minute village against which civilization and what gets called progress still beat themselves in vain, that Oliver and his colleagues found something to work with and justify some six gallons of petrol. For, called to the microphone, the farrier, with the minimum of fuss, opened his mouth and sang. . . .

It is an unhappy fact that the recording on paper of any song conveys next to nothing of its quality: in print, the ballad, even be it by Schubert himself, becomes flat, pedestrian, stripped of the haunting transfiguration of its music, whether florid, or as in this case, of the purity and simplicity of the winding stream, moving by many a calm loop, by sudden roulade of water and small cascade to its appointed goal.

And helped by nothing but a fiddler, who was also the cow-herd, they sang and played together in an accord which was as instinctive as it was untrained.

> In spring and in spring
> When weather falls warm
> The coney in burrow
> Shall come to no harm.
>
> The fox in his lair,
> The hare in his form,
> The rook in the furrow
> Shall come to no harm.
>
> For in spring and in spring
> No crossbow of yeoman,
> No arrow from bowman
> Doth fright or alarm:
>
> And the fox in his lair,
> The rook in the furrow
> The coney in burrow
> Shall come to no harm.
>
> For in spring and in spring
> The Great Ones forswear us
> Our living do spare us
> And let us to calm;
>
> And the Small Ones in lair,
> And the Small Ones in burrow
> And the Small Ones in furrow
> Shall come to no harm.

It was when Oliver replaced the performers at the microphone and had reached that peroration, ' — and I'm sure we all thank Mr. Ronsell and Mr. Norman very much indeed for letting us hear such a — a delightful and typical song of the old country-side — ', that, happening to glance round, he suddenly found that all the villagers, noiselessly and as though by preconcerted signal, had got up and left.

Shy, probably. But O.K. for sound.

3

In a semi-detached villa at Pinner a wife was saying with the maximum of resentment and ungracious embarrassment at her own susceptibility to a tune, 'Life's too short to keep up this row, Arthur. I'm sorry if you are'.

In a house in Great Portland Street a well-known conductor hurried from his pedestal radio, clashed back the lid of his Bechstein, and sat, humming, reconstructing chords and transcribing until six o'clock in the morning. He played through the manuscript sheets for half an hour more, would get the actual words later, send his secretary to do the rounds of the music publishers, and if that failed, to rummaging in the British Museum, and if *that* was no go pack him off straight to Rohan. Or the B.B.C. might have a copy?

But at six-thirty, a.m., he regretfully tore up his night's output. 'It's no use. I'm not a countryman and that sort of music is only safe in the hands of peasants. I've made the usual mistake: over-orchestrated it, made it sophisticated and cityfied and so confoundedly pretty that it'll go the way of the Londonderry Air. All *I'm* fit for is to conduct Act Three of *Aïda*.'

In a bed-sitting-room in Hamburg an elderly teacher of the violin with a tragic amount of time on his hands these days walked the narrow limits of his shelter playing the Rohan melody. The landlord — incredibly kind to one who could no longer be meticulous about rent — had allowed Hans Schaeffer to come in and listen to his wireless on the previous night.

In spring and in spring

softly played Herr Schaeffer. And now he would never see England at all, except in his mind, nor the people he felt so drawn to, and the heaven-kind atmosphere of a country with a will to peace . . . Even in that medieval song the sportsmanship of the English was as alive to-day, giving to the humblest victim of rifle and snare a close-time from treachery and destruction that the dear Fatherland had some-how abandoned even towards humanity.

And let us to calm . . .

No, he'd got that wrong. It was in that phrase that, unlike the preceding verses, the penultimate word took an insolent turn from the sharp to the natural, a typical twist of Early English music . . . that, too, was probably like the English themselves, whose charac-ters he sensed; if they wanted a minor or a major or a natural they took it, daringly, illegitimately, but with the minimum of uproar and threat, and great, unconscious effectiveness . . . he could see those little bouncing hares, the glossy rook pecking his diet in a richly upturned furrow under a shrill blue sky.

Too late, now. It wasn't only the fare that must be hoarded, pfennig by pfennig, but this business of passports and permits.

No. You didn't leave your country on debts and promises. The little foxes. He had heard that they were red, and stank, poor babes, so that the dogs could trail them the easier.

But he would write to his only English acquaintances: two pupils he had once had, of a colossal intelligence but no musical feeling at all. Their touch! Oh God, Thou Almighty one! Of all in-struments, the violin (oh word most lovely in itself, shapely and slender) demanded the best. He would write at once, remembering himself and expressing his delight in the village song, his unreason-able nostalgia for a land he had never seen.

It was about fifteen months later that the Gestapo arrested Hans Schaeffer on the ground of his pro-English sympathies. Only they called them 'Anti-Nazi'.

When they had shot him, they ransacked his room for what it might yield of plunder, to find that his pro-English sympathies, his violin and a picture-postcard of some unknown hamlet were about the sum of his possessions.

CHAPTER IX

1

EVELYN ROUNDELAY had found that of all the villages within walking or bicycling distance Rohan was her ewe lamb.

At first, armed with any excuse that occurred to her, and later as the inhabitants came to know her, with nothing but herself and her shy and open enjoyment of their company, she seldom let a week go by without a glimpse of it.

Rohan's population was one hundred and ninety-five souls, and dwindling every year. The majority of the villagers were, like Nursie, of an incredible age, and there was a sprinkling of the middle-aged of a generation too set in its ways to desire change or advancement to the towns, and of these the farrier and cowman were typical examples. Their hamlet, Lady Roundelay was to discover, they called Roon, just as she was to find that it took years of practice to understand their speech which is a mixture of the Shire dialect and of anglicized Norman-French.

She met it first while admiring a border of love-in-a-mist at the blacksmith's, and he had agreed, saying 'It is a gentle flower'. Charmed with the adjective she brought it back to Delaye, and Edmund Roundelay had explained that 'gentle' was no graceful whimsy of tribute but a bastard version *of gentille*, which charmed her the more. If a thing pleased the people of Rohan they said they were 'well content': if alluding to their homes, they said 'my toat', which (her husband again translating) signified *toit,* the roof-tree. A favourite expression of surprise was 'Cordew!' and the womenfolk referred to their husbands as 'the mary'. Women suspected of too great a liking for the tankard were 'sullards', local wits were 'spiritual' (confusing as an adjective when allied to a broadly comic song), those known to be gossips were 'onditts' whereas a 'gossip' could also signify a godmother.

King George the Sixth was quite simply referred to as 'Leroy', which sounded over-familiar until you got used to it, and at first hearing ('We wish Leroy would visit Roon') had betrayed Lady Roundelay into the politely vague rejoinder 'Is he a relation of yours? I shall look forward to meeting him'.

She had returned discouraged and fuming to her husband. 'I believe they do it on purpose!' Sir Edmund chuckled. 'Of course they do. You wouldn't want them to turn it on like a tap for you as if you were a tripper. Rohan is one of those villages (there's at least one more in England which says 'by my halidom' to this day) which has never changed. It's a fragment of arrested history, and', here he gave his wife a faint grin, 'it *has* come to my ears that you are spoken of as "a very beldam".'

His wife's instinctive shout of protest was quenched as she considered. 'Oh, I see.'

'Exactly. A pretty lady and a very handsome tribute, believe me.'

'But . . . look here . . . what about sullards and children being petty, and men being mary —oh! I *see. Mari*. But the other things?'

'Sullard: a sot, from *soularde*; actually it's a bit of argot that may have been added to their vocabulary a century or so later. Petty is of course a reference to the smallest of the family in height.'

'Ohh . . . and is an "onditt" and *on dit?*'

'You're coming along nicely. Rohan itself derives not only from Normandy but from Brittany and owes its existence to your ancestor-by-marriage and his band of retainers.'

'Cordew!' exclaimed the latest Lady Rohan de l'Oeux. She had got Rohan quite badly on the brain.

2

She found that it was not really much good to bring presents to favourites, such as the grandmother of her kitchenmaid, Sue Privett, for, whatever she took over to the village, one calendar week would elapse, and then to the great door of the back kitchen of Delaye a Rohan man would present himself, doffing cap and laying at the feet (never giving into the hands) of whomsoever opened the door to him a bunch of flowers, a brace of pheasants in their plumage, a porter cake of a plummy richness indescribable into which half a bottle of stout had been stirred, 'for the dame of Delaye'. But, Lady Roundelay thought, it was perhaps to the Squire that the greatest plum fell: for the village of Rohan paid unto him annually Petty Serjeantry in the form of one yellow rosebud and a billet of applewood 'of not less than one eighth of an elle'.

The baker, who knew no book-keeping, kept instead a great wooden bowl of sticks, one for each household, and notched their accounts with a knife, as is done in some villages of Brittany to this day.

Evelyn had discovered long before the B.B.C. did that the farrier had a voice. But she gave him two years before she openly asked him to sing to her. Just while he worked. And although his innate courtesy ruled out such loose unmannerliness before Lady Roundelay, it was from him that she first heard the Rohan melody, 'Roy Stephen his tree', 'Fat Nut-filled Squirrell' and that artless trifle which begins:

> Hart on thy pointed feet
> The beechmast tapping
> In thy echapping
> Hasten for life is sweet.

At Harvest-tide, the village brought in the doll, fashioned from the last gleanings and laid in the church overnight.

On Harvest Monday the Rohan villagers meet in a tithe barn to dance among themselves, steps of which they had forgotten the half and which are indiscriminately spoken of as 'brannels'.

To these merrymakings the outside world was not invited unless related by blood or marriage.

After the Delaye-Rohan broadcast, a certain newspaper, there being a passing slump in scandals, Crises, bathing belles, murders and film stars stepping off the *Queen Mary* at Southampton in the very act of declaring that the London policemen were wonderful and our King a Great Guy, sent down a special representative to Rohan, who, seeing a lighted outbuilding and being bored with his Norminster hotel, gladly entered to encourage the yokels. He had a blurred impression of couples, old and middleaged, weaving by lanternlight in some unknown dance, and was (even he of Fleet street) confounded to find himself quite suddenly in total darkness. Flashing his torch, and blinking, he saw that the barn was empty.

Even the Editor was unable to turn that incident to favour or to prettiness, as one forlorn hope of a caption after another flitted through his brain.

MYSTERY IN RURAL BARN

Who Were The Dancers of Rohan?

(No. Sounded like Maria Martin.)

VILLAGE INSULTS THE DAILY WIRE

(No. Too political. The paper, God knew, thanks to Hitler, was already festooned with ultimata and avenues being explored and doors still left open and rays of hope and slight slackening of the tension and pressure being applied and patience being exhausted, varied by appeasement and a stray *fait accompli* and strong representations to unpronounceable persons with un-spellable names in countries which were small portions of vowel entirely surrounded by consonants.)

WHO ARE THE SECRET DANCERS?

Norman Village Keeps Its Secret.

(No. Can't have two secrets in head- and cross-line.)

FORBIDDEN DANCERS.

(Too Chinese.)

STRANGE RITE IN NORMAN HAMLET.

What Is It?

(Well — what was it? If *The Wire* couldn't tell its readers the column was n.b.g.)

Damn the village.

3

He swung round on his chair. 'Then you got nothing at all, Eastbourne?'

'Nothing to work on,' answered the man who had been sent to cover Rohan.

'But what about the morning after?'

Eastbourne smiled. 'I did the rounds of what appeared to be the principal cottages; I somehow got the notion I'd gate-crashed the party and thought that an apology might give us *some* copy.'

'And — ?'

'Do you remember that part in *Doctor Nicola* when he gets tripped up on a question by one of the monks in the lamaserai?

Well, the Rohan folk assured me that, as there had been no festivity, I could not have delighted them with my honourable presence, and therefore no perfumed apologies were called for, or words to that effect.'

The Editor gazed and muttered 'Good God' before returning to his littered desk. 'England's a rum place . . . a *very* rum place . . . oh, Eastbourne . . . about this evacuation of kids if war should break out —'

'D' you believe it?'

'It's a dead cert, looks like. The Government's just beginning to lose its head and is being influenced by friend Adolf's methods to an extent it doesn't realize. Hitler, whatever you may think of him, has been a success so far. This scheme of billeting is England's first attempt to ape his tactics and Sovietize the British home.'

'There'd be a revolution in any other country.'

'Yes, but not here. The Government knows us just well enough to count on that. What it doesn't foresee is that the scheme is going to have some very nasty repercussions at the next General Election, that, and the confiscation of property idea which is getting into the air.'

'War conditions are no fair test of any government.'

'Tah! The voters won't look at it that way. All they'll see is a chance of booting out M.P.s who let them in for measures their constituents were violently opposed to. They got away with the evacuation idea in the September Crisis because it was only infinitesimal, and being premature as events proved, the country got no idea of what it might work out like because the schools were back before they started, almost.'

'Well, we can down it in the *Wire*. I should enjoy letting myself go on the subject, personally.'

'You won't get the chance.'

'No, I suppose Tatchett'll handle that.'

'Eastbourne, we had a staff conference last night, and the Chief is coming out strong in favour of the scheme.'

' *What?* He'll be on the wrong side of the fence if he does — or has he got wind that the *Cable* is against it? The Chief'd be against washing your neck if the *Daily Cable* advocated it. Why *are* they always at each other's throats?'

'A politer term for it is "healthy competition".'

'Anyway, what's the idea?'

'Just what a friend of mine asked me last night. I told him that in Fleet Street one learnt not to ask why certain newspapers take a violent stand for or against anything; you either don't get told, or stay on a paper so long that you know all the answers. It can be sincere. It's usually a Peerage: sometimes it's exhibitionism-wanting to be "different" and discussed; sometimes it's because the proprietors own interests in war or other material and production, or because they want to show up a rival who doesn't, or because some relative of theirs in public life has made a bloomer. I'm not alluding of course to England's Big Four publications, such as *The Times*, but to some of the papers like the one I edit, the kind that the upper-middle classes call Lower-class, the aristocracy calls Gutter, and we're trained to call Popular.'

'Which of the reasons is it this time?'

The Editor of *The Daily Wire* looked pensive, and suddenly giggled. 'A misunderstanding. Of course, we wrap our motives up in six sheets of the thickest brown paper, but from what I know of the Chief, plus having a friend or two in our good rival's offices, I gather that when this billeting scheme first came on the air, the proprietors of the *Wire* and the *Cable* did some quick thinking. You see they both own large houses in the country . . . the next move was to find out what line the other meant to take about it. They circled round each other like prizefighters for weeks — that was the time when both papers went all non-committal about evacuation, and we had to bump out our columns with photos of Waacs and Wrens and old Princess Henrietta Maria beaming at a sandbag, and keep our readers' noses steadily to the grindstone of possible rationing, and so on, and leaders headed "Whence, Goebbels?" and "Whither Hitler?" and "Why Czechoslovakia?" and "Wherefore Munich?", plus stating that every day and in every way we were fitter and fitter and fitter. . . .

'That was a very curious period, trying with the help of the B.B.C. simultaneously to warn the public to be prepared and at the same time to allay panic by hinting that there was nothing to be prepared for. . . .

'Well, then the *Cable's* proprietor happened to take another house further inland in case of raids, and our Chief got wind that he was moving out. He sent a reporter down to do a bit of snooping, and this chap actually saw the furniture being put into pantechnicons. That seemed conclusive, and just as the Chief ordered, supervised and printed a sarcastic stinger on the subject of lack of civic feeling — no names, of course: just a pontifical essay on public spirit and selfish obstructionism — he found out that the *Cable's* boss had only been precautionary, that he's dead against billeting and is now free to say so, while we, in our columns, are committed to the loving and fostering of several million children for an indefinite period. Even The Woman's Page has been dragged in and poor old Theodosia is preparing a grand idea for the women of England by which they sew their fingers to the bone at their own expense for the needy, send their work to us, and we get all the credit.'

Eastbourne hung on to a chair and looked swoony, then his body shook.

'Hah, hah!' he began. 'Oh ha ha ha HAR! . . . oh! *Did* she tell her readers that it would be a patriotic as well as pleasant occupation for the long winter evenings ahead of us?'

'But, naturally. She even told us all that this black-out might make theatre-going difficult —'

'Oh, *ha* — !'

'Can you guess why, Eastbourne? Because the streets would be unlit.'

'Oh ha ha ha!'

'And *then* she said that every day gained for peace meant one less day of war.'

Eastbourne mopped his eyes. 'Oh — I *must* marry that woman.'

'And now, as you've let me down over this Rohan business, go and earn your keep.'

'But I haven't a feature in my head, except my nose.'

'Then go and look out of the window. The whole secret of journalism lies in the capacity to make a mountain out of a molehill at a moment's notice.'

CHAPTER X

ROHAN MIGHT and did exclude a London newspaper from its social occasions, but it was Lady Roundelay, also uninvited, who experienced a keener disappointment that was almost childish. Take it all round, her greatest victory had been over Ronsell and his songs. But if she had mentally assessed the farrier as a character of the gentle-giant type, slow to move and pitiful to bird and beast, she revised her idea when he sang her The Running Song.

Writing of it to her sister, she said: 'It's somehow horrible. There's a kind of appalling jocosity running all through it which makes it worse, a matter-of-fact acceptance of cruelty — even a grim little pun, something about the cheapness of life and "two bodies for a *noble*". This man sang it without any attempt a phrasing or concert-platform tricks. It just poured from him. Quite why I found it so repellent I don't know; it's got very few notes and they're all in the minor, and the rhythm is a son of sprinting staccato especially in the repeated lines (*Ra*-tata-*tat*-tat-*tat*) like hail pattering on a glass roof and about as chilling. Oh, *why* can't I write down music, or even *describe* it? "The Running Song" oughtn't to be striking: even I can hear that it doesn't scan, is a law unto itself, and that the key line (*"Run* running *run*-ner run") is schoolboyish. Possibly its dreadfulness is just due to the fact that it's all wrong from the lyricist's point of view: no neat verse and chorus with everything tied up in an effective bow at the end. As it is, it's just a tussock of raw suffering. I can't send you the words unless Ronsell will sing it often again, but I'm haunted by the tune and catch myself humming it at odd moments about the house. Edmund says he never heard it at all, only of it, and that it's only one of hundreds they know at Rohan, and even at Delaye, but it's quite beastly.'

2

This is The Running Song of Rohan:

> Run, running runner, run,
> The horses o'ertake you
> Though breath shall forsake you,

Run, running runner, run.
Run, running runner, run,
The hoofbeats are gaining,
Lungs bursting and straining:
Run, running runner, run.

Run, running runner, run,
Is there sweat on your breast?
(They are nearing the crest)
Run, running runner, run.
Bodies are cheap, are cheap,
One body for a noble,
Two bodies for a noble,
Three bodies for a noble
(Run, running runner, run).
A furlong, a mile, to go
With sight that is dim
Is your pace getting slow?
Run, running runner, run!

On your lips there is froth, is froth,
(Run north, and run northward):
Does your travail make east
That your killer may feast?
Or make south? Is that blood on your mouth?

Is it flowing?
Are you slowing?
Is it heavy the going?
(Run, running runner, run)
    Run
    Run
    Run
(*Run, running runner, run!*)

3

Evelyn had walked home from Rohan curiously oppres sed, her simple faith in Ronsell, the farrier, distinctly shaken. It was, she thought, as though over the years he had been concealing his real nature from her. Treacherous, almost . . . or at least unfriendly. Or was it a proof of trust, finally arrived at and achieved by her own fostering and interest? If you deliberately sought out medieval England you must take the rough with the smooth, and, loving still, be prepared to welter with it in bloody cruelty and that supreme injustice which is the fashioning of weapons against the helpless and disarmed, the birds and beasts who learned, in time, to fear humanity as its natural enemy.

The pity of it!

There was, of course, she reasoned, no logic in the sentimentalist: he returned wet-eyed with pity to a dinner of roast venison or pheasant which he enjoyed extremely, which, indeed, mollified his vicarious suffering entirely until next time, when sheer chance brought him up against some beastliness to the animal that was, unhappily, available as a spectacle at all times.

One must eat. And even vegetables contained the same life principle. The Running Song should have recognized that . . . have harrowed one a little less in the indecency of the mental picture it evoked of that death-before-death. . . .

It never once occurred to Evelyn Roundelay that The Running Song of Rohan might refer to a victim that was neither winged nor four-footed.

4

Nor could she have foreseen the effect of the song upon her daughter Angela.

As Evelyn had told her sister, she caught herself at odd moments humming the song about the house. She could not, on looking back, remember when Angela had first heard the song save that it was in the spring. Angela was so much from home that a considerable period could have elapsed before, casually, unwittingly, mother had passed it on to child. But Evelyn remembered the outcome only too well.

They had been together in the garden, were strolling by the little marble temple where in bad weather the peacock lurked; and, as one so often does over trifles which precede something of moment, Evelyn could even recall the subject of their conversation which ended in her own humming of The Running Song — some nonsense about the peacock being like a discontented inmate in a boarding-house ('He'd be the type who'd dispute every item and mark his bottle of ginger ale so that the down-trodden waitress didn't get any,' she had said), and stooping to stick a plant, to tap the green tooth of a bulb as they walked towards the house, she began to hum. Angela stopped short. 'What's that tune?' She spoke sharply, for her.

'It's called "The Running Song".'

'Ohhh . . .' it was half acknowledgment, half acquiescence in the remembered details of some forgotten disturbance. Then, 'Yes . . . yes. It would be'.

Evelyn had missed the possible significance of that as she answered, 'It's a Rohan song. I find it rather awful, but quite haunting, with a certain fascination of its own'. In her enthusiasm, she enlarged upon the song, quoting fragments, whole memorized lines, while Angela looked sick, listening as though compelled by some uncomprehended duty.

'These medieval songs ought to be saved, somehow. As things are, their preservation is at the mercy of memory, and of elderly memory at that; they're all getting on in years, at Rohan,' Evelyn said.

'Medieval . . . no. It's not that,' Angela answered, correcting one abstractedly yet with authority, her mother, piecing together the memory of that morning, recollected.

'You think it was of later date? Why?'

Angela looked harassed as she groped. 'I don't know. It's the way I feel about it,' and then urgently, 'We needn't hear it again, ever, need we?'

It was, Evelyn recognized afterwards, the oblique appeal that is all of direct request which some daughters feel free to make to parents.

'Never, if I can remember,' Evelyn answered, still obtuse and, as always, ready to respect a whim. 'I hate it, myself, rather, as I told auntie Kathy. It gets hold of one so, and the fact that it's only a song doesn't lessen the tension. In the same way, one can be roused to fury by a purely fictional account of cruelty to an animal in any novel. The fact that it never really happened doesn't help one an atom.'

'No. Not an atom. . . .'

'And it's like that over The Running Song; we shall never be able to pin down the actual hunt which it tells of, if indeed one special and particular hunt ever did — it's far more likely that it was scribbled by some tosspot who'd never been able to afford for himself what in those days was still a gentleman's pastime, and who worked off his bloodlust by popularizing it in verse, if you can call it verse. It's a symbol of the misery of any poor hunted beast — '

And it was then that Angela had looked at her mother as if Evelyn for the first time had failed her utterly, leaving Angela alone to shoulder some burden.

And she had begun to tremble all over.

Evelyn took a chilled hand in her own. 'My ducky, don't you feel well? We'll go in, it's beastly cold out. There's — nothing *the matter*, is there?' Angela would understand that particular vagueness, must have long realized that she herself was of a different texture from, say, Margaret, and that the family colloquialism which called it 'something the matter' could in her own case range from a cold in the head to (on one former occasion at least) a sheer instance of unhappy and unwelcome prevision.

Angela was obviously straining towards normality, almost, it seemed, seeking to apologize to her mother for some failure to conform to family standards, some disability of the nature of which she was, as obviously, in the dark. It was, Evelyn rapidly calculated, no use closing with her and asking what the trouble was. Quite patently, Angela didn't know, any more than she knew what, years ago, had made her shiver in that upstairs bedroom with its window-pane and scrawled epitaph. Both she and Angela were unpleasantly affected by The Running Song, Angela to a greater degree. Then why worry?

5

It was while they both stood there on the path in mutual helplessness that what might be regarded as a solution of a sort had presented itself. For over the box hedge they saw the head of Sue Privett, hurrying towards them.

The little creature was also shivering, had been, Lady Roundelay supposed, too respectful to snatch a coat from behind the kitchen door. . . .

'Yes, m'lady?'

'Hullo, Sue. What is it?'

'I understood Miss Angela wanted me, m'lady.'

'No. She's been out here with me.'

The kitchenmaid looked unconvinced, Angela bewildered and relieved. Evelyn said, 'You hadn't a message for Sue, had you, dear?'

'No, mother.'

'You'd better trot back to the fire, Sue.'

Sue Privett hesitated. 'I'm very sorry, m'lady. I was quite sure I heard Miss Angela calling out. To me.'

'No. And you couldn't have heard from the kitchen if she had.'

Sue's training held.

'No, m'lady,' agreed the kitchenmaid, woodenly, and turned away obediently.

Angela started forward. 'I —I think I'll go back with Sue. It's *warm* in the kitchen.'

Evelyn was adequate. 'Yes, off you go, and tell cook to give you both a glass of hot milk.'

The two girls ran together towards the house.

Evelyn, watching them, was hoping that the pin which had pricked her when Angela abandoned her own mother in favour of a servant, wasn't resentment. Mothers, as she herself had told Basil Winchcombe, could be quite lamentably insufficient, and from the day she had recognized that fact Evelyn had determined never to assume that any act or word of her son or daughters should, by her, be treated as a final expression of character, but merely as a temporary quirk of development. To overstress a passing phase was to make the mistake common to too many families. 'And when one is reduced to philosophizing', she told herself, as she too moved away from the marble temple, 'it's nearly always a sign that one is in the last ditch, and trying to bamboozle oneself out of it.'

CHAPTER XI

1

AND OF THESE THINGS Evelyn Roundelay still thought, as she dusted the drawing-room, for Delaye was once more going through a period of domestic stress, and only one of the village girls available, this time, who was housemaiding abovestairs, helped by Sue Privett.

To the views from the three long windows Evelyn resolutely shut her eyes; a drawing-room was very well in its place, but on a morning of early September in the country, your place definitely wasn't in it; but at least dusting, which is probably the most imbecile employment in the world, left your mind free to chew its cud.

There was no doubt that, however quick and well-organized your dusting might be, the drawing-room was too full of knick-knacks. It wasn't only the pearl and enamel comfit boxes (queer that they'd been handled by a murdered predecessor), but the contributions of a contemporary. For whenever he was at a loose end, or was extra-galled by Nursie and the aunts, Maxwell Dunston retired into an improvised studio which had once been the family coach house, and, unexpectedly to Lady Roundelay, painted endless views of Delaye. For bad pictures they could have been much worse, but their frames all had to be dusted. Cousin Maxwell was too shy to paint nature as she was from the grounds themselves, and his efforts, to ensure privacy and avoid gardener or boy glancing over his shoulder (or the ultimate calamity that an encouraging ejaculation from Jessie, Amy or Sapphy would have been) were from memory. In time, these works of art were so numerous as to threaten to assume a serious aesthetic problem, and Lady Roundelay gave away as many as possible both as personal presents and to the local bazaars and sales of work. Unfortunately, people, faced with the alternatives of hand-painted sachets and lavender ladies with china heads, bought Maxwell's output, which so frequently came back to Evelyn and Margaret as Christmas presents from their innocent donors, that a proportion of his pictures was always in the house. The marble temple had made three returns already. . . .

Evelyn herself could date a great number of the pictures by the topical fury by which they had been inspired.

There were the marble temple (War Loan's Conversion to three-and-a-half per cent): the avenue at sunset (first Socialist Government): the kitchen garden in spring (admittance of women to the annexe of The Athenaeum), while Sir Edmund could, of course, go back much earlier, and had once told his wife that the unfinished sunk garden was Mrs. Pankhurst and the militants. Cousin Maxwell's present canvas — the stables at noon with the peacock in the foreground — was his reaction to Hitler and the Nazis. General Elections were apt to culminate in canvases that, if uncontrolled, would overflow into other rooms as well, and God knew, thought Evelyn Roundelay as she feather-brushed, what the future of the world might bring on to the walls, for there was another acute Crisis on at the moment, and England had made a singularly bad convalescence from the September one a year ago, so that everybody was beginning to say that a war would be an evil lesser than this ever-lasting trade depression, nerve-wrack and general uncertainty. But she still liked Maxwell, though, she saw, he was far more coherent and concise even in paint when in indignation. At calm, particularly at meal times, he was a little prone to committing, or being committed to, long jokes at which you laughed much too soon. Evelyn and her children, when the latter were of an age proper to the exchange of such confidences, found that they all secretly likened his locutions to mechanical transport. Evelyn herself saw his jokes as a lorry negotiating a hairpin bend: a slow progress . . . a sudden backfire to a forgotten incident that must find its allotted place . . . a creaking advance, and then it came! It came!

Her son, Stacey, agreed about the hairpin bend, but ached to get out and shove behind to accelerate the dénouement, while Margaret sympathized with her old great-cousin's vocal gears and longed to apply the brake. Angela once said that she saw his conversation as the mills of God, grinding its material remorselessly yet with the maximum of delay.

The Roundelays knew when jokes or reminiscence might be imminent, for then Major Dunston emitted a preliminary noise that resembled a swarm of large mosquitoes, and which seems to be a peculiarity of retired army men.

'Mmmmmmmm-mmmmm,' cousin Max would begin, 'Old Coleman's — mmmmm — on the ramp again. I remember — ha ha

— ha ha — him coming to my father — ha — and saying — hahaha-haha — that he — ha ha ha! —'

Sometimes, quite monstrously, Evelyn's husband would join in and abet Maxwell, and the two old men, flushed, their lean cheeks damp with tears, ha-ha'd and hooted themselves to a standstill. Well . . . they were kinsmen, with shared memories, but it was on these occasions that Evelyn seriously wondered if, after all, she herself was deficient of any sense of humour: on these occasions that, with a queer pang, she suddenly saw the whole tableful, except her children, quite objectively, and asked herself what she was doing in that galley. Who *were* these people? What combination of circumstances had connived to set her at this board? And then her mind clicked and they all sank back into the subjective, explained, liked, with all they stood for. . . .

Marriage, she pondered, however contented, was probably like that. It was a great tribute to Edmund that it was only when Max was on the stump that she felt the disparity between her own age and her husband's. Edmund would be sixty-one next winter, and she was now that baffling age, fifty, which roughly meant that you were still young enough for anything and old enough to know better.

People said that your children were a steadying influence. So they might be, socially, but never emotionally. No family, probably, ever saves a woman from susceptibility, because women are born romantic idealists or they couldn't weather the sidelines of marriage for six weeks. As it was, for women of Evelyn's type, the early years of marriage, at once more thrilling and repellent than the later; were a constant struggle to preserve the romantic element by calling the grosser side of it by any name but the correct one, a constant tussle to explain away to yourself the incompatible.

And marriage, of course, shut the door of adventure in your face until death, and *that* meant another struggle not to become even superficially attracted by any other man, lest, out of pure contrariness and knowing you mustn't succumb, the surface attraction developed into something deeper. And that was a thought so alarming that you went off to the Lacquer Room and darned socks and hemmed handkerchiefs to send to Stacey at school.

In the early years, Evelyn had even made a dreadful little gamble with herself which she involuntarily indulged in at meal times and which her sister Helen would doubtless diagnose as a compulsion neurosis. It concerned the exact and unthinkable moment at which she might suddenly cease to love Edmund. Love was such a delicate thing: a state of mind, largely, so that there seemed no real reason why at any minute it might not vanish like a puff of smoke, leaving you, so to speak, with a perfect mountain of unwanted and unsaleable effects, human and material, on your hands. And so, at table, she would sit internally muttering 'I shall stop loving Edmund while Musgrave hands the potatoes to aunt Amy . . . no? Still caring for him? Then it will be as Musgrave goes to the sideboard (one — two — three — four)', or 'I shall continue to love Edmund *unless* Maxwell makes a joke or tells a story before we all get up.'

It had been Helen, fluent, wise, as unmarried young women so frequently are, who had anticipated Evelyn's state of mind and laid it out on the bed for her eldest sister's inspection during her own first visit to Delaye. Strictly, of course, as an abstraction: brides were apt, Helen knew, to sprout sudden loyalties and reticences which were very tiresome while they lasted and to overcome which they must, within reason, be helped. 'I'm always sorry', Helen had remarked, 'for women like us who, in the last resort, would be kept perfectly happy on kisses. But unfortunately by the time most husbands have left off pestering you with sex, they've also left off wanting to kiss you. The business runs together, with them, and it never does, with us. They're just opportunists, and it doesn't even work out from the family point of view, because men go on for ever, while women cease to be able to oblige far sooner. Which is about the only way in which that arch-muddler, nature, protects 'em. So nobody is *ever* being kissed at the right time.'

Over Edmund Roundelay, at least, Helen Calcott was wrong. He had been charmed when he and Evelyn achieved three children, but there was no getting over the fact that since he and Evelyn had, without discussion, abandoned the purely sex relationship, they had become far better friends, companions and allies. It was, Evelyn supposed, that for the first time they saw each other fairly, as they really were, without all that hypocritic hocus-pocus, those conventional intimacies which could be so dismaying coming at the end of a day which had included a squabble or a serious difference of opinion about the children, or a session depressed and cautionary on his side, vindicatory and statistical on hers, about the household expenses. It was, she had come to suspect, this horrible attempt to reconcile the grandiose with the petty that was the downfall of matrimony. And it was a downfall because, acting on the hocus-pocus plan, this aspect of things was kept from you by even the kindest of mothers until you were married, when it was hoped it was too late to do anything about it. Helen had once said that they managed these things better in the East, where the houris of the harem weren't expected to combine allurement with the market price of rump steak.

2

Thoughts of her sister led Evelyn Roundelay by placid, dusting stages (did one *whang* a feather broom out of the window to clean it or just shake it? She had never met the things save in Bath-Comedy novels until she came to Delaye) to Angela, who was at present concluding a visit to her aunts in Hereford Square and acquiring in the process, one passionately hoped, a more robust outlook on life.

Perhaps Evelyn, in her mental catalogue of blessings and contentments, had been a little too sweeping, for what, in Angela, passed with Edmund as just uncertain physical health, Evelyn perceived to go deeper and to rank among those psychologic upsets about which doctors could do little even in these days of sight-restoring and skin grafting. Kathleen, from her letters to her sister Evelyn, evidently thought so too.

'She's fearfully reserved, you know, and yet can be extraordinarily perceptive: the kind of girl who doesn't seem to talk very much but who listens a lot, and without appearing to take one in at all suddenly shows you by some remark that she's more than followed your character, and has known what you were feeling all the time. Oh, nothing the *least* rude. All your kids are polite, and we're all fond of them . . .'

Evidently, perception ran also on the Calcott side of the family, for Kathleen's letter had put into words what Evelyn felt to be true. It was the Roundelay reserve that stood in the way of progress.

And that brought Evelyn's thoughts back to her last autumnal garden party, a year ago.

She herself had stood under a tree admiring the effect of the burnt colours of September, the pink sun, the suggestion of mist — even the heathery tones of the tweed suits of her guests as they talked and laughed and exclaimed at the peacock, who had elected to show himself (he was a chancy bird), while Musgrave moved among them all with his tray.

Angela had joined her mother, who made some comment upon the scene, and Angela looked, too, and said slowly, 'It's awful . . . it's not a party at all. It *is* a scene, like the theatre, you know, when they show you this sort of thing to heighten something bad to come.'

'My *dear*!'

'Only in the theatre the party is usually in the summer, to look gayer and more sunny.' And then, urgently, 'You'd better go and speak to that man over there, the nice-looking one.'

'But — he's not *thinking* of going. It's only half-past four.' That had apparently confused Angela for the moment. But she said, 'Yes, but you won't see him again. Who is he?'

'Darling, he's always on tap! Though we haven't known him many months. You must have just missed each other, with your visits and his work. He's a great dear, is Charlie Carfrae, and going into the Air Force. He's on leave from Cranwell — '

And six months later the name of Flight-Lieutenant Charles Carfrae had appeared among those missing, believed killed, while on a reconnaissance flight over the North Sea.

3

It was at this moment that the attentions of Lady Roundelay to the knick-knacks were shattered by a loud and corncrake screech. She dropped her feather broom, emitted a mild 'damnation!' and, raking the room with her eye, found that the peacock had had the temerity to fly up to a very window-ledge, from which he regarded her with a sarcastic bead.

'Go away! Yes, I know you're a dream of loveliness, but go away all the same.'

Steps sounded in the hall outside. 'Oh, Musgrave! *Do* turn the peacock out. He's come right *in*.'

The butler located the trouble and advanced upon it, making sotto voce reproaches and shooing gestures. 'Get out! Out you go (augh!), it's very difficult to know what to do, m'lady. Should I get a broom from the housemaid's cupboard?'

'Yes, anything. And poke him hard. We really *can't* have this.'

Musgrave left the room, relieved that her ladyship had not entered into further particulars . . . The peacock waited. When the manservant (one felt he was thinking of Musgrave in that way) had returned with a long broom commonly reserved for dealing with the immense staircase windows, the creature, head tilted and critical to the last, turned tail and, taking his time flumped to the roseborder below. It was enough. He had made a fool of Musgrave. The latter, his occupation gone, apparently stranded without any suitable exit line, triumphed at the eleventh second over the broom and situation, and murmuring 'Did you ladyship require anything further?' gently quitted the arena.

CHAPTER XII

1

HAD YOU MADE a tour of the household, and, assuming the impossible, that you were upon confidential terms with all of them, from little Sue Privett to the master himself, you would have discovered that the peacock was disregarded by none, and that their feelings about him were widely different and of varying degrees of intensity.

Taking the family first: Sir Edmund, tolerant of all creatures furred or feathered, forgave the bird's maraudings, his furious advances upon the poultry-yard, spiteful beak wide with ire, because a peacock seemed to go with the general surroundings and pleased the stranger within the gates.

Lady Roundelay took little notice of the creature, only regretting the quality of his voice.

Margaret Roundelay sometimes said 'Hullo, you', as she gardened, and wondered if his chronic ill-temper were due to lack of a mate; her brother would have preferred guinea fowls who at least laid and could be later roast, and said so.

The sight of the peacock upon the lawn roused in the old ladies an atavistic urge to get a closer view of him which Miss Amy and Miss Sapphy, back in their rooms, explained to each other coldly on post-cards was no doubt due to Mamma's love of jewellery, and resulted, while on the lawn slowly drinking him in from every angle in a perfect mutual ignoring, in frequent colds that had to be dosed by Lady Roundelay.

On those occasions when Angela was at home, she of all the family wasted time and breath in attempts to humanize the gorgeous vision. She would save fruit and bread, steal chicken meal and Indian corn in efforts to establish some friendly contact, racking her brains for their scant knowledge of what diet peacocks preferred. Sometimes, with bated breath, it seemed to her that a partial success was in sight: then, at worst, it looked as though the bird was merely doubtful. Committed to its taming and confidence, this made Angela unhappy. It was terrible to fail with a helpless thing . . . his character was beside the point: it was, she came to believe, an effect and not a cause. He had been ill-treated? But that was unlikely. Peacocks, even now are still the appurtenances of a certain degree of financial standing and as for ill-treatment, how correct a peacock? You can't slap him, and being only semi-domesticated, depriving him of food as a punishment is futile. He could fend for himself.

Once, as a last resort, she had saved half of her breakfast egg to tempt him. The cook had boiled it rather hard, that morning. And the bird had seemed to dim before her eyes, his own brilliant sight to cloud (with what?) and he had attacked her for the first time, digging once and deeply into her wrist.

2

With the staff, Musgrave and the peacock headed the list with a straightforward mutual detestation, a feeling which was, if possible, intensified by an occasional habit the bird had of making for one of the back doors and promenading the long length of kitchen and scullery, choosing by some unknown sense the time at which the servants were sitting about enjoying their mid-morning meal — for snack it could not be called. At these times, Musgrave, about to retire to the pantry with his own portion, would (he hoped unnoticed by the other servants) accelerate his pace lest the peacock from an apparently large repertoire should find yet another means of causing him to lose his dignity.

Except that the cook was conventionally shocked by the discovery of anything in its wrong place, being of the type that automatically turns any sleeping cat off any chair however shabby and unwanted, there was no active emotion generated between the peacock and herself. At worst they looked upon each other as necessary evils, although she had once exclaimed on finding the bird surveying her struggles with a refractory oven that it almost looked as though that brute enjoyed seeing a person working herself to a shadow.

There are degrees even in ill-humour: so, with the upper and under housemaid, the tension was of a fluctuating quality. On the whole, they all left each other alone, though even the staff had begun to notice that the peacock was distinctly more inimical to those housemaids who had served at Delaye for any period of time than he was to the stopgap village help. . . .

The girls themselves were slightly nervous in his presence (one's ankles), but would cluster together delightedly to watch the creature's really superb rages whenever the master was about. This, it was felt, was the real thing. For then, with beak ajar and gleaming eye, that miracle of construction which is a peacock unfolded piece by piece before their gaze.

First the barred wings lifted, then from his saddle rose erect a plaque of bronze, then upswept the iridescent fan cleaving to this support, and then, centrepiece to blue-green pride studded with discs of bluer blue and greener green, each quilled feather tipped with a softly-waving arrow-head of dust-colour, the peacock was equipped for venom, and, still in his hatred, would by some un-guessable process contrive to rattle quite audibly his each delicate quill until every feather was jarred.

Dickon, the gardener, was alternately teased by and facetious to-wards the bird's appearances. In facetiousness he followed that uni-versal practice of the working-class in addressing the object of his banter by the latest topical surname, regardless of any poor side-is-sue of relevancy; thus if the peacock merely appeared and watched him he became Hitler, but when outraged at the unerring flair shown by the trespasser for the more delicate produce, its cultivator would upbraid the ex-chancellor of Germany in broad Normanshire. To-wards the grower of these tit-bits the peacock, on his side, though watchful, was largely neutral as he was to Nursie, who being housed on the third storey and practically room-bound very seldom saw him at all. They had met, of course, in a past in which Nursie's age was a little less what is bafflingly known as 'tidy', but the encounters were negligible. Nursie just stood there addressing him as Chook, Chook, Chook, while the peacock merely inspected the old dependent (one felt he was thinking of Nursie in those terms).

3

But in that house the peacock had one ally, one faithful champion.

For him, Sue Privett could brave even the cook or Mr. Mus-grave: towards him she had never shown the slightest fear. For him she also would save tit-bits from her own meals, and when; she, peeping out of the kitchen windows on highest tiptoe, glimpsed him in the shrubbery, she would glance round, but with the minimum of caution, lest the eye of an upper servant be on her, and run to meet him at the great side door.

At times of her permitted leisure, the staff itself had noticed that the bird even appeared to advance to meet her, though that, they all agreed, must be a coincidence, and that the nasty brute must have been meaning to come in to parade the kitchens in any case. But (a housemaid had seen it happen) the peacock had once taken food from Sue's very hand, pecking it as tame as you like, and actually (here the domestic credulity collapsed) letting her stroke its neck.

4

It was Sue Privett who had first come running to the cry of Miss Angela when the peacock bit her. Miss Angela had stopped making any noise when Sue hurried to her (the gentry never carried on before anyone) but her face was very white and there was blood on her wrist, at sight of which the little kitchenmaid's face turned as white. The peacock stood his ground. Sue turned on him.

'Why, you bad boy! Whatever are you thinking of?' The bird, head tilted, seemed to consider this and emitted a feeble squawk. 'Yes, you may well say you're sorry.' And then Sue forgot all etiquette. 'What did you do, Miss?'

Loss of faith, her nerves jangled, Angela's voice was sharp. 'Do? Nothing. Just gave him some food.'

'You should've sent for me, Miss, to find out what 'e likes.' Angela was stung. 'I *only* gave him some of my own breakfast — ' Sue was clumsily winding a clean glasscloth round Miss Angela's wrist. 'He didn't ought to've minded that. He knows you and I.'

'Well, it seems he *did* mind. He struck at me the moment I held out the bit of hardboiled egg.'

As she looked at her the hands of the other girl were stilled.

'He wouldn't touch *that*, Miss.'

'But he's never pecked *you* — '

'I've never offered 'im egg, Miss Angela.'

'Then how d'you know he doesn't like it?'

It may have been the exasperation in her mistress's voice that caused Sue to begin to go to pieces herself. 'I — well — I *know* 'e won't eat it.' Her voice rose. 'It won't *never* be any good givin' it to 'im.'

'Well . . . thanks, Sue.'

Angela Roundelay slowly passed on into the house by the main door. She was trembling a little, longing for the privacy of the house, but one didn't break down before servants.

Back in the scullery, Sue Privett, her filched glasscloth and the use to which it had been put having been promptly discovered and scolded, suddenly became the centre of attention by turning a shade whiter and tumbling on to a chair. The cook, always hoping against hope that the girl had got herself into trouble with one of the village lads, felt that she had been defrauded when Sue in a muffled sort of voice conveyed to those present that it was Miss Angela's wrist that'd turned her green. And then she said a thing whose oddness passed right over the head of her audience.

'I never could abear the sight of blood, nor my Mum couldn't nor my Gran neither, not if it were unkindly come by.'

5

A few months later there had been another small episode, on the day that the peacock trespassed into the drawing-room. For, discussing it at luncheon, Sir Edmund suggested that the peacock be offered to the Severns, whose estate was separated from Delaye by the public road to Delaye village and Norminster alone.

Severn kept peacocks, didn't he? and this creature was the sole survivor of what peacocks Delaye had ever harboured. The poor brute probably wanted — hum — company. And what price getting Severn to send a man over to fetch the peacock and then we'd be quit of him? Sir Edmund would telephone in person.

The squire of Delaye was more than agreeable. They had at the moment — ah — rather too many peahens, and quite ... quite ... and what price the present world situation? Looked pretty nasty. On the brink, if you ask me. There's one thing: if we're really for it it'll free us all at last to say what we really think about friend Adolf. Oh, entirely so, but what Edmund Roundelay felt was that even the British gutter Press behaved better than they did in — oh well, it *was* a relatively New World, of course, with no traditions ... look at the way they handled that business about Mrs. — well, hope to see you soon. G'bye.

And that same evening at sunset, a servant — it should, hierarchically speaking, have been an under gardener but it happened to be his half day off so a young footman was detailed for the job — presented himself in the grounds of Delaye and began a resentful, harried but still deferential hunt for the accursèd fowl.

It was Sue Privett, all unwittingly if a little surprised, who put the footman on the right track. 'He likes the lil' temple come the light goes', and there that the bird was found, taking the sunset, at his ease, and there that, six seconds later, a very unearthly screeching set up of which the household took small notice, peacocks being like that, but which brought Sue Privett running, against all etiquette and precedent and to the upset of the culinary routine, across the pleasure grounds. She was a swift mover.

At sight of the green and blue armful and of Joe Dale's beaded face in which ill-humour and professional outrage were equally obvious she drew up short. It was when the footman started running towards the avenue, asylum, and decency that bird and girl set up their mutual outcries.

'Mr. Dale! Put 'im down. 'E won't let you hold 'im.' The footman slowed his slogging to retort 'I can see that, can't I?'

'You're making 'im misruble, put 'im *down*!'

'I've my orders — '

'What orders? I tell you, 'e won't let nobody touch 'im but me.'

'Oh . . . well then, *you* take 'im. 'E's 'cavy, but it's only over to squire's.'

'*What?*'

The man was riled to shouting point. 'They want 'im over at Severn's. Sir Edmund's getting rid of 'im — '

But he spoke to the air, for the kitchenmaid was scudding back to the house.

6

It was in a sense a scene, and Lady Roundelay who coped with it, kind, a little impatient, largely in the dark. Servants always got hysteric at trifles.

'But my dear child, really you must allow the master to know best. The peacock is very pretty, I know, but he's a horrid nuisance, not only in the kitchen garden but in the house as well. Mrs. Hatchett tells me he comes into the kitchens, he's bitten Miss Angela, and to-day he came right into the drawing-room.' The maid was sullen with obstinacy. ' 'E does no real harm, m'lady, a bit here an' a bit there, p'raps, and I know there was Miss Angela's wrist, but she offended 'im, like.'

'She what?'

Sue looked confused. 'Please, m'lady, she fed 'im what 'e don't eat an' won't look at.'

'Well, that's all past and done with — '

'If you could see your way, m'lady . . . 'e'd miss *me* . . . a word to the master — '

'But we don't *want* him, Sue. I'm sorry if he's your pet' (for some reason the girl winced at this), 'but can't you look at it from the poor thing's point of view? He must be fearfully lonely here, that's probably why he's so unfriendly to everybody.'

'*Unfriendly?*' Sue clenched her hands in her apron and answered slowly, 'If it's for 'is good, m'lady — '

Lady Roundelay was brisk and thankful. 'I'm sure it is. And he'll have plenty of company of his own kind, and' (here she allowed herself to indulge in the whimsical as sop to her kitchen-maid) 'plenty of lady friends to play with.'

Servants were an incalculable race. For at this bright remark, Sue Privett's eyes dilated, and an extraordinary look came over her face as she moved off to her own quarters. Thinking it over as she returned to the dining-room, Evelyn Roundelay incredulously ran the impression to earth.

Resentment. Sue resented the peahens.

She related the incident to Angela, half laughing, half impatient, and Angela said nothing, but looked troubled.

7

And after all Sue had nothing to fear. For next morning the peacock paced over the road from Severn Court and displayed himself as usual upon the front lawn of Delaye.

Three times was a manservant sent to fetch him, thrice was he removed, screeching, and thrice punctually reappeared upon the following day.

The squire and Sir Edmund admitted defeat and the heart of Sue Privett was content.

CHAPTER XIII

1

ANGELA ROUNDELAY'S well of pity for the peacock had not dried as a result of her bitten wrist, it was, rather, replenished by the latest development. But two days after the third return and the unwilling reinstatement of the peacock in her father's home she had a shock. The happening, baldly stated, was trivial on the face of it. But she sensed that the face of it was a misleading one, knew that it alienated her. Something was wrong, somewhere, or if not wrong, which implied ill-doing, un-right.

The incident itself could easily be viewed in a humorous light in the retailing; seen, it wasn't funny at all. It could be translated and explained by many a precedent of understanding between human and animal, and that, too, failed to satisfy.

Angela had strolled into the grounds before tea, a field that you approached through the coppice where the gardener's boy brought home logs and kindling on a barrow. There was nobody on the estate in sight, that afternoon: the men were at tea. She had come here by instinct, out of her programme, to rediscover Delaye after a London visit to her aunts, to own once more the tangs, the silences that even a baby wood can give you, asking only in return that you stir your feet for the russet smell of beech-mast and use your eyes for a shrivelled last-year nut lying by some sparse outbreak of bluebell or primrose, if it were Spring. This was September, season of wood smoke and browning nut, unready as yet. It was only the second of September. . . .

And then in the field she saw them, Sue and the peacock, strolling together.

Angela, leaning on a bough to watch, was moved at first glance to an inexplicable pleasure, a vicarious sensation of triumphant exhilaration on their behalf until something about the spectacle misgave her. She was at that moment in the plight of those who feel a grief to which they are not officially entitled, and which, of all woe, is hardest to endure. Almost, in some antick manner, she was self-convicted of eavesdropping. . . .

Round the field went bird and kitchenmaid, quite obviously taking a walk. It was a pretty sight . . . if you came to it fresh . . . The peacock helped out the idea of a deliberate stroll by failing as all creatures do sooner or later to drop behind and peck and stray, or rush ahead towards some unseen attraction, edible or enemy. Quite literally, he was out for a walk, and quite incomprehensibly Angela Roundelay received the impression that this was not their first outing.

Sue, she noted, was wearing her village-made best. Her day off, Angela supposed. Then, why hadn't she started earlier? It was already tea-time and Sue was still on the estate . . . She turned to go, very quietly, but the peacock heard her, and wheeled. Angela, discovered, did the only possible thing, and waved. Sue hurried across the field, the peacock hastily mincing at her side. They stood in talk for a minute or so, the maid recovering poise as her young lady spoke of the afternoon, the wood, and the sights of London.

As Angela was leaving, Sue, emboldened, remarked 'Say good-bye to Miss Angela, my lad, and tell 'er you're sorry about what you did', and the peacock, poised for evasion if danger signalled, its eyes bright, fearful but steady, stretched out its neck and for a moment put its head upon her hand, its neat and twinkling crest brushing her fingers.

CHAPTER XIV

1

IT WAS PLEASANT in the garden on a hot autumn morning, even on Sundays, and that, thought Evelyn Roundelay, was a distinct feat for any garden to achieve, especially where, as at Delaye, your ear could catch blurred intermittent quanglings carried by the lazy breeze from the peal of three bells from the village church. Bells, unless they were behind the doors of very small shops, were a depressing sound and the Reverend Basil Winch-combe himself had once denounced them roundly on the ground that they were an abuse of privilege, and that, carried to its logical and fair conclusion, every pub ought to own a peal as well to announce its time of opening. Bells, he had summed up, should be relegated solely to melodrama of post-1914 vintage, and moving scene round village cenotaph, while hero stands at attention very bronzed and loyal to the strains of the National Anthem and the German spy suavely smiles from behind the pump, muttering Gott Strafe England in the accents of Kennington Road, or to those hayfield-cum-production numbers of revue, when the leading lady on the chorus enquiring 'But where is our Harvest Queen?' leaps from a hay wain with genuine straws adhering to her rural gown as conceived by Furbelow of South Molton Street.

The question was, thought Lady Roundelay, weeding the beet root beds, did one love the job or was it boring, exhausting and disheartening? In common with most translated townswomen she didn't know but was irresistibly drawn to the earth. Without the comings and goings of Dickon and the boy the garden fell half undressed: which meant that if you did good work on the beds there was no voice to praise however grudgingly, but also meant that should you commit agricultural gaffes there was no professional eye to see and expose them.

2

In the hall Miss Jessie was ready for church. One must allow twenty minutes to reach the village. Once more she regretted that the transport question ruled out worship at Norminster cathedral.

There was a motor bus from Delaye village that would get her in in time, but the returning bus would not set her down outside the public house at Delaye until two o'clock so that one was always the best part of an hour late for luncheon, counting the walk back. Evelyn was very kind about this, but Edmund and Maxwell never liked it, and then the staff expected to get away earlier on Sundays.

'Oh, aunt Jessie, *do* go! Do do something you want to, *sometimes*! Think of Nora and The Doll's House and just walk out!' Evelyn had exclaimed over the years, but aunt Jessie, she saw, offered an unlikely surface for Ibsenite pokings-up and was of the scourging generation that elevated duty to the status of a vice and whose life was earmarked as one long unintelligent sacrifice to heaven really only knew what, an arrangement which as usual pleased nobody and probably bored God stiff into the bargain, 'and honestly', Lady Roundelay often thought, after yet another time-wasting and sticky verbal session in which aunt Jessie abandoned her own will for the Almighty's or anyone else's in face of all opposition, 'I'd *tip* the postman to seduce her!'

Raising her aching back Evelyn flung her cardigan over a bough, selected an apple and ate it.

How, she wondered once more, had old Jessie got 'struck so'? What, so to speak, had been the original impetus which had propelled her into the everlasting arms of goodness? Was it possible she didn't know the tonic, the uplift, the cleansing that a deliberate occasional fall from any grace you prefer could be? Was it possible to go through life never once having allowed yourself to spend just more than your means, kiss the improper person, eat to excess or drink the drop too much? It was: it must be, and Jessie was the living proof. She didn't even resemble old Sapphy or Amy in their existence of a nullity that was at least social, neither did she share the inherited lust of jewels which had in their case acted as a preservative and kept them still of the world. Even Jessie's reactions to the peacock were unknown, if she felt any, nor had the Roundelays, if one came to think of it, ever noted any kind of emotion shown by the peacock towards Miss Jessie. It really seemed as though the creature knew all about the essential cipherdom that was her portion, and refrained of system from wasting powder and shot upon her.

3

It was, after all, the social Miss Sapphire Roundelay who achieved the cathedral that morning, unexpectedly, but also precariously and by the skin of her teeth as were so many of her outings. The Severns had telephoned at the last moment offering a lift in their car to the Roundelays and too late to save Miss Jessie. Many small dilemmas then presented themselves for solution. Miss Sapphy wasn't ready: had not dressed in her Sunday best: Lady Roundelay might wish to attend the service? Or Margaret, or Angela? Amethyst her sister Sapphire ruled out at once, too flustered to be harried by her own slight deviation from the scrupulous, but there was no time to send message or write postcard to her room to enquire. Edmund was as usual all over the place — every day was a Sunday to him, or rather, no day was, including Sunday, Jessie had often regretted, and Maxwell wouldn't turn out if you paid him. Also, his hands were probably all over paint; he was engaged upon a painting of the façade of the house this time, he was so angry about the invasion of Czechoslovakia.

Musgrave added to Miss Sapphire's distress his own exasperation at her ditherings while he waited, receiver in hand. ('Augh . . . if you could give Mrs. Severn a definite answer, Miss Sophia — '). That meant Sapphire was once more in disgrace with the butler and she almost screamed 'Then — yes. Yes. Tell her I'll come, and of course my thanks. *Oh* dear — '

4

The service was well attended — Doctor Mimms-Welwyn himself was preaching, to-day, but, as always with the vast edifice, beautifully, leisurely planned, there seemed to be room and to spare for all in spite of the serried hundreds.

In the aisles vergers glided, at the great doors and in the side chapels tourists and hikers, shorted, blowzy and brawny, the females of their species with blown hair tied up in gipsy handkerchiefs, loitered whispering. Amplifiers fixed to Norman pillars carried the prayers and psalms as an intensified volume of sound in which all words were drowned; the choir, as always, conveying to the eye an impression of numeric insufficiency, as always assuaged the ear as the sexless boy voices rose and penetrated to the remotest corner.

> Glory be to the Father
> And — to the Son —

The congregation prepared to settle for the second Lesson. And it was then that the Archbishop himself was seen by some to take a slip of paper from Canon Minter. He read it swiftly, paused fractionally, and murmured to the clergyman advancing upon the lectern. Coming to the altar steps the Archbishop spoke:

'I have to tell you all that, this morning, war was declared between England and Germany. Let us pray.'

On their knees, they listened, some of them more to their own thoughts.

'Oh Lord God of battles, strengthen our hands from now onwards, lead us not into the temptation of hatred and bitterness: arm with the conviction of the righteousness of our cause those who will meet the enemy face to face: comfort those of us who are left: uphold the weak and defenceless: guide us to a peace which is not alone of the earth but of Thy Holy Spirit and bring us to an everlasting glory that shall be humble and worthy in Thy sight.'

To her pain and distaste (a public place) old Miss Sapphire Roundelay was crying. She wept a little for the griefs she would never know, the loss of husband, the hazard of son . . . the absence of personal partaking in this the latest holocaust of which she, at over seventy, had seen so many.

Boring inwards, her mind searching its material of pity, she wept a little for Stacey, her nephew's heir, and even for that agelong silence which she and Amethyst had observed towards each other.

Amy had borrowed a necklace for the Hunt Ball in Norminster without asking, as sisters sometimes do; but it was that Florentine ornament bought on her honeymoon in Italy by Mamma, a chain curiously worked in pinchbeck plaques studded with blister pearls and emeralds and said to have belonged to Bianca Capelli. Sapphire had not seen it upon her sister's neck in the converted cloakroom at the Guild Hall — an ex-committee room with baize boards still upon the walls and inkpots ranged out of the way along the Gibbons mantelpiece that people came miles to see. Amethyst had let the trinket burst upon her in the very ballroom . . . and Vernon Severn was to be at the occasion . . . the father of that present squire of Delaye whose wife now stood beside her while the organ clarioned and the voices soared.

Our hope in years to come —

Mrs. Severn, a nice woman, middle-aged herself, now.

The necklace had suited Sapphire, it was, she thought, quaint: it was noticeable: it created conversation that, with men especially, led on to other, warmer topics. And she had been, thanks to Amy, reduced to her garnets which clashed abominably with the pink coats of her partners, with Severn's pink . . . The fact that his intentions might be non-existent and his affections elsewhere she had never allowed herself to face; she clung to the belief that the Capelli necklet would have clinched matters. It was her story, her secret dignity, realized, she sometimes hoped, by the family.

Amy had of course not stopped speaking at once, had, indeed, persisted in her efforts to re-establish the old footing for weeks until Sapphire wore her down . . . the matter was never threshed out between them. Impossible in the circumstances. One had one's pride to consider: one doesn't admit that particular type of defeat.

And our eternal home.

The written messages that they exchanged were a semi-healing of the breach, their mutual silences in each other's company at table and about the house a sufficing gesture, an adherence to the letter of alienation.

Furtively mopping her eyes as they knelt for the Benediction Sapphire mentally circled round the scene of the reconciliation. She would go up to Amy's room . . . or perhaps they would meet in the garden —

The congregation was bathed in a sudden whim of sunlight, struggling to them through man-made obstacle. The famous Apostles Window was a network of scaffolding, the fourteenth-century glass had been removed and hidden some weeks ago, no one knew where. Some said to the cellars of the Archbishop's palace at Normansmead, some to the crypt, others that it had been buried on

Harold's Barrow, that hill outside the city where the gold torque had been dug up and Roman pottery, as the townsfolk said, was six a penny.

The congregation dispersed slowly; there was always a delay during the valedictory intoning in the vestry and the main doors were kept closed, their accesses roped off with crimson, until the final smothered Amen.

Miss Sapphire and the Severns waited to reach their car by the North door which faced Morionyard. Over the whole city an extra-Sabbatic stillness hung. But Miss Sapphy, happy to be escorted, seeing life, with friends, even glimpsing a neighbour here and there, was recovering poise. There was the drive home to be looked forward to, and a good luncheon; social threads might be gathered up which, later on in the month, would lead to an engagement, an afternoon out. Alicia Severn was looking quite cheerful so that one need not give lip-service to the dreadfulness of war. The people were dispersing gravely, but as those who at least shoulder a familiar burden. . . .

Alicia Severn said, 'Well, it's come, and I must say it's a relief. We've danced too long on the rim of a volcano.'

It was little Mrs. Galbraith who found the party and came up to Miss Roundelay and the squire's wife white and anxious.

'My cats, you know. I shall have them all put to sleep, of course.' The squire's wife was pitiful. 'Send them over to Severn. We'll do our best for the poor beasties.' Mrs. Galbraith shook her head as she gave husky thanks. 'It's no good. The air-raids . . . gas . . . to see them choking . . . and I can't afford those pneumatic-floor'd kennels the animal Societies are advertising.' Miss Sapphire's mind returned, while Mrs. Galbraith flitted off to catch the motor bus, to the contemplated rapprochement with Amy. She had given way, she felt, in the cathedral, had been impulsive. A reconciliation would make such talk among the family, might even lead to an exposure of the original *casus belli*, and that must *never* come out. And she and Amy would make uphill work of it at first, perhaps for the remainder of their time. Sadly shy, both. Better hold one's tongue. But she would write Amy a nice account of the eventful service and the memorable occasion.

Jauntily stepping into the car Miss Sapphy was herself again.

5

In the village church of Delaye the Reverend Basil Winchcombe spoke to the familiarly sparse-filled pews. The people were indoors, he supposed, listening to the continuously relaid news from White-hall on their wireless sets. His eyes rested a second on the trickle of shop-keepers, the publican's wife, the Vicar's servants, the decent, *déclassé* climbers and their families who called themselves gentleman farmers, and his standby in the other principal pew (for the Severns for some reason had deserted him this morning), Miss Jacinth Roundelay, the one they all called 'Jessie'.

To them he spoke from the pulpit, scrapping at the last minute the sermon that he had worked upon with some enthusiasm if little expectation (it derived from the slaying by the jawbone of an ass, which he had always privately regarded as yet another piece of symbolism, in this case representing malicious gossip).

'"*I come not to bring peace: but a sword.*"'

'It seems that once again we're at war. I cannot in honesty preach to you about the duty of forgiveness and I am not going to suggest we turn the other cheek, or love our enemies. Some hates are holy things. Keep that hate alive in your minds and hearts as you go about your jobs, only keep it impersonal as you would your feeling about kicking a blind dog.

'It is a very strange thought to me to realize that so many of the young fellows here to-day have never known a war. I only had six months of it, myself. But I want to tell those of you who may be called up that you mustn't be too ready to believe all you've read about it. One lot writes and says it was all blood and filth and the other lot that it was all high heroism and high jinks and concerts and pretty girls. Neither side is entirely right. There's monotony to face, and stage waits when the action sags and the field kitchens get lost and your letters and parcels don't reach you and you can't get a wash. That searches one out worse than going over the top.

'Before we all go home and make our plans, I want to say that I wish you boys all the luck in the world, and that I've put in my application for draft as army chaplain, and I am hoping very much it may be with the Normanshires. We haven't always understood each other, you and I. I believe this will be our chance. The curtain's up on a very big show this time, if I'm not mistaken. Don't belittle it, but don't get stage fright. And may God guard us all.'

CHAPTER XV

1

IT WAS BY the usual devious routes that Delaye received the news.

According to the milkman, England had been at war three days ago, but the postman thought not, adducing evidence of his eyes, that the Normanshires were still in barracks because his nephew, who was a Lance Corporal, had popped in to tea only yesterday. The fact that the Guild Hall was sandbagged out of all recognition was of course nothing to go by; it had been, for weeks, and half of the sandbags had burst already and the fleas (said the Lance Corporal) were getting something shocking and when it wasn't fleas it was dogs. And that, concluded the British Army, is what comes of being too prepared. Nex' time p'raps we should be a bit more backward in coming forward.

It was from their butler that the Roundelays had the news, as was right and proper. For had not Musgrave broken to them the tidings of war in 1914? and had he not, if it came to that, imparted the information that we were at war with the Boers to the late Mr. and Mrs. Roundelay, and Madam, being an excitable lady, had screamed and tugged at her pearl bracelet until it broke and scattered all over the boudoir floor, and cried out something about pearls for tears, which even as a young man Musgrave had regretted as being unworthy of the family as he stooped (stooping came easier in those days) to pick them up. And so, this Sunday morning, the old man plodded house and grounds seeking his family.

It was, he pondered, perhaps all for the best. For days and days there had been tension and strain at Delaye: someone always commencing to fidget round about eleven o'clock for the arrival of the newspapers: somebody always going down the avenue to see if the white roll of world events had been dropped like a bomb inside the lodge gates: the whole family except Nursie and Miss Amy converging to peer over each other's shoulders, weighing possibilities, breathing again as once more disaster was averted by a hairsbreadth before dispersing about their business and letting Musgrave get on with his. Very unsettling. He had even seen the whole family in the first kitchen, drawn like hounds to fox by the scent of printers' ink, one day, when the papers had got put on the table there, and passing on the news to housemaid and cook — anyone. They'd even all sat down together and had their elevenses that morning, master and man, mistress and maid . . . it had passed off wonderfully well, though Musgrave might have to deal with aftermaths if any of the staff got above and beyond as a result. Even the gardener's boy had been included, standing about on the flagstones, grinning and bashful in his loamy boots, his face in a mug of tea, until Musgrave had set him to handing cake to the ladies, *and* seeing that he passed the plate the proper side, too. There was no need to go all to pieces because Germany had.

Musgrave himself heard the news at the Severns: their butler, Mr. Cocker, had long given him a standing invitation to listen-in to the family wireless which years ago the squire had had extended to the servants' hall. Musgrave and Cocker enjoyed a mutual liking and esteem; upon no point of butlerhood had they yet faulted each other and now were never likely to. Their age, restriction of transport and local amenity had thrown them together upon their days off duty.

This Sunday, Musgrave, standing in the passage that led from dining-room to kitchens, ran his mind's eye over possible neglect of any point of routine before proceeding down the avenue. The table was, as usual on this more informal day, already laid for luncheon: no callers were to be expected before afternoon, if then: the housemaids having gone home, he had instructed Sue Privett to keep all doors open against the telephone ringing and to be sharp and quick to distribute any incoming messages. You never knew. Not that they were to be looked for just now. The line to Norminister had been uncertain for days and trunk calls to and from London were at present affairs of hours-long waits and no assurance of a connection at the end of them. It was owing to the officers being recalled to Norminster, Mr. Cocker said.

His conscience clear, Musgrave made his way to Severn Court. He wished a little that he had been able on this warm morning to wear the alpaca jacket in which in his pantry he cleaned his silver, or took the air in the grounds, but a call in other halls was no occasion for slackness. Bad form.

Sitting with the staff he listened gravely to Mr. Chamberlain.

'From eleven o'clock this morning we have been at war with Germany.' The reception was poor, interspersed with cracklings, indistinctness, sudden silences redeemed by the apologies of announcer and the sound of that old gramophone record of the peal of bells from some ancient City church. A setter dozed by the fireplace sprawled over by a large cat, property of Mrs. Canning the housekeeper. The vegetable maid nervously stooped to stroke them. This was being one of those betwixt- and-between occasions when you didn't know where to put your face or what to do with your hands. Social without being sociable. Like a funeral tea. She wondered if, in spite of the occasion and his higher domestic rating, she dare catch the eye of Joe Dale; but Mr. Dale was sweet on that Sue Privett, or Bessie didn't know the signs: came back with that peacock from Delaye in a high old temper and ever since had burst out about Sue, what a proper plucked 'un she was and how she understood animals in a way she really didn't ought, in the hall. But he was only a great gomeril of a lad that Bessie had heard Mr. Cocker himself tell Mrs. Canning would never make a footman and ought to be on the land. Otherwise, a match with Joe might lead on. Footmen became butlers in time, and on retiring took neat little publics, or got pensioned. And, gomeril or no, Joe *was* a man. . . .

They were all present to-day. She wondered when it was going to end, this sitting familiar with the upper servants at an unnatural time of day. Already Mrs. Canning was frowning at her slightly for fidgeting: the housekeeper's stays creaked a little under her black silk dress.

The wireless suddenly burst into the National Anthem and they all rose instantly to their feet and stood, serious and selfconscious, until the apparatus was silent. Mrs. Canning, looking at the oleograph of Queen Victoria over the dresser, said, 'We did better in her reign, bless her'.

'A great loss, Mrs. Canning. One felt it personally, in a manner of speaking,' answered Mr. Musgrave. Mr. Cocker hesitated, 'One doesn't quite like to suggest — but after all there's no harm — will you smoke, Mr. Musgrave?'

The tension relaxed. 'You'll stay lunch, Mr. Musgrave?'

'You're most good, very kind indeed, but I must be getting back to the family. Well . . . this is a bad business, but I am glad we heard the worst together.'

The housekeeper extended him her hand. 'Old friends, Mr. Musgrave. No one better. Now girls, it's time you were getting on with your work. I'll give you a hand with the trifle, Cook, as we're rather behind, to-day.'

2

Musgrave found Sir Edmund in the fold yard re-stapling a gate.

'I'm sorry to say, Sir, that we are at war,' and waited, poultry clucking round his boots, for he knew not what. There was young Mr. Stacey, now . . .

'Oh? Ah . . . Well — it was only to be expected, Musgrave. It'll send up the price of feed again, I'm 'fraid. Is lunch ready?' Musgrave plodded to the kitchen gardens. There was no need to tell Miss Sapphy or Miss Jessie who had gone to church and would have heard: that left her ladyship, the Major, Miss Amy, the young ladies, and Nursie, Mrs. Hatchett and Sue.

Lady Roundelay, gingerly putting grimed hands into her cardigan sleeves, said, 'Oh, Musgrave . . .! Oh, *damn* Hitler. Oh lor. Oh — well — ' and walked with him to the house.

Miss Margaret said, 'I must make a note to get the Guides some First Aid classes.'

Miss Amy, turning out a drawer in her bedroom, looked almost as scared as on that afternoon when she had arrived at the Palace for the Archbishop's garden party without her pocket handkerchief, and keened 'What can we *do* about it? They are sure to mistake the house for the barracks . . . does the master know? Do you think one should send one's valuables to the Bank? Would they take jewellery or only silver? But perhaps as they know us all so well . . . and they're *shut* on Sundays! Or are they open, do you think, as it's war time? Is anyone going in to Norminster to-morrow? There are the cellars, of course. They're down very *far*. I hardly think a bomb would reach them. We must all keep out of the garden. Dickon mustn't risk coming over — better call Lady Roundelay in at *once*, Musgrave!' And she had stood by her window anxiously watching for the return of

Miss Sapphy and Miss Jessie, whom, since eleven o'clock a.m., she might never see again.

A rather distressing incident, to Musgrave, and he sighed and reassured and aughed, and even took a couple of handsome shoe buckles of old French paste to the alleged security of his pantry.

Nursie was pottering in her room when Musgrave cautiously tapped at the door. He had consulted with Lady Roundelay as to the advisability of shocking the old woman with the news, but her ladyship (a most sensible woman, herself, always, in his admiring opinion) remarked that Nursie, already not quite right in the head, would have forgotten it in ten minutes and that that was one of the compensations of age. 'And in any case we can't keep it from her for ever. She'll have to learn to wear her gasmask, and senile though she may be, she isn't so far gone yet as to believe that it's a cure for asthma, or a new game, or anything of that sort.'

'Well, Nurse!' (lightly and cheerfully does it, for the old woman: a smile, even, and perhaps a little joke) 'It seems we're having another war.'

Nursie said, ' *I* don't hear anything. And I don't *smell* anything, either. What's happened to the beef?'

(These old people !) Musgrave contained himself with an effort.

'There is no beef,' he retorted austerely, and departed in a Maeterlinckian aura.

The Major was painting in the coach house. At the darkening of his canvas caused by the bulky figure in the doorway he refrained, it being a fellow male, from the otherwise instant and instinctive concealment of his picture, which, so profound was his exasperation with Hitler, was coming rather extra well.

'Is it war or the telephone?' he rasped.

'(Augh!) War, I'm afraid, Major.'

'Then I needn't wash my hands yet.' The gills of Major Dunston crimsoned and he added to the façade of Delaye a perfectly non-existent lilac bush.

Mrs. Hatchett, supervising the kitchen-maid's dishing up of luncheon, said, 'It's to be hoped this war won't make more work in the kitchen. If it goes on as long as the last one I shall have to think about making a change.'

Sue's eyes grew big as, cook being in the second kitchen by now, she asked shyly, 'Was Miss Angela very upset like, Mr. Musgrave?' Musgrave was paternal in view of events and the day being already at sixes and sevens. 'She didn't say much, not much. Never one to show her feelings,' he instructed the maid who knew that already better than he. 'We must remember that Miss Angela was doubtless thinking of Mr. Stacey — '

'Will — will 'e 'ave to go, Mr. Musgrave?'

'Naturally. And now I am going to sound the gong.'

3

The Roundelays were at lunch.

Musgrave, stooped to the cellaret, noted that the Major's burgundy was running low —

' — us good, for Jesus' sake'

concluded Miss Jessie.

— but he *had* mentioned it to the Major who perhaps had phoned Stone?

'If that fellow Goebbels — ' began Sir Edmund.

'Such an odd name. I never can spell it,' brightly capped Miss Sapphy. 'Oh, there! I've left my — but all things must be forgiven me to-day.' She was gone. Miss Jessie looked resigned. On this warm day the ever-open door that marked the wake of Miss Sapphy was pleasant rather than otherwise, but Musgrave with gentle ostentation shut it upon Miss Sophy as a protest and a species of debit note against the winter.

'I've been out of all the fun to-day,' remarked Evelyn Roundelay, 'beetroot bed.'

'We might think of putting those beds to sugar beet,' affirmed her husband. 'Where's the joint?' The butler murmured. Her ladyship rescued him. 'Couldn't get through to the butcher, my dear. If I'd gone on trying it would have cost the price of the sirloin. We shall have to live out of the garden and the shop till things get normal. It's at times like this I'd give my soul for a store cupboard. You might try — cold tongue, aunt Amy?'

'Is there a choice, dear? If not, of course, it — '

'Yes, ham or sardines and salad.'

'Then — I think — if it's all the same, perhaps the tongue.'

' — you might try to get us a rabbit, Edmund, this evening. Such a bore the shooting's let.'

'Jolly glad of the money,' said Sir Edmund.

'Oh, rather. And if it's true the buses to Norminster have all been altered — they have, haven't they, Musgrave?'

'Yes, my lady, and (at present, that is) the time-tables changed.'

'Confound 'em! That's the worst of a monopoly. Well . . . there's your bicycle, Margaret, but one can't bring home the week's stores on the handle bars.'

'There's the Severns' car.'

'Yes, we may have to cadge one lift, but one doesn't like — but I suppose the tradesmen will send?'

Major Dunston shook his head. 'Half of their cars impounded by the Government, they've even taken over Greensleave's van. How they expect tradesmen to get a living . . . and no compensation, that I've heard of. It's daylight robbery. And now it seems the Socialists have thrown in their lot with the Government.'

'Well, that was decent of them.'

'*Decent?* My dear lady, it's not decency, it's an eye on the next General Election. These fellows see that if they raised a stink at this crisis they'd get in dutch with even the best elements in their own party, so they're taking the long view. It's about the most dangerous thing that could have happened, actually, though it's disguised as public spirit. Quite good tongue, this.'

Musgrave was murmuring. 'My lady, Nursie . . . very much upset over there being no roast.'

'Oh *dear*! Angela, be a dear and run up. We *must* be firm with her. Tell her we've got none, either. If she'd only get a little more dotty we might persuade her that a sardine was a sirloin.'

'"But beef is rare within these oxless isles",' chuckled Sir Edmund gently. 'I wonder what Byron would have made of Nursie.'

'I hope nobody's waited for me,' announced Miss Sapphy flinging open the door and resuming her seat. 'Oh, Angela! Quite a collision. What ho, she bumps. What a popular song that was. Vulgar, but popular.'

'Same thing,' grunted Sir Edmund, 'the vulgar tongue — '

'Tongue,' confirmed Miss Amy. 'No, no more, thank you. Margaret, your aunt Sapphy has dropped her handkerchief.'

'Aunt Sapphy, aunt Amy says your hanky's on the floor.'

'Thank you, dear.'

'I say, mother, I had a letter yesterday from Ortrud Bohm, that German girl I was at school with — '

Lady Roundelay smote the table with her fist. 'No! No she doesn't! My heart bleeds for the German Jews as much as anybody's but I can*not* face a pale fugitive running tear-stained in what she stands up in down *this* avenue. I've read horrors until I'm sick and I know everything the Nazis have done and I can't cope with being wept over and having the old home in Hamburg or wherever it is described brick by brick and hearing that *Mein Vater* was suddenly not there and hasn't been seen since, and that the *Liebe Mutter* was raped before her eyes and my German wouldn't stand the strain. I can only say *Bitte* and *Danke Sehr* and *Sauerkraut* and *Mein Kampf,* and I won't, I won't, I WON'T!'

'God, no,' confirmed Sir Edmund. 'If she comes, I go.'

Margaret finished her ham. 'I was only going to tell you what she wrote and she's not Jewish, you know. . . . She says that she's joined the Youth Movement and her brother's in the army and he's got a commission he couldn't have hoped for in peace time as the Bohms aren't *geboren,* you know, and that they're not half so sniffed at as they used to be when they were only in trade, and she's really seeing some men at last and is having the time of her life. She actually used some German words, so that really looks as though she might even marry now she sees it's no good being so frightfully British. She was the one who came into the class once in a tartan skirt.'

'Gosh . . . well, sorry I spoke. I hope she hooks some *oberleutnant* — what happened in church to-day, aunt Jessie?'

Miss Jessie compressed her lips. 'Mr. Winchcombe preached,' she answered thinly.

'Good!'

'I didn't think so.'

'Why?'

Miss Jessie, a little offended at being pressed to give chapter and verse for an instinct and at all times inarticulate, selected, 'It was unsuitable. Not a sermon at all.'

'Bless him,' said Evelyn. Internally she was girding 'You silly old frump. I wish I'd been there!' She said aloud, 'What about you, aunt Sapphy?'

'Oh, my dear, it was a spectacle, a real spectacle. *Most* impressive, and the Archbishop giving the news himself — we had a high old time. I *know* you'll laugh, but I was reduced to tears. Quite a swamp.'

Miss Amy shot her a furtive glance. She had seen tear marks on her face at table, and Sapphy didn't cry for nothing. This Judas-like betrayal of her own feelings as a public piece of social chit-chat riled Miss Amy. If you had a grief, stick to it. But Sapphy had always been rather like that, a fribble Mamma called her, and she ought to know, only Mamma had done it on the grand scale and been known as 'dashing'. It closed Miss Amy's heart the tighter.

When Musgrave had left Miss Amy after bringing the news about war she had been filled with a kind of awe, a certain excitement too after the immediate shock. Possibilities opened up of an armistice with her sister and of all that implied. No more dodging and watchfulness and timing and feeling left out by Sapphy and Jessie, who only paired together *faut de mieux*; sisters they all might be, but of the three Amy and Sapphy were of the blood . . . she knew; closest in character, most similar in aim and taste and conviction and will-to-pleasure. Jessie didn't understand or want pleasure because she was religious. It was because she was plain; competition and participation were wiped out at the start, and she saved her face that nobody else thought worth saving by fixing herself on higher things that nobody was in a position to dispute. Amy and Sapphy had often talked it over together in girlhood days, before Sapphy had started that awful not speaking to one. Pleasant days . . . of outdoor games and knowing one excelled, and Sapphy with her music and the young men round the piano; outings in which rivalries if any were offset by the companionship and the reassurance that a sister stood beside you braving the same social occasion. Borrowing each other's finery —Mamma had always been a bit chary with her own. And then, out of the blue, everything stopped between her and Sapphy. And it was over such a piece of stuff and nonsense, too: one had run the eye of conscience so closely over the probabilities all these years that they really fined down to two: that Amy had said to a Mr. Marmaduke Fletcher — of a neighbouring family —

that Sapphy wasn't free to play tennis one afternoon when she was, only Amy wanted to protect her sister's almost certain performance on the court from exposure, because Mr. Fletcher and herself were crack players, or that Amy had eaten all the sausages one morning, thinking Sapphy had already had her breakfast in bed. One could approximately date the sausage episode because it was the morning after the Norminster Hunt Ball and breakfast in bed was a treat and a ritual and not commonly encouraged by Mamma who did any late lying there was in the family; and Amy had felt so bucked with the winter day and the overnight festivity that she'd come down for the meal. She had apologized fifty years ago for both tennis and sausages but it had only made Sapphy angrier. Regarding the sausages she had said that were not such a suggestion almost an insult it would be laughable, and as for the tennis, she had almost stamped her foot and cried that it was preposterous and that Mr. Fletcher's company was nothing on this earth to her, in the tone of voice which finally convinced her sister that the exact opposite was the case.

And now we were at war again, and Amy longing to cling to everyone, even friends, let alone Sapphy, and sense of injustice and exasperation had taken hold, stronger with keeping.

Well . . . it mightn't answer, even if one swallowed one's pride. There would be such a lot to unlearn and remember: not only that one now might say things to Sapphy, but trifles like being free to go downstairs with her and not passing messages through the great-nieces. Quite a worry to memorize! And besides, if they did make it up so late in life it would have seemed to have wasted the years more than ever. They might as well go through with it, now. See it out. Take a line and stick to it. And — what would the servants think if they became friends?

But all the same, one was any moment now in the hands of God, and at any second a bomb might fall through the ceiling Jessie, as was only fair, was probably feeling the least nervous because she was used to being in God's hands, but Amy came to them fresh . . . and even God's hands needed time to settle down in.

She began to babble. 'Evelyn, you won't go into the garden again – '

'No. Too tired.'

'It can't be safe. So exposed. And Dickon. Someone ought to go to the village to give him and the boy a chance not to come any more.'

Sir Edmund looked up. 'Eh? What's the matter with him?'

'Well — the raids. And don't you think we ought to move from our rooms rather more on to the *ground* floor?'

'If an incendiary bomb gets us we're done for wherever we sleep,' grunted Major Dunston; 'too big a space between the roof and attic ceilings to extinguish it. Have we a stirrup pump, Edmund?'

'Two. Use 'em for cleaning the fowl-house.'

'Ah. Takes two to work 'em properly, of course. Better move 'em in, I suppose.'

'Oh, I suppose so.'

'But if the *roof* isn't safe,' persisted aunt Amy, 'even a stirrup-cup — a stomach-pump — '

Evelyn laughed. The Major twitched with irritation. 'And what about the fire-engine? So far from here to Norminster . . .'

'Keep your hair on, aunt,' grated Sir Edmund. 'There's precious little to be done, in houses like this right off the beaten track, except keep your head and hope for the best.'

'But — '

'Aunt Amy, please!' Evelyn shot an apprehensive glance at her husband; she hated him to be worried and Delaye was a problem so vast and intricate that one thought about it as little as possible.

'Yes . . . yes, but they all seem to expect the raids to begin at once.'

'Oh no. They — '

Bang!

Past the window fell a hail of débris with assorted clashes, throwing up as finale a generous spattered star of yellow upon the panes. Miss Jessie started and bent her head, her lips moving silently. Miss Amy screamed. Miss Sapphy for the first time in her life called out, 'Oh my God!' and ducked under the table as Musgrave hurried in and the men and Margaret rose to investigate, while Lady Roundelay looked resigned. This was all of a piece with the whole morning. It was Margaret who found her voice.

'It's Nursie's tray,' she explained. 'She didn't like her lunch, I suppose. I think practically everything's broken except a spoon on the gravel. That's soup on the window.'

Musgrave confirmed. 'A little left over that Mrs. Hatchett thought could be spared, Miss. Not enough for the dining-room. I'll send out Sue.'

CHAPTER XVI

1

THE FAMILY DISPERSED, Lady Roundelay to the Lacquer Room to get away from everybody, an anti-social move which she dispassionately regarded as a sensible precaution, Major Dunston to the coach house, Sir Edmund to his stapling in the sun-filled quiet of the fold-yard. He was passed by Margaret on the way to fetch her bicycle from the old harness room; it was, she felt, up to her to keep a hand on the village pulse, she would sound the parents about those First Aid classes and knock up the school-master at his house which adjoined the playground. Nothing like immediate co-operation.

Mrs. Hatchett went into the kitchen gardens and consumed late raspberries, though it is to be admitted that she occasionally dropped a few into the basin in the crook of her arm. In his pantry, Musgrave, relaxed in alpaca jacket and adjusting the spectacles whose help he still refused himself when in the dining-room, re-read his mother's letters. In the lounge hall, Miss Jessie, upright in a profusely carved ebony chair with a pine-apple painfully grinding into her back, read through the Parish Magazine from Send For Our Brochure of Designs in Aberdeen Granite via the Vicar's weekly address to parishioners: ('Dear People, once again the Harvest Festival draws near reminding us in its kindly abundance, of God's goodwill towards us. This year, darkened as is its close by threats of war — ', the Vicar's words had gone to Press four days ago and were, though helpful, already out of date) to the advertisement of The Ecclesiastical Supply Co. (Telegrams: Religiocentric) which offered Communion cups in plated silver with washable lining, which Miss Jessie thought self-indulgent and ever so slightly profane. One shouldn't think of the body's health at such a time. If Christ had been afraid of germs where would the Church of England be?

In their bedrooms, Miss Sapphy and Miss Amy respectively leant out of her window to scan the sky for enemy aircraft and the avenue for callers, and sat in the extreme middle of the room as precaution against what the Germans might think of to send through the windows, a plan whose only drawback was that should emergency arise one was rather far from the embroidered bell-pull that would summon Musgrave.

Miss Sapphy was soon to be rewarded by a sign of life: Margaret, wheeling her bicycle across the gravel drive by the front lawn. She leant out. 'Margaret, you're not going out! Alone?'

'Village,' shouted her great-niece, and indeed, Margaret thought, preparing to mount, it was a jolly good thing war had broken out on Sunday. Week-days were usually busy ones at Delaye and everyone — particularly the servants — would have had time to get used to the idea and let off steam among themselves.

'But — are you all *right?* Aren't you nervous?'

'What could happen between here and the village?' shouted Margaret in common with thousands of other outgoing relatives all over England who trusted implicitly in the security of their familiar routes because they were familiar.

'Have you told your mother? But I will. Oh, dear — I don't *like* it for you.'

'Back for tea,' shouted Margaret.

Miss Sapphy sighed and stood dithering in indecision. The sky was a big place, of course, particularly that stretch between house and village . . . and all those great trees in the parks and pastureland made it more sheltered . . . and there were the neighbours on the way and the Vicarage to run in to . . . or Mr. Winchcombe might see Margaret home . . . you were always safer with a man. And there was dear Edmund coming round the shrubbery, his disgraceful but reassuring old pockets full of hammers and nails and goodness knew what.

'Edmund!'

'Hey?'

'*Must* you work right *outside* the house?'

'Fencing.' He did not even pause in his retreat.

'*Where?*' anxiously screamed aunt Sapphy.

'Fold-yard.'

'Couldn't you do something under *cover* until we know rather more where we are?'

'What?' (Damn the women.)

From the hall Miss Jessie heard the voices of sister and nephew and came out on to the flight of steps. On such a day and in times like these you never knew . . . service to others . . . though it was very pleasant in the hall. 'Can I do anything for you, Edmund?'

'Oh good Gad no, no thanks. Better go in and rest.' Miss Amy's ears were also competent and her window now framed her head, timorously peering. 'What is it? What's happened?' Her nephew disappeared round the angle of the house. This was intolerable. The fold-yard was now out of the question. He might be followed. Entering the outer kitchen by the side door and unhooking another coat from the boot-room he descended to the cellars. Nobody would pursue him there, the cellars had always stood for safety. Safety. Well, now he was down here he might as well vet the prospects in case there should be an air raid during the war.

The walls were thick but the whitewash and stone flooring made the great echoing place impracticable, unless you sank a small fortune in oil-stoves, or piped for gas, and with a crowd of old women in their night gear . . . But it might be possible to — It was at this point that the eye of Edmund Roundelay fell upon the old household accounts books and the question of air raid precaution was shelved. Drawing up the disused kitchen chair on which he had sat, records on knees, so often and happily in the past, he plunged into that volume dated 1788-1806. The book opened by this time almost invariably at the same entry — the eighteenth century was a favourite period. To-day, something of later date towards the end of the book slid from the covers and fell to the flagstones. He stooped to the thick yellowed slip of paper. There were one or two loose pages, he knew: this was smaller, put in evidently as emendation. It was nothing much, but annoying that the entries should not run consecutively.

'NOTA BENE', requested the thin, elegant handwriting: *To date from the 19th January, 1792, the Sum of One Crown paid af wage in Lieu of Notice to Polly Privett, Kitchen maid, difmiffed suddenly.*

Sir Edmund pondered. So a Privett had got the sack in the eighteenth century. He supposed that even in those days the domestic was beginning to get out of hand, though he would like to know wherein a mere kitchenmaid could have so presumed as to have got herself 'difmiffed' with five shillings in her pocket. Sue Privett was a direct descendant of this Polly: the week's gap probably represented the only break in that line of service. He turned back the pages. Yes. Here we were. One week later, the entry of the wage of Susan Privett. He smiled at the business-like burying of the hatchet, this tacit condoning of Polly's misdemeanour in her instant replacement by Susan. Someone at Delaye had an eye to good Privett service.

His absent gaze lighted on the brickwork recesses in which on their tan lay those bottles of Frontenac and Sillery. But one somehow didn't associate a Privett with tipsiness, even in that hard-drinking age.

Three storeys above his head Miss Amy returned to her chair and Miss Sapphy dithered again, mentally marshalling the possible objects upon which to expend her affection, and sudden sense of loyalty and enveloping world-pity. There was Maxwell who was splendid, as an old soldier, or Mrs. Hatchett, pathetic because she was a servant among strangers in national calamity or Evelyn who was the mother of a son, or even Angela as the sister of a brother, or the dog who might be gassed or killed when doing his unpaid duty of retrieving. That was a very moving thought. Or one might actually get the tea for Musgrave — only one didn't know where the things were kept . . .

With tears in her eyes Miss Sapphire Roundelay planned benevolences.

In her room, Nursie had put herself to bed. She was in disgrace, and knew it, and bed or the corner was associated in her mind with expiation. She smelt a strong odour of Coventry in the offing, guessed that her tea would be brought up by a servant instead of Margaret or Angela; she was at the same time bed or no, twitching with exultation at her deed. The middle-day dinner had been no meal for a person who liked butcher's meat and the tray had gone out of window without a hitch. That would learn them a lesson. Later would come the fussing over her and the extra attention, and she would, perhaps, find herself quite sorry about it. The afternoon was being very long and she might get up now and tell them so. But it was very warmish, the weather was, and Nursie hadn't got down all them stairs in she couldn't remember when. She wondered if she could? She'd do anything she set *her* mind to. To-morrow would do.

Her sleep-sodden eye, ere it closed, fixed upon one of her photographs framed in whelk-shells and dried seaweed: Stacey Roundelay at ten years old. She told it, 'Ah, Master Kenneth *you* never gave Nursie any trouble. Kenneth. Kenneth Culling that was his full name. Broom Water, Hillingdon. . . .

2

The washing up of the luncheon dishes was finished at last and Sue Privett free now until seven o'clock when she must give Mr. Musgrave a hand with the fetching and carrying of cold supper to the dining-room. She did not go to her bedroom on the attic storey to-day, or even take off her apron. There might be mucky work ahead of her. A nuisance that the master was in the fold-yard, doing work the gentry didn't ought to, and the coach house had the Major inside painting his pictures. Quite different it looked now from the old days, Sue's grandmother, coming over from Rohan to spend an afternoon at Delaye, had once told her; even Sue's mother could remember the time when the coach house *was* a coach house and the great family coach of the Roundelays had stood much where the Major sat now, fiddling with his paints. A very handsome turn-out the coach was, Gran said, with hand lamps in the sockets that glittered like gold. She'd even, as a young maid herself, seen it in use once, rolling down the avenue, but it'd been given up in her time, and the master — that would be the father of the old ladies — had bought a gig. The coach itself had been sold dirt cheap to a livery stables the other side of the county.

Sue was anxious. It wasn't only that this war might worry Miss Angela and trouble her ladyship about Mr. Stacey, but because of the peacock who might be scared away when the bombs began to fall, as Mrs. Hatchett said they would almost at once. Cook had been awful about it, talking about Jehovah and the wrath to come and Abraham's bosom, and asking that something she called 'this cup' might be taken from her, though she was drinking water out of a tumbler and the kettle hadn't even boiled for the after-lunch tea. Even Mr. Musgrave had got a bit short, and turned her off by asking her for some raspberries for the dining-room. Even the old ladies were taking on a bit, it seemed. And birds were scary of all guns. The dog didn't mind them, but he was a gun dog, broke to it, but even he carried on alarmingly on the Fifth of November when there was fireworks, so that Miss Margaret always had to shut him up. *He* knew the difference. But a bird wouldn't. Guns meant death to birds. . . .

Sue must try and contrive a shelter for the peacock that he would know and settle down in if danger threatened, and there seemed nothing for it but the little temple. Nobody ever used; it, not to say sat there, and the round roof was strong enough; it was the open spaces between the pillars that'd need filling in for safety, *and* warmth, with the winter coming on. The temple would give him his freedom, too, even if Mr. Dickon allowed him, he'd be miserable shut up, nights, in an outhouse.

There was old hay still in the mangers — no horses left to eat it, and straw in plenty in the granary for a bed. Sue, by rights, should ask the master or her ladyship for permission to take it and make the temple secure, but she was a little shy of the master since that time he'd wanted her pet to go to Severn Court, had never really felt the same towards him, kind as he was. And her ladyship didn't understand, either. There was Miss Angela. Sue would ask *her*.

Miss Angela she found at last, reading in the Turret Room, the old schoolroom that was; she looked pleased and said it was a good idea, and even could she help? 'Of course the poor thing must be kept warm, Sue. I think you'll find a lot of old hangings and unwanted stuff in the upstairs drawers, but better show them to me first in case they can't be spared.'

All over the house Sue flitted. There were cupboards and presses in the servants' sleeping quarters full, as Lady Roundelay sometimes said, of heaven really only knew what, and that in wet weather she occasionally inspected, though she had not yet examined a quarter of all the accumulations of years. But there was, she told visitors, a certain fascination in the business; you literally never knew what you might find, or what, should you be hasty with latch, bolt or button, would tumble out on to your head. She herself had once received a smart rap on the temple from a rusted crossbow that became dislodged upon her accidentally pulling a wooden pillar that turned out to be a whole panel, and which nobody could have suspected opened at all, though her husband knew all about it. Once, Evelyn had unearthed from an iron-bound chest in a passage a fool's motley, faded and crumpled, whose little bells still faintly tinkled when shaken. She had called it a Jester's dress and been corrected by Edmund, who said that the confusion of Jester with Fool was a very common error and would have been regarded as an insult in the sixteenth century by the serious, hired wit of rank superior to the capering clown who was sometimes retained by even private families of high social standing. And once she and Angela had unpacked and shaken out in the odour of orris root an elaborate eighteenth-century gown, property of that fated square peg in the round hole of Delaye, the French Marguerite Roundelay who had died by a compatriot's hand from sweeping through the situation as Rohan de l'Oeux, and whom Angela so strongly resembled in her small, dark fragility, if the portrait of Marguerite in the Lacquer Room was anything to go by.

Angela had tried on the gown to please her mother, and looked charming in it, and a little apprehensive, though death had not touched its fabric . . . it had never known the Paris of the Terror but remained safe at Delaye, Evelyn said, hinting circuitously. One had to handle Angela with care.

Dustily Sue rummaged comforts for the peacock: the strengthening of the temple itself she must contrive later, if the family seemed to be getting used to its changed appearance, filled in as Sue planned. It wouldn't look nice, of course, but looks weren't everything, in war.

From attic and basement she took what seemed discarded. One empty bedroom had produced from a built-in cupboard what looked like a man's shirt made of some stuff she didn't recognize, but so coarse — holes, too — and so stained on the front that it was really no good to anyone except perhaps cut up for scrubbers. Someone'd laundered it badly, all splashed with ironmould, like that. . . .

Sue Privett had always liked this room with the writing on the pane. It was only one of the servants' bedrooms and not even a large one like some of the others which, she had heard, were once filled with servants sleeping three and four together, before staff was cut down. It had a nice view of the garden, too; it would be wonderful to own it and furnish it as you liked. One could be happy sitting there, away from the kitchen and everybody. There had, Sue knew, always been a Privett at Delaye. She liked to fancy that a great-great-great-aunt or grandmother had been put in that room. The bedstead was grand; much too big for the room and not valuable, probably, or it'd be downstairs in one of the principal bedrooms. Must be something the matter with it. Sue could not know that the meat of one era was the poison of the next, or that French taste, horrorstruck at its tilt with the elephantine however valuable, homesick for gilt and lovers'-knots however incongruous when combined with a rosbif English husband, had effected at least one alteration in banishing the splendid Carolean tester to a servant's attic, or that in her turn the dashing Mrs. (Frances) Roundelay would reject, as tending to underline the whole marital question and if possible to stem the tide of daughters, the gilt Louis bed which was now upended in a lumber room in favour of Spanish walnut, upon which, to date, the untheoretic Miss Jessie nightly lay.

Sue could not dawdle in that top storey bedroom to-day, but she sometimes ran in with dustpan and brush to give it a bit of a clean up when, by rights, she ought to be belowstairs running errands for Mrs. Hatchett.

3

To the pile of stuffs laid out on the table in the Turret Room Miss Angela said Yes, Yes, Yes, I should think so, or that she wasn't sure about this and Sue had better ask her ladyship about the other. Sue spread the stained shirt. Angela scanned it.

'That's surely not one of Sir Edmund's?'

'Oh *no*, Miss Angela, he wouldn't never wear such an old thing.'

'Where did you get it from?'

'The room with the writing on the pane, that "Heryn I dye".' Angela snatched her hand away from the shirt. '"Herein". It means "in here".'

'Yes, Miss.'

'Oh, take it, take it away and tear it up.'

That was funny: it was what Sue had decided to do. That back breadth was whole and would stop a gap to keep the wind away. All that afternoon she laboured in the temple, tieing, tearing, folding, littering the circular floor with straw and hay until the sun set over the poplars bordering the Home field and the rooks returned clamouring. If the family made a fuss there was the coppice. The peacock might settle there though Sue didn't fancy it for him. Too damp.

It was while she was hurrying to the house that, casually, the great blue bird joined her, and she stopped to explain her action. Sue often told the chaffing servants that he understood all she said, in any case more than they knew.

'You see, dearie, we're at war, and you don't want t'be bombed by no Germans. They may come over any time now trying to kill us all in our beds.' The bird's eye gleamed as he listened. 'An' you mustn't be afraid if you see the house all dark an' think I'm not there. It's cos we mayn't show any light or the Germans could see to hit us better.'

She stroked his saddle and left him.

CHAPTER XVII

1

THE GONG SOUNDED for supper. Margaret, changed and ready, switched off the light — she must really speak to mother about the whole question of lighting and warn her to read the riot act over the servants, if necessary — ran downstairs, witnessed the emergence from her room of aunt Amy and her withdrawal on sighting aunt Sapphy. But to-night, for Margaret, the descent could be unbroken, for Nursie was under a cloud and didn't deserve a good-night visit.

From the passage on the lower storey aunt Jessie appeared, was advanced upon as usual by aunt Amy, hoping to make the dining-room in her company, who, this time, was doubly foiled by seeing her sister Sapphire in the company not only of Margaret but of Jessie as well, and as usual followed them after the necessary interval, during which Jessie made her nightly remark to her great-niece as to her little visit to Nursie.

At eight-forty-five Musgrave brought in coffee to the drawing-room; Miss Sapphy went to her table and poured out her solitaire marbles of habit, though she felt exceptionally talkative, while Miss Jessie, her Parish Magazine already consumed, got out her knitting and Miss Amy wondered what she herself should read. Edmund had *The Sunday Times* and Maxwell didn't seem to have anything, but was smoking in a silence that looked angry and Evelyn had flung herself on to the sofa and seemed to be half asleep. Margaret was busier than ever over her Guides' affairs and Angela at her usual place by the window, her feet on her favourite footstool. Evelyn through half-shut eyes was thinking 'She never gives the impression of idling even when she's doing nothing. Personality? Or just immense power of receptivity?'

Edmund cast his paper on to the floor, lit pipe and said, 'About this black-out business . . . it says here they're going to fine us pretty hot for lights showing. Are we all right?'

'The shutters ought to do the trick, with the curtains. But we shall *stifle* on warm evenings.'

'I'm too warm now,' capped Miss Sapphy, thankfully discarding her marbles for conversation, 'quite hottentot! Can't we have something a little less shut?'

'Yes, if you care to pay a hundred pound fine,' grunted her nephew. Aunt Sapphy laughed heartily, Miss Jessie chittered general commiseration and Miss Amy exclaimed 'A hundred pounds! There!' Edmund Roundelay unwillingly supposed aloud that they'd better look into the matter and vet the shutters and curtains from the outside of the house. Major Dunston said 'Want any help?' in a tone markedly deterrent to acceptance. Margaret got up. 'I'll do one side and you do the other, father.' Miss Sapphy called after them, 'You'd better take a lantern, Edmund, or you may fall *down*!' Evelyn, faintly groaning, reminded her that it was no use taking a forbidden light to look for forbidden lights, to which Miss Amy responded that she quite saw and that lights showed up so much more clearly in darkness and that she did hope that Edmund and Margaret would be all right as poachers were now in season. Major Dunston muttered, 'Oh good God!' but the invocation availed him nothing, for Sapphy and Amy suddenly elected for extreme femininity and dependence on masculine omniscience and worked steadily at him for the next six minutes to know how long the war would last and when or if the raids would begin. After all, he had been in the army and if that couldn't produce inside information nothing could. Also, men liked to be drawn out about their work and hobbies. The sisters were both pleasantly alarmed at the departure of Edmund and Margaret at such an hour to safeguard the house. It made a change. Made the drawing-room seem more cosy.

The sudden, reiterated raucous yells from somewhere outside in the night stirred Evelyn to remark, 'That confounded peacock! What's started *him* off? At a distance, it's exactly like laughter. Listen . . . there!'

'*Ha ha ha ha ha haha haha!*'

'If he's going to start *that*,' vaguely threatened Lady Roundelay. In her seat by the window Angela shivered in the warm air made warmer by closed shutters and curtains.

Sir Edmund and Margaret returned. 'You brave people! Well?' challenged aunt Sapphy. Her nephew addressed himself to his wife. 'Dining-room windows all right, I got Musgrave to turn on the lights inside and go over the house turning everything else on. Bathroom doubtful. It's that geyser vent that leaves about a foot of light showing all along the top.'

'Oh lor,' complained his lady. 'I suppose I shall have to set to and make a valance. Damn Hitler.'

'Servants' bedrooms all right on my side, most of 'em empty of course. The kitchen shutters won't do; quarter-inch of light showing through the join.'

'Oh *lor.*' Evelyn turned to her daughter. 'What about you?' Margaret referred to the notes she had made in the garden.

'Hatchett's bedroom light is much too near the window — '

'Then she'll have to use candles — '

'She won't like that,' prophesied the Major. 'You know what servants are, Evelyn.'

'I do. From now on, the war is entirely my fault.'

'Nursie was a blaze. She hadn't even drawn her curtains, but of course she couldn't know — '

'That old woman,' began Sir Edmund, 'going to be a fearful problem, ask me. We can't give her candles or a lamp or she'll set the place on fire.'

'One of us'll have to unscrew her Osram every night — '

'That'll be awful fun for somebody, and what about the winter? She can't sit in the dark from tea to bedtime.' Evelyn said, 'I see myself going into Norminster to-morrow there never to cease buying dark material and electric candles, and coming home weighed down like a carthorse. Somebody'll *have* to come with me. And I shall be sewing till the end of time.'

'Going to cost a pretty penny,' fretted her husband, 'and nothing to show for it.' Miss Jessie, knitting, made no offer of help. Sewing for the house wasn't working for the poor and the house was Evelyn's province as the bills were Edmund's. Aunt Sapphy exclaimed that she'd like to come and she could change books for everybody and they might have coffee at Dolly's, 'and if it will *help,* Edmund, I'll of course go without a light at *all* in my room. Just something to undress by, and as for baths, couldn't we all have them in the daytime, or every other night — '

' — and the staircase windows are *impossible*,' concluded Margaret, 'one can see the hall and landing lights quite clearly through the curtains.'

'Well, that about finishes *us*,' announced her mother, 'those curtains are twelve-foot long if they're an inch. We'll have to scrap the hall and landing lights and manage on torches and candles.'

Margaret sat down and began to make shopping lists. The family simmered. Evelyn asked Margaret if she had seen the peacock. 'He was making the most infernal racket just now, like a maniac laughing.'

'Yes, he was outside the dining-room windows when I joined up with father.' Angela commented, 'Not in the temple, then? Sue's made him up a shelter there.'

'No, right up by the house.'

'Did he come from the temple?'

'No, from the shrubbery as far as I can remember.'

Angela was thoughtful. 'I wonder if he's been to his shelter yet?'

'Trust *him* to make himself comfortable.'

Sir Edmund knocked out his pipe. 'Talking of Sue, I came across a rather nice entry in the accounts books this afternoon. That Polly Privett who was here in the French Revolution seems to have got the sack. A week's money and no notice.'

The response was tepid. It was aunt Sapphy who pounced. 'I thought you were in the fold-yard!' Her nephew, recollecting the cause of his escape to the cellar, changed the subject. But he had had one listener in his younger daughter, stilled, mentally turning over the item. Her father was speaking again, if to her relief or disappointment Angela hardly knew.

'Max, oughtn't we to be doing something about your mother?' Evelyn, from a haze of calculation of costs of torches and material, unwillingly supported her husband. 'I'll ask her down here, if you think — '

'Good Gad, no,' rapped Major Dunston, 'she'll be all right. If the Mater'd wanted a funk-hole she'd've asked for it.'

'She mightn't have, you know, nice feelings, and all that.' Sir Edmund looked shriven. 'Well . . . if you think she's all right . . . I must say I couldn't stand having the Lost Tribes pumped into me with all our other worries.'

'It's The Second Coming, now. She scrapped the L.T.s years ago. It's been The New Messiah for some time. Goes to meetings full of Indian pansies. Beats me.'

Miss Jessie compressed her lips and rose. It was a great pity that Chrissy, one's own sister, should make a travesty of sacred subjects and lay herself open to getting talked about like that. Maxwell was far from young, but he was still only a nephew. About the actual question of this New Messiah of Chrissy's, Jessie herself refused to be drawn into discussion though she had once written to her sister and pointed out that we had one already therefore there could not be another. Surely Chrissy would understand all the things behind that reminder: that one had not been able, of reverence, to bring oneself to write? That if there were two, what was to be done with the first one, and where did religion stand if Christ was, after all, the wrong one? Though to decorate the meetings with pansies was a pretty idea enough. Thoughts. . . .

'Well — good night, everybody.'

Evelyn roused herself. 'What? Oh, good night.'

'Going up?' brightly enquired Sapphy.

'Don't forget the lights,' came from the interior of the wing-chair containing Edmund Roundelay. Miss Sapphy was valiant. 'I'll come with you.' Miss Amy, relieved, for now she too could seek her bed, was wondering what difference it would make if Chrissy did choose to escape from the dangers of London and come to Delaye. On whose side would she range herself about the tennis (or the sausages)? One really hardly knew Chrissy. Or she might like Jessie best, they being both in religion.

Evelyn, wearily stumbling upstairs in the dark after having twice lost her bearings entirely and embraced the same armoire in the hall, was thinking.

It had been a queer day. And that recurrent number eleven had cropped up again in this war, after twenty-five years.

The Armistice: the eleventh hour of the eleventh day of the eleventh month.

And now an Ultimatum which expired at eleven o'clock.

'From eleven o'clock this morning we have been at war with Germany.' 'Some peace which came at the eleventh hour.' No. That wasn't either of the wars; it was what Basil Winch-combe had said about that top room with the writing on the window-pane.

2

There was moonlight on the lawn.

Angela, pressed against the window of her room, waited, strained with listening. But there was no more eldritch laughter. Yet he came.

Round the corner from the shrubbery the peacock swept, taking the stage as she watched: Slowly, deliberately — or were peacocks always leisured in the process? — he displayed himself and paraded the lawn, sometimes pausing to look up at the sky.

Waiting? Listening? The exact word eluded her until it came with an impact of incredulity and a dismay that was not lessened by her own self-ridicule.

Guiding. No. *Signalling.* Pitting his wit against the darkened mass that was Delaye, moving with the moon's light that his betraying colours might be seen at their most glittering. Where there were peacocks there was human life. Where there was life there could be death. And he knew it.

Heryn I dye. Thomas Picocke.

Angela groped her way to the bed. She was striving against belief that she must see that room again, and alone. That shirt which Sue had brought in had come from there.

Angela lay in a woebegone confusion, her brain milling its questions.

Assuming that her fantastic impression of the bird's signals to the sky was correct, what about Sue, and Angela herself? He wished them no harm, he was apparently devoted, in his way, to the maid, though he had bitten Angela. Why? Because she had offered him some hard-boiled egg.

That got one nowhere.

She had seen him walking out with Sue. What did that recall? A servants' phrase. 'Walking out.' Even in mental desolation Angela almost smiled. Yet it hadn't been amusing at the time.

Run, running runner, run . . .

From nowhere the sickeningly familiar line slid into her brain.

CHAPTER XVIII

1

EVEN NOW, when remembering the following day, Evelyn Roundelay will say with placid irony, 'Oh, there was something for everyone: even a dash of low comedy for those who can appreciate it.'

It began before breakfast, with aunt Jessie tripping down the short flight of stairs that led to the lavatory, and slightly straining her ankle. The fact that she had contrived to do it in daylight added fuel to Lady Roundelay's exasperation; achieved in the black-out a more reasonable aura would have surrounded the affair. Then, the postman arrived so late that nobody could read their letters before the day's round began — extra tiresome, as there seemed to be about thirty for every member of the family; Angela came to table looking tired out, and aunt Sapphy had not forgotten her overnight intention of coming in to Norminster where Evelyn, swiftly planning, meant to lose her. It could be done, and had been, in the past. You just went to the furnishing fabric department of Tatfield and Winter, told Sapphy to go and buy what she wanted — and vanished through the further door facing the Guild Hall. Subsequent explanations offered endless choice and permutations when, two hours later, you rejoined her at the bus stop. Sometimes the *amende déshonorable* had to be made over the table if they unluckily chose the same restaurant for luncheon. All outings and so all eating places were a treat to aunt Sapphy, although she had not failed to be cozened by Dolly's, which, fortunately, she couldn't often afford. Aunt Amy ate wherever she was advised, while aunt Jessie consumed a chastened scone anywhere and subdued the flesh at a cost of sevenpence halfpenny, counting tip to the waitress.

Evelyn had once told Basil Winchcombe that in the early years of her acquaintance with aunt Jessie she had tried to establish relations by giving her fish on Fridays during Lent, but the gesture had not, so to speak, appeared to ring any Sanctus bell with her new in-law. The curate considered. 'That, of course, isn't amusing', he assured Lady Roundelay, 'but it happens to suit me,' and laughed till he cried.

The family had barely begun its eggs and bacon before the telephone rang. Margaret returned from the hall. 'The blacksmith wants to know if we've all got our gas-masks.'

'What's that to do with him?'

'They've asked him to be District Warden and he doesn't know what it'll involve, yet, and he says if we haven't got them, the schoolroom will be open at seven to-night for fitting and distribution.'

'Kind. But how do we get there and back? Does he expect us to take Nursie in a wheelbarrow, and all go without dinner? And what about aunt Sapphy and aunt Amy and aunt Jessie?' queried Sir Edmund.

'Well,' considered Lady Roundelay, 'I think we've all got ours, if I can remember where we put 'em. They weren't fitted, just handed out a year ago after the September Crisis. I suppose they're all right.' She turned to the butler. 'What about you and the maids, Musgrave?'

'Er — I 'ave my respirator, m'lady. I and Mr. Severn's man, Cocker, went over to the village when they was first given out. Mrs. Hatchett says she'd prefer not to 'ave one and the maids all say they can't breathe in theirs.'

Evelyn had expected that; according to the remembered accounts of her neighbours, nearly all servants made a similar declaration. To the domestic mind, not to be able to breathe in your gas-mask conferred an unassailable gentility.

'We shan't want 'em out here,' pronounced the Major, upsetting the public-spirited homily to the staff that Lady Roundelay was preparing to emit, 'they can't send gas down in sufficient volume — '

'Mother, I *must* go back to the phone.'

'Yes. Tell your boy friend — I dunno!'

Margaret, in the hall, could be heard enquiring what defects were to be looked for in gas-masks. She returned with a written list.

'The rubber can perish; the cellulose eye-pieces crack: the cotton come unsewn: the valve be dried, cockled or missing: the rubber band be too high if it's a Medium and too low if it's a Large (or be missing), the three safety-pins missing, and the nose-piece battered. If you'll collect them all, mother, I'll vet them by this list, only I don't know where to look for the valve.'

'Thing like a gramophone record in the inside on top of the nose-piece,' supplied Major Dunston, taking another rasher.

'Where's yours, aunt Sapphy?'

'My dear, I don't believe I *know*.'

'Well, may I go and look?'

'Yes, of course, *anything* — but not among the hats. I do feel practically certain where I didn't put it.'

'What's the use of 'em if you haven't been fitted?' groused the Major, 'mine's O.K. because I know something about 'em from the last war, and when this fellow at the schools gave me a Large because I'm a man I ticked him off and took a Medium. It's the shape of a face as much as size of head. Stands to reason if someone's got a face like a pear — '

'You *are* funny!' said aunt Sapphy.

'A pear,' confirmed aunt Amy.

''Reminds me: if you have time, Evelyn, I'd be glad of another tube of Prussian Blue —'

'Oh, my dear Max!'

'That sounds *most* unpatriotic!' Aunt Sapphy looked facetious.

'Aunt Jessie, what about your mask?'

'I have none.'

Evelyn was wondering if this statement of dearth was a manifestation of trust in divine Providence, and was ready with a reminder that heaven helps those who help themselves, when aunt Jessie explained that on the afternoon, last year, that she had walked over to Delaye to see about it, the distributing centre was closed and then the Crisis was over.

'Well, we shall all have to try and go down in turn, though heaven knows how. If we aren't properly fitted out it's so bad for the servants.'

'"*Quis custodiet ipsos custodes*",' murmured Sir Edmund, handing his cup.

'Mmmmmm-mmm . . .' began the Major, 'd'you remember that fellow at school in old Prendergast's form — Barclay? Burbury? No. Barton. Barton. And that morning — ha ha ha! — he translated — ha ha! — translated his bit've Pliny — '

But even at this immature stage Edmund Roundelay joined in and the scholastic *conte* hocketed very deviously to its close while Miss Sapphy and Miss Amy sought, like eager hens, what grains of enlightenment they could peck and Lady Roundelay waited in an affectionate fume.

'What about Nursie, mother?'

'I did take a mask for her out of an unappetizing heap at the time, but of course she couldn't be fitted, and frankly I don't see any use in trying.'

' 'Nother thing,' said Major Dunston, 'we shan't hear the sirens all this way out if there *is* a raid.'

'Where are they?' asked Evelyn. 'Do you know, Musgrave?'

'Mr. Severn's man, Cocker, tells me one is at the Norminster barracks, m'lady: it appears the postman's nephew is stationed there . . .'

'Over five miles away,' gloated the Major.

'But the postman thinks, sir, that in the event of a raid we shall all be warned by the local Wardens.'

'Splendid. And how are they to get here in the dark?'

'Some 'as bicycles I presume, sir.'

'They'll be a lot of good over ploughed fields. What about the outlying farms? Half of 'em aren't on the phone and if there is a raid the line'll be the first thing to go.'

'"Blest pair of syrens",' mused Sir Edmund, and chuckled.

'It — does seem a little difficult, sir,' despondently agreed Musgrave.

'Well . . . it's all being quite an experience,' revelled Miss Sapphy, 'I expect we shall look back on this morning, one day, and have a good laugh.'

'May I remove your plate, Miss Sophia?'

A woman who could joke, however ignorantly, about war, thought Musgrave as he bore his tray along the passage to the kitchens, was of course preferable to one who cried out and panicked, but a man couldn't help feeling jarred by it through anxiety about the family he served and the safety of Delaye.

Miss Sapphy was so annoyed that she said, 'I think Musgrave is looking very *old* this morning.' Evelyn got up. 'Well, we'd better be making a start, aunt Sapphy, if you really want to come, though I don't advise it; it'll be one long scrimmage round and I don't even know when we can come back — '

'Oh, *that* won't trouble me, my dear, I shall be able to help, so. And if we miss a bus we can always lunch out — '

Margaret handed a list to her mother. 'That's what's wanted, and I'll go to Delaye on my bike and get in this morning's food. You can't carry everything. One of the Guides'll be waiting at the pub to give you a hand. Don't tip her. Bring her some sweets.'

'Bless you! But you won't raise anything fit to eat in Delaye. You'll all have to make do on a ham omelet and cheese and fruit for lunch, and anything tinned Margaret can find. Edmund, if you and Max can't face it, ask the Severns to give you a meal.'

'Good Gad!' Her husband looked astonished. 'Too much to do. Can't go changing m'clothes all day.'

' — and tell Dickon to kill four fowls, they'll do for the middle of the week.'

Margaret said, 'Cousin Max, if you understand about these gas-masks couldn't you fit us all?' He shook his head. 'No good, my dear girl, we used Service pattern, not like these Civilian contraptions. Shouldn't care to take the responsibility.'

'But you'll take your masks *with* you into Norminster. They must, mustn't they, Edmund?' keened aunt Amy. 'I mean, it would be *something* to put on.'

'Hey? Oh, I suppose so. Extra thing to carry, though. Well, I must be off. Evelyn, you might just find out as you're going in why Ezor's haven't sent up that size I ordered.'

'What size? Oh, *size*.' It later appeared that Evelyn, together with the size and the Major's Prussian Blue, might find time to price uncurled ostrich feathers in Tatfield and Winter (aunt Amy), purchase a copy of *The Church Times*, and a card of slate-grey darning wool (aunt Jessie), and bring back a postal order for one-and-nine-pence (very respectful request sent via Musgrave, bearing the sum itself, from Mrs. Hatchett).

Even as Lady Roundelay stood in the hall waiting for Miss Sapphy the telephone rang. Receiver in hand she called up the staircase well, 'Aunt Sapphy, we must be going. Delaye. Yes . . . ?' The voice of Basil Winchcombe said, 'Oh, it *is* you, Lady Roundelay. I say, *have* you heard? The Archbish' has been threatened with twenty-five expectant mothers billeted on him.'

'My *dear* . . . well . . . he'll be able to Church them cheap. But of course it's not true.'

'No, really, I'm serious. He's turned the whole matter over to his secretary and issued an encyclical, Papal Bull, or what not, to the effect that he will accommodate a similar number of boys at Normansmead if sent under suitable supervision. They'll be put in the South wing of the Palace, trained for his private chapel and he won't even see them. I'm sorry the story tails off so, but the first part was such that I had to ring you.'

'But, they won't *really* do things like that, will they? I mean, it can't be done.'

Certainly, Normanshire had heard a year ago through its newspapers and wireless sets of an evacuation scheme by which innumerable strangers of no credentials at all were to invade the homes of private householders, where, the B.B.C. announcer brightly concluded, he was sure they would very soon become household pets (some listeners swear he said Pests), but the enormity of the idea was so vast, violating as it did the very principles of privacy and individual liberty, demolishing at one blow that rule of life that the Englishman's home is his castle, that, indignation and apprehension having passed with the Crisis, the county went back to its affairs, social, domestic and agricultural and thought of it no more. Some things are too bad to be true, and the word evacuation was one which they only associated with the worming of their dogs.

'Well, so long as they leave *us* alone . . . can you imagine a mob of children here? They'd drive my husband and the Major distracted, and the old ladies, and my cook would give notice at once and then where'd we be?' And, indeed, the idea was so preposterous, looked at from any angle, that Lady Roundelay was not perturbed. 'I suppose people aren't forced to take in these children and mothers?'

'That's what the whole village wants to know. It appears to boil down to this: that the scheme is voluntary for the receptionist until the need to put it into operation arises, when it becomes compulsory, though at no time is it compulsory to the evacuee.'

'But that's not fair.'

'It's British hypocrisy. The Government daren't take the onus of forcing us to accept a measure that can only be universally unpopular, so it is leaving us in doubt on the matter, and diffusing an idea of leaving the choice to us. They've already begun to praise the reception areas in the newspapers for joyfully co-operating in a scheme they mean to fine us heavily for if we refuse to. Why, old Burrowes has two girls of nine and twelve billeted on him — '

'*Burrowes?* But he's bedridden and on the Old Age Pension and only has a village woman to come and feed him and clean up twice a day for half an hour — '

'Well, there it is; the only person who's been definitely exempted is Miss Tybonnet at the post-office, who's overwhelmed with extra work over the billeting money and at it till ten o'clock at night. The poor woman looks a perfect wreck . . . I say, Lady Roundelay, what about your son?'

'Oh, he'll be off soon, I suppose.'

'One does feel so savage about it . . . is Sir Edmund taking it hard?'

'He hasn't said anything, you know.'

'No. One doesn't, does one? It's always been a theory of mine that eldest and only sons ought to be exempted entirely except for Home Defence, particularly in the case of the old name and the historic house. Too much is at stake; it's race suicide of the worst type.'

'I know . . . and what about you, Basil?'

'I'm down to go out as Padre but don't expect to hear just immediately. I went over to the barracks yesterday afternoon after children's service to see if I could be doing anything in the meantime. All I got the offer of was to guard one of the bridges in Norminster.'

'What against?'

'Two old men fishing for dace and the language of the bargees, apparently. I shall be issued with an armlet of sorts and a rifle that I rather fancy I shan't be allowed to fire in emergency because I'm not in the army. Otherwise it's a picked position.'

'"Have you had quiet watch?"' bantered Evelyn.

'"Not a mouse stirring." Crosses Left,' responded Winchcombe.

'Mice?' exclaimed Miss Sapphy on the staircase. 'Don't say we have *mice!*'

2

That was at nine-forty-five. At eleven-ten, Evelyn Roundelay and Miss Sapphy were still waiting outside the public house at Delaye for the ten-thirty bus to Norminster. Miss Sapphy watched the cottages, the vicarage field, and a dog, while Lady Roundelay rather thought that a tin advertisement of Leney's Ales would be found written on her heart. When another ten minutes brought no reassuring red and cream monster to fill the road, she was impelled to make an odious pun about the advertisement.

The Léner Quartette
Leney's Quart Tot

Greatly daring, she sat at last upon the bench outside the pub for the first time in her married life. It would, of course, be all over the village by the afternoon that she had taken to drink, but was worth it. Aunt Sapphy sank down too, and said she'd 'fancy' a glass of sherry and her niece-in-law was struck as much by the common-sense of the idea as by its impossibility. It took a really good woman like Sapphy to have no sense of social nuances whatsoever. To her, a dubious speakeasy and the cocktail bar of the Criterion would be equally an outing. Occasionally aunt Sapphy would alternatively suggest their walking on and letting the bus overtake them or giving it up and walking back home, to which Evelyn, worried, responded that if they walked on the bus might fail to see their signals and if it didn't come at all they couldn't walk to Norminster, and that if they went home the bus would arrive two minutes after their backs were turned.

Occasionally, villagers came up to condole with the ladies of Delaye about the war, of which they had much to say, but of the bus time-table no information of any kind. At her end of the bench Miss Sapphy held a small levee, happily receiving personal enquiries and greetings, and dispensing answers as to the rest of the family with great volubility and fundamental lack of knowledge of her subject.

From the window of the saloon bar the landlord looked down something sourly upon the backs of Lady Roundelay and Miss Sapphire, for did not Major Dunston deal with Stone for his wine? And the fact that the landlord did not stock wine himself, there being no demand for it, still left the whole question of beers and spirits unsettled. Six dozen of ginger-beers and lemonades for the school and Guide Treats at Delaye twice a year was neither here nor there. Deliberately he flicked half an inch of cigarette ash on to the unconscious floral toque of Miss Roundelay. Higherderangers. A very dressy flower. Same as what Queen Mary favoured for *her* rats.

At the moment that Lady Roundelay had given up watching for the bus and while The Leney Quart Tot was dangerously in the ascendant, the bus arrived, and the conductor — not what Miss Sapphy described as 'the same man' — alighted for a few minutes to answer questions about the war posed him by two loitering villagers and an avid crone at an upper window. It was felt that coming as the conductor had from a market town ten miles away, the news, if not better, might be different.

The bus contained five strangers, two soldiers, four gipsies who sang uninterruptedly on the back seat to which for hygienic reasons they were relegated, and Mrs. Holland who greeted the Delaye party as one shipwrecked, asked if they thought that the luncheons at Greensleave's would have 'gone off owing to all this' and sympathetically grieved over the putting to sleep of all Mrs. Galbraith's cats. At the next stop, outside the bungalow of Mrs. Galbraith, Champion Milk of Magnesia was seen, taking gluttonous bites out of his pad in the verandah, was cheered by the driver ('Eh, Maggie, lad!') while his mistress waved to the Roundelays and Mrs. Holland, and Evelyn marvelled at the times which had induced in herself, a disliker of Persian cats, regarding them as she did as boring animated hearthrugs, a warm pleasure and relief that the Persians of Mrs. Galbraith were still alive.

In Norminster, the streets seemed to be extra congested, and a tanned policeman wearing a tin hat with a reversed chin-strap binding the back of his head that caused him to resemble a determined but fashionable dowager, dealt with the traffic, receiving in the process a succession of raps from the official respirator carriers that the townsfolk self-consciously, and with smiles to complete strangers, had slung to their backs, and which gave, until you looked at their clothes, an impression wholly misleading of a race meeting. There was not, to Lady Roundelay's immeasurable relief, a run on the Bank. Business was as usual. It was only at the chemist's and in Woolworth's that an unmistakable queue had assembled for Keating's Powder, ringworm ointment, toilet paraffin and carbolic soap that the feast might be more joyful and the guests be more contented, and the Government safeguard several hundreds of thousands of children from the cities at the expense of their hosts by infecting those in the rural districts.

In Tatfield and Winter's, Evelyn lost Miss Sapphy without a hitch by the lure of Miss Amy's (uncurled) ostrich feathers. It was to be about her only achievement; for with mounting consternation Lady Roundelay discovered that in regard to the laying in of blacking-out material and torches three-quarters of the city also had the same idea, and to-day, typically, belatedly, apprehensively, good-naturedly were trying to take those precautions which had been open to them for weeks past, and found themselves paying inflated prices for black paper through which straws could be shot, repellent megaphones of cardboard for the shielding of electric lights, and patent bulb-darkeners whose feature was the giving of a black-out so complete inside the house that the family, having attached them, could not see one inch in front of their noses, though the bills from the electric light company remained as bright as ever. But despite the faintly beleaguered atmosphere and the feeling that every man's hand was against you what time the last yard of black cardboard was snapped up under your nose, humour of our rough island quality still held.

The search for torches took Lady Roundelay to Boots, W. H. Smith, Marks and Spencer, The British Home Stores, Woolworth's, three chemists, four bicycle and six wireless and radio accessories shops. Some had three batteries left which fitted no torch in the establishment, the rest had a magnificent display of torches and no batteries at all, although as mitigation to her tour she was at various times offered bicycle lamps, a pedestal light costing half a guinea and a ship's lantern.

It was for the moment evidently hopeless; they must just be as careful as they could at Delaye and wait until the emergency rush was over. Delaye, reasoned its mistress, stood in its own grounds half a mile back from the high road and the Wardens and police, if any, would not have time to come all that distance to scold even if they could see through the trees, so it really left the house safe from everything but the Germans, who would with luck give very little trouble, far less, certainly, than Nursie and the cook. It would be catastrophic to be fined, and Edmund dreaded falling dividends worse than falling bombs. Meanwhile the torch-cum-paper chase developed into an affair in which, on passing Mrs. Holland or other friends in the act of vanishing into shops, Evelyn cried out 'No use! I've tried there myself!' or was called to over a hurrying shoulder, 'They say Flaxman's still got a few.'

At 1.20, Evelyn sighted Miss Sapphy turning into Dolly's and herself promptly collapsed into Greensleave's.

The bus home to Delaye village already contained Mrs. Holland and Miss Sapphy and by some unexplained whim left Norminster so punctually that Evelyn nearly missed it and the butcher's boy panting up with the Roundelay meat entirely did, until by taking a short cut and pedalling wildly he intercepted the bus at the next stop, and the joint was passed from hand to hand until it reached Lady Roundelay — a not unfamiliar routine.

It was at about this time that in her room at Delaye, Nursie, her luncheon consumed, prepared to embark upon the small adventure of a journey downstairs. She meant to see what the family was up to and what the house looked like. According to her reception by any Roundelay by her encountered would depend her own attitude towards the tray she had thrown out of the window yesterday. It might be an apology from Nursie or it might be a good talking-to. Nursie couldn't tell. Certainly the midday dinner, she pondered, had been very poor again — no butcher's meat, only an egg mess and some bits and pieces bought by Margaret from the village, according to Sue Privett who brought in the tray; on the other hand, Nursie had been hasty, yesterday, so that equalled matters. She'd see.

Like a parrot over his cage, Nursie laboriously handed herself down the staircase.

3

At the Mill House the bus conductor threw out a roll of newspapers, causing Miss Sapphy who had seen nothing at all so far except a month-old copy of *The Screen Pictorial* in Dolly's to speculate aloud as to the nature of the latest news on what she described as 'the headlinings'; at Mrs. Galbraith's bungalow the bus stopped to deliver an unmistakable bundle of fish, a carton labelled 'Pussipurr' (which looked as though the Persians were to be spared), stopped again to eject Mrs. Holland who diminished across a footpath and at the post-office slowed up to cast a roll of black-out paper into the small front garden.

At the public house, where Leney's Ales at last meant nothing to Lady Roundelay, they being now overlaid by filleted plaice and two cups of coffee, a Girl Guide, faithful and bored unto death, received her share of parcels from the ladies of Delaye and with them slowly achieved the two miles to the lodge gates against which Lady Roundelay leant exhausted while Miss Sapphy recklessly sat on the post.

'Come on, aunt Sapphy. I'm parching for my tea.'

They straggled up the avenue to find a small crowd by the front door which, sighting them, broke up, surrounded them and began the discussion with renewed energy.

Tired as she was, Evelyn still found vitality for dismay in the fact that her husband had been drawn into whatever was going on.

'Ah, my dear, we seem to be in a bit of a fix. This gentleman is the district Billeting Officer — '

Evelyn's heart flopped and she said the instinctive thing.

'We're tired out. We *must* have some tea.'

Musgrave, his face lined with anxiety, disappeared up the steps, even as Evelyn's eye, beginning to focus more clearly, took in the presence of Mrs. Hatchett, a housemaid, the gardener and her elder daughter on the drive.

Margaret said stoutly, 'I've told him how we're placed.' The officer who looked overworked and disillusioned, remarked 'You will not be expected to receive evacuated persons for three days; you've by now received your notification of my call, I presume?'

'I — I never saw it; it may have come this morning, but I haven't had one second even to read my private letters . . . are private houses compelled to take in strangers, Mr — I'm afraid I don't know your name?'

'Mallet. You will be allowed to billet boys or girls, or mothers accompanying young children,' evaded the official. 'You are down for fifteen children accompanied by two teachers, or ten mothers with babies, or twenty boys or girls.'

Lady Roundelay felt her face growing green as fragmentary aspects of the family's future for an indefinite period shot into her brain. The chairs brought by Musgrave arrived timely indeed. From hers, she opened a faltering case for the defence while her daughter vanished up the steps.

'I don't think you can possibly realize how impossible this is. I have not sufficient bedding or bedsteads for one quarter of such a number; my four spare rooms are practically dismantled, and one of those is my son's, who may be home any day, now. My staff is barely adequate to our own needs, catering is never easy — oh go on, Edmund.' For it was a lamentable fact that oratory, the true and telling argument, was never at call, at any rate in her own case. She had, for years now, ceased to aim any higher than declaring bazaars open, the prepared word, rehearse it as she might, escaped her on the platform offering no substitute, where, she had discovered, one's breath vanished as well, and one's voice came from one what sounded like an octave higher than normal. Edmund, she reckoned, might not be domestically plausible in the way that only a woman can be, and to another woman, who will understand and foresee to the last dreary saucepan and bicker round the oven the hinterlands of hades which such a scheme must open up (which was no doubt why the Government had sent a man, who could shelter behind a very real obtuseness), but Edmund was a J.P. and they had the gift of the gab of a kind, and in a major crisis of this nature any words are better than none.

He was saying, 'I'm sorry, it's quite out of the question. This household is largely composed of old women — '

'*Well!*' exclaimed Miss Sapphy, from her chair. Evelyn bent to her. ('Oh, aunt Sapphy, *please* don't mind. Don't say anything. *Please* be an old woman until this man goes.')

Margaret ran down the steps and muttered in her mother's ear.

'I've been on the telephone to Doctor Elmslie. I told him your nerves wouldn't stand it and father can't be badgered like this and can't he give you a medical certificate — '

'You marvel!'

' — but he says he's had fifteen similar requests already and has had to turn them down.'

'Oh, my God,' murmured Lady Roundelay.

Musgrave was at her side with tea. 'Oh, . . . Musgrave! What *are* we to do?' The butler shook his head. 'It's beyond me, my lady . . . if I might suggest, though: could you not invite relatives in place of these persons? The Misses Calcott — Mrs. Dunston — that would fill three of the spare rooms, and if Mr. Stacey comes 'ome — '

'Yes, yes. We'll have to do that.'

The announcement was instantly scotched by Mr. Mallet. It appeared that application for the housing of relatives should have been put in in writing and that in plain English the Government had, by now, reached a stage of pessimism with regard to last-minute exhibitions of hospitable concern by blood relations for each other's safety. 'Also, I understand that practically the whole of the top floor is vacant.'

'There are four vacant rooms in the servants' quarters, but if we did take these people, where would they eat? There's no gas or water laid on on the top storey, and what about fires in winter? My maids already have all they can do, in this big place — '

'That would be a matter of arrangement.'

'Who with? And where are their separate lots of coal to be stored? There aren't even fireplaces in most of those attic bedrooms.'

'I won't have any strangers messing up my floors,' announced the cook.

'Please, Mrs. Hatchett!' Evelyn was torn between exasperation at the parochial objection and wholehearted gratitude for the forthright ultimatum. Her husband remarked kindly, 'These old country houses aren't hotels, you know. One can't adapt 'em at no notice even if one had the capital. Another thing: do you realize that all my life I've set my face against even the admission of paying trippers to see the place under escort for three hours once a week in the summer months. There are valuables here — pictures, tapestries, and what not — that would be in very serious jeopardy if you let a parcel of children loose among 'em.'

'Then you'd better take the mothers with babies. All you will be expected to do for them is to give them reasonable facilities for cooking, access to water and lavatory, and their room.'

Miss Sapphy's cup was arrested at her Ups. 'My dear man, what should we do with a houseful of crying babies?'

'Then, what about girls?'

'I won't have a pack of youngsters in my gardens,' rasped Dickon, 'pulling the flowers, tramplin' the beds, throwin' stones at the fruit an' breakin' the boughs. We've 'ad some in village already an' two gardens wrecked. No better than savages, some o' them town brats.'

'And suppose they get ill?' asked Lady Roundelay, 'are we expected to nurse them?'

'There is the local hospital — '

' — seven miles off. Who gets 'em down there? We've no car and the hospital will be chocabloc in ten days, even if they don't turn it over to the military authorities. Our doctor lives five miles away and will be booked to the eyes from now on.'

'That will no doubt be attended to — '

'Who by? Be reasonable, my dear fellow.' But Mr. Mallet was not there to be reasonable but to represent the British Government.

'The children would, of course, be at school for the greater part of the day,' he solaced.

'How are they to get there?' asked Margaret. 'Do you expect them to walk four miles a day in the winter?'

'And what about their luncheon?' added her mother.

'That matter is under consideration. It is hoped to set up communal eating places — '

'Tah! "Hoped"!' joined in Sir Edmund, 'meanwhile, they haven't got 'em. So that makes six miles a day, coming back here for lunch — '

' — unless my maids cut eighty sandwiches every morning, allowing four per head,' concluded his wife.

'Lady Shelter is taking twenty children,' began Mr. Mallet improvingly, but Sir Edmund cut in with, 'It's not my habit to discuss the private affairs of my neighbours, but I have to remind you that the Shelters have a staff of eight resident servants and five thousand a year — '

'Wonderful parties,' confirmed Miss Sapphy, putting down her cup on to the lawn.

' — but even if I had the same I should still challenge the right of the Government or anybody else to upset my home and my family and put me to incalculable incidental expense in the process — '

'That's what I say,' agreed Mrs. Hatchett.

' — because a problem hasn't been properly tackled. We may live in the country but we read the newspapers and the Government has been given every opportunity for a year now to run this billeting scheme fairly and sensibly; it's been deluged with letters of caution, protest and prognostication from the womenfolk whom it will most affect; it's been offered the free advice and co-operation of such fellows as this Butlin who's had a lifetime of experience in building holiday camps at wholesale rates, and what does it do? Turns him down cold and expects the country and people like ourselves to clear up a mess for them that never need have existed. Well . . . sorry we can't help you out, Mr. — um — Mitchell — er — Masters. 'Fraid landowners have no time to waste these days, y'know. Where's tea, Evelyn? 'Offer you a cup, I hope, sir?'

Mr. Mallet reddened. He had had an appalling day, ranging from tears to threats and abuse. He had helplessly placed a girl of nine in the care of a hard-faced woman who admitted she hated all children: had put, willy-nilly, two more into an unventilated cottage where the elder would have to share bed with an asthmatic of seventy-two, he had even suspected a case of whooping-cough in the boy he had installed with a young married couple with a six-months-old baby . . . his own underclothes felt prophetically acrawl . . . at a hamlet called Rohan, there had been no scenes, no violence or abuse, but a silent listening — and Mr. Mallet had found himself unexpectedly outside the village again in the company of two tall men who spoke in an odd manner, and with the conviction that he would not trouble Rohan further in the matter. . . .

And here, at Delaye, was a feast of pure reason and politeness to wind up the day.

'I'm afraid I can't let it go at that, sir. I must definitely put you down for — '

To his despair, yet another female appeared from the hall doors, one of those old women they'd spoken of.

Tottering, mowing, Nursie advanced sideways down the stone steps, each felt-clad boot placed in her descent as in the second position of dancing.

'I've come to see what you're all doing and why my tea hasn't been brought up,' she panted.

'Come along, Nurse,' urged Musgrave in an undertone, attempting like a sheep-dog to round her up.

'Don't touch me!' Her eye fell on the empty cups dotted about the turf. 'There *is* tea! They've had it!'

'T'tt . . . (augh),' murmured the butler.

'Go along upstairs, Nursie, and you'll get your tea. Mrs. Hatchett, will you see to her? You and Margery will be wanting your own.' Unwillingly cook and housemaid moved away, but without Nursie. They drew the line at tackling her in that mood. Above the group a bedroom window opened and the alarmed head of Miss Amy peeped forth.

'What is it? Has anything *happened*?'

'Don't come down it's all right oh my God' answered Lady Roundelay, without a comma. Once more Musgrave reentered the house, giving as he went a meaning glance at that Mr. Mallet; his own immediate roaring upon the gong might act as a hint, though Musgrave expected little of social perception from one whom he had instantly summed up as a half-sir.

'No tea,' ruminated Nursie, 'and no meat for dinner to-day *or* yesterday — '

'Go along in, Nursie, I don't know what's come over you.'

Lady Roundelay spoke with rare sharpness. Nursie instantly began to cry. 'And stop that nonsense. When we have twenty children landed on us will be time enough to complain.'

'Twenty children,' retorted Nursie. 'I can manage *them*. I've managed 'em all my life and I can manage 'em till I'm gone.' She advanced upon Mr. Mallet. 'You remember Kenneth? You're Kenneth's father. Very like him, you are. Where's Kenneth?'

'No . . . no,' disclaimed Mr. Mallet, retreating, and treading upon the joint that the Girl Guide had set down on the grass.

'He never gave Nursie any trouble, though a terror for skinning his knees and diarrhoea in the summer — ' Nursie inspected the unwieldy bundle through which a betraying bone protruded. 'Meat! They had it all along and not a morsel for me . . .'

She clung to Mr. Mallet's arm, tottering with unaccustomed excitement, exertion and ire. 'I'm over ninety,' she confided.

'Yes. Quite so . . .'

'I've worked all my life and now *this*. I've seen King William in London and don't you believe it when they tell you I never. No. No butcher's meat at *all*, so I threw my tray out of window.'

Mr. Mallet disengaged himself with some difficulty and lowering his voice said to Lady Roundelay, 'I hadn't been informed there was a *mental* case here.'

Evelyn did some rapid thinking. If this meant that Delaye was to be permanently exempted from evacuees, then Nursie was not only insane but on occasion dangerous: if, on the other hand, the mental faculties of Nursie were only to act as a numeric reducer of strangers, then the family would be the first to resent the imputation of derangement on behalf of the poor dear old woman, damn and confound her. She selected 'She is not, so far, violent.'

'No, no . . . but with children about, or nursing mothers . . . I think we must remove you from the list of receptionists.'

'Oh, yes?' Lady Roundelay hoped that her voice was sounding casual. 'Then, if we can't offer you any tea, I *think—* '

But Delaye had not yet quite finished with Mr. Mallet, and supplied him as tailpiece with a spectacle so essentially improbable that, he told friends afterwards, had he been a Roman Catholic he would have crossed himself. For suddenly and quite silently across the drive and down the avenue came a young man running, white-faced, his cheeks spattered with blood. In pursuit, plumage furled, neck extended, skimmed a peacock. There were, perhaps, six yards between them.

The old woman they called 'Nursie' sidled up to him and confided, 'It's a peacock. Peacock. Chook! chook! chook!'

Lady Roundelay, her eyes glazing, asked of the autumnal air, '*What* is the Severn's footman doing in our grounds?'

Mr. Mallet leaked away. He does not remember saying goodbye to anyone.

CHAPTER XIX

1

To BE IN the hall again, sheltered in its coolness of gleaming wood, was heaven. After four cups of tea Evelyn could even rise to speech from overlong, dazed and unintelligent listening to that of the family.

'These fellows — ' began Sir Edmund, but his eye caught and held by an article on the training of bassets in *Field Fare*, left his denunciation incompleted.

'Guide there all right?' asked Margaret, eating cake. Her mother nodded. 'Nice child. Forgot her sweets, though.'

'Doesn't matter. To-morrow.'

Aunt Sapphy was impressive with Maxwell Dunston. 'And if you'll believe me — twenty children! Here!'

'Might as well let Moscow have England and be done with it. Glad I missed that. I'd give 'em pack-drill. Show 'em hell. 'Kick this chap's backside for tuppence.'

'And he said Nursie was dotty.'

'Well, here's to her.' Major Dunston slowly drank his tea; he was still crimson with incredulous fury.

'Musgrave suggested filling up with your mother and Helen and Kathleen,' Lady Roundelay at length managed to inform him.

'The Mater? Oh, she wouldn't care for that, I daresay. Anyway . . . question doesn't arise now, thank God.'

'I quite thought something had *happened*,' contributed Miss Amy.

'It had!'

Evelyn's eyes roved the family. Aunt Jessie seemed to have said nothing since they all assembled, and Evelyn expected that quite soon she herself might summon enough energy to enquire about her strained ankle which Jessie was as usual bearing with unendearing fortitude.

Idly, Evelyn scanned two communications which had arrived by the second post. The first was from an illegible signature writing from a printed address that conveyed nothing to her whatsoever, and was headed:

NATIONAL VOLUNTARY DEFENCE SERVICES
Norminster

It informed her that her kind offer of sorting and grading apples had been noted, but that at present the N.V.D.S. was awaiting further instructions from The Board of Agriculture before putting the scheme into operation. The second was a postcard printed in two colours bearing the facsimile autograph of Mr. Walter Elliot. It thanked her warmly for her generous co-operation in the Evacuation Scheme. Lady Roundelay leant back and closed her eyes. 'It's no use,' she murmured, 'we must just let all this roll over our heads.

Musgrave was at her side. 'The telephone, my lady. Lady Shelter sends her kindest regards and wishes to know if you would care to help her with the canteen she is organizing —'

'My kindest regards, Musgrave, and I'd rather remain friends with her.'

'Hah!' said the Major.

'Tell her — oh, I don't know.'

'I'll attend to it, m'lady.'

From the outer hall Musgrave was heard to inform Lady Shelter, with Lady Roundelay's kindest regards, that her ladyship was as yet a little undecided as to what form her war work would take.

The effort to get upstairs to the relief of changed clothes and shoes still seemed to Evelyn one of the impossibilities, and she sat on, postponing it. Angela was really looking very unwell, worse if anything, than in the morning. She had come in rather late for tea, her mother now remembered. And quite suddenly she also remembered what, on a normal day, could not have been so long overlooked.

'By the way, what *was* the Severn's footman doing here?'

Her husband looked up. 'Hey? D'you mean Joe Dale?'

'Well, if that's his name that's the one I mean. And the peacock was after him.'

'Damn that bird.'

Angela spoke, unwillingly. 'Dale had been for a walk with Sue. I — I saw them go.'

'Oh. Sets the wind in that quarter? Well, hope we don't lose her. He's the world's worst manservant, Severn tells me,' her father commented, 'still, suppose he'll be called up any day, now.'

'Is she fond of him?' Evelyn was thinking that of all the family Angela would be in closest touch with current developments in that particular direction. For the past few years Angela and Sue had been friends; the tie of youth, she supposed, and their mutual interest in the peacock. Given easier financial circumstances one would like to promote Sue as personal maid to Angela and Margaret.

Angela shifted. 'No, I should say decidedly no.'

'But he's keen on her?'

'Oh, yes.'

'No chance, then, of her leaving us?'

'Sue says that if she marries it will be a Rohan man; it's her village, you see. There's the telephone again.' Angela's face relaxed in relief at the shrilling of the bell. Margaret called from the hall, 'Father! It's Mr. Severn. Says he wants to speak to you personally.'

'Ah, damn,' murmured Sir Edmund, and went unwillingly. He was back in five minutes. 'Severn's very peeved about young Dale. It seems that the chap came home in a regular state, blown and his face bloody and a nasty jab just over the left eye. He says he can't get a straight answer out of Dale, just that he was "walking out" as he put it with one of our maids and the peacock attacked him. I've offered to settle the doctor's bill, but as I pointed out to Severn, if his man comes on to my land he does so at his own risk, and he knows as well as any of us that that bird's a bad-tempered brute. Had to agree, and we left it at that.'

'Poor fellow!' vaguely sympathized Miss Amy. 'First it's Jessie's ankle and now another accident. Quite an unfortunate day.'

'And a war on the top of everything,' capped Miss Sapphy, addressing Margaret.

'Well,' decided Evelyn, 'we don't want the chance of this recurring, and if Sue isn't going to marry the youth I think I'd better give her a hint. What d'you say, Angela?' Angela was obviously thinking, hard. 'Yes. I quite agree. They'd both prefer that.' The ambiguous statement passed over her mother's exhausted head. It was Margaret who asked, 'How d'you mean "they"? Dale or the peacock!' Angela said swiftly, 'Dale, of course,' and saw too late where that opinion led her, adding confusedly, 'I didn't mean "they", of course, I meant "she", Sue, would prefer it.'

For so straightforward an issue, her mistress thought when she sent for her before dinner, Sue Privett was being singularly tiresome — giving way submissively over the major point of relinquishing the society of an admirer where vanity should have made her unwilling to concede it, and closing down, Lady Roundelay suspected, over the relative triviality of the peacock's attack upon her young man.

Yes, they had been for a walk, it was at Dale's request and Sue didn't see no harm in it. —

'There isn't any. Go on, Sue.'

And then, and then as he was going back to Squire's the peacock struck at him, like.

'But why?' Sue couldn't say, she was sure.

'Had Dale been teasing him?'

Yes, yes he had. That was it.

Evelyn, at a loss, scenting an eager grasp at a lie, said at random, 'That was stupid of him.'

'Yes, m'lady.'

'What did he do?'

Sue was unprepared for that, hesitated, 'Oh, poked him, m'lady.'

'H'm . . . well, never mind. The master will make that right with Dale and Mr. Severn.'

'Thank you, m'lady.'

'And, of course, it's quite possible that your very naughty pet remembered that it was Dale who tried to take him back to Severn Court.'

The ingenuous face of Lady Roundelay's kitchenmaid radiated admiration as she gasped, 'Oh *yes*, m'lady. That was it.'

'What a fool I am,' thought Evelyn. 'That, in the Law Courts, is what's called "leading" a witness. And I fancy Sue sensed it.'

2

After dinner Evelyn read her letters. They included nine affectionate enquiries, lovable, disturbing and pathetic, after her safety and plans, the tenor of which was 'Do let us, if possible, keep in touch', and two hints of varying strength from friends that in case London became too hot to hold them Delaye would be a delightful asylum; one circled round the nice point of payment, the other's feelings were too nice to envisage anything but free board, lodging, light, heat and laundry. Tactful evasion of both correspondents must be thought out later.

Her son wrote from his Agricultural College.

Stacey Roundelay didn't see the point of coming home just to 'cumber the earth' until he'd wangled a commission somewhere, and all this was pretty tedious, wasn't it, in view of what his training had cost the family, and it remained to hope that when this business was all over one might be able to pull one's weight at Delaye and take some of the grind off father . . . and his mother wasn't to worry. Stacey supposed that it was true, as she said, that his generation had no future to speak of and had rather contrived to miss the feeling of security enjoyed by hers, but that 'his lot' had lived so much under the shadow of the last war and in anticipation of the next that he supposed they were case-hardened and broke to unsettled feelings, 'and of course we haven't even the glamour-of-ignorance that the 1914 lot had; we're merely jaded, at once sans Jingoism or experience . . . and they haven't got Delaye to bolster them up.' From which philosophy Stacey's mother derived little comfort. Her son was now twenty-eight and not even engaged. . . .

It was the mordant comments of Maxwell Dunston that braced her.

"Way the authorities are truckling, and bribing men into the army is a scandal, making a pack of mollycoddles out of 'em, over-feeding 'em, lowering the marriage age at which they can begin drawing family allowances . . . of course there'll be a crop of war weddings and then half these fellows'll get picked off and their widows'll come on public assistance for life, and probably not one boy-child in ten to show for it. As for this democratization of the army, it won't work and it isn't right that it should. I tell you, war is no time for the all-men-are-equal brigade's experiments. It never occurs to anyone that the young men of our class are investments for the country who've been pretty costly ones for their parents, and who are best fitted for leadership by education, heredity and instinct. But we've practically got to the stage now when we've got to apologize for not dropping our aitches, wearing a whole suit of clothes and having an income higher than a bus conductor's. You mark my words: Stacey's going to have the fight of his life to get a commission, and if they get wind that he knows something about agriculture and forestry they'll put him to any job on earth but the one he's specialized in.'

Evelyn's sisters had both written. Kathleen Calcott said:

'London is looking very unbecoming and odd and you can walk for miles without seeing one inch of khaki or hearing a single band. Too prepared, I suppose. At every street corner people are shovelling sand into bags; elderly Edwardian matrons in toques stop as a matter of course, drop handbags and umbrellas and shovel too, all over their neat stockings. We had an air raid warning in church yesterday just after the P.M.'s speech, but nobody turned a hair; they thought it was something gone wrong with the organ, and in short, we played the ukulele till the ship went down. As a matter of fact there is no bomb born of woman that could shake South Kensington's complacent stagnation. It's rather fine really, like putting on a dinner jacket every night for one cobra and a cactus in the wilds of Boggley-Wallah.

'The war already strikes one as being in a different category altogether from any other we've weathered; there's really no political or religious issue, when you get down to brass tacks, but a most simple and dramatic tussle between good and evil — like the Fairy Queen and the Demon in a pantomime, and that's why nobody here, I think, is seriously worried except by the trifling side-issues it'll raise, and the outcome, because of this, seems so foregone that it's only a matter of hanging on and enduring it all.

'If you're short of torches, I'm told in some of the shops that they're expecting a consignment of American batteries. They'll cost 11d., I hear — about three-quarters more than the proper price, so America wins the war once again, at the beginning of it, this time, instead of the end. Meanwhile, I guess and surmise and 'low our cue is to be terribly polite about the U.S.A. for some months yet, with plenteous reference to *The Mayflower,* our roots in a common soil and great traditions of liberty, so wise up your cheer-squads to whoop it up for Gopher Prairie, fair city of hundred per-cent, two-fisted, red-blooded, up-and-coming reg-lar fellows.

'The London theatres are to be closed until further notice, so the distress among the poor wretches will be acuter than usual. There seems to be no war work really wanted for my likes, so I wrote in to "Ensa" offering to do odd clerical jobs for them. I thought a theatrical atmosphere would be cheering for the duration, but Lord love you! they've no use for me, so the Ensa's a lemon, as it were, and I shall just have to wait until something turns up. There don't seem to be any work depots open, either, because there aren't any casualties, and what canteens there are have waiting-lists yards long. I did have three days in one started by a Kensington friend of ours, but the moment she got it on its feet the authorities closed it as being superfluous. The current pastime seems to be clearing the hospitals of civilian patients who can't get nursed anywhere else in order to make room for soldiers who aren't arriving.

'A universal eagerness to serve in any capacity together with an almost entire lack of openings has resulted in car-owners pasting announcements across their windscreens bearing information that, except in the case of "Doctor", results in the butcher's becoming promoted to "Essential Foodstuffs", the chemist delivering headache powders to "Medical Supplies, Urgent", while the rest fill up with obscure combinations of initials in which the only absentees seem to be W.C., B.F., R.S.V.P., P.P.C., and D.T., and yesterday one diehard who had no connection with anything was reduced to "Don't Indulge In Careless Talk". I'm now waiting for Barker's and Debenham's vans to roll by marked "Vital Satins" and "W.O. Ospreys".

'Saw in a newspaper that there is an idea that women may have to be conscripted. This was followed in another by a sermonette to the effect that we shall be doing good National Service by staying at home and keeping the gas-fires burning, and by the announcement of the closing of even the waiting-list for Wrens and Land Girls.

'No plague of catchwords and comic songs, thank God! So far, we're existing on the old crop left over from the last war. *Don't* feel you've got to ask us to Delaye, m'dear. In any case, Helen couldn't get away just now, having become an Air Raid Warning!'

Helen Calcott supplemented this news item:

'Am doing (voluntary) A.R.P., and gosh! how they put one through the mangle! Eight lectures, a bomb demonstration, an exam and go through the gas chamber. My experience in winning my badge (officially valued at 2s.) was as follows:

'Having attended the lectures, during one of which (on types of bomb) the lecturer told us that the criss-cross of gummed paper on the windows of the Town Hall and in the room in which we sat were very pretty but no good at all against splinters, we were told to await instructions as to where to go for the exam. When I'd finished waiting for mine, I flogged to the nearest A.R.P. Post where I was received by a long young man who, I heard later, is a dramatist, and by him was told to attend at a school at 8 o'clock, p.m. I filled in a form giving name and age, was told this should have been done before the first lecture, to which I replied that the Town Hall had never even shown me one when I enrolled. Next morning, totally different Warden from another Post rang up cancelling my school assignation and telling me to ask for an Admiral at the Town Hall in the afternoon at 2.30. He, it seemed, would catechize me alone. Having assimilated this unnatural combination of water, gas, air and fire, I arrived, was told to see a perfectly different name (Admiral idea evidently scrapped) and was put through my paces by a nice old bird who would be a dream as Charles The Second at a fancy dress ball who asked me questions and was kind enough to supply most of the answers. Then told me that women were not being used in our Sector as patrols, which is what I had joined for.

'The bomb demonstration took place in a draughty goods-yard and we dispersed shivering, covered with magnesium powder and filled with the conviction that no precaution of an amateur nature is of the smallest use against incendiaries or H.E.'s. The former dam' thing goes clean through a sheet of metal, a bucket of water and another bucket; the noise, on the other hand, is unexpectedly little, I've heard many a firework that makes far more.

'The gas chamber is a small brick house in the goods-yard with a red light over the door, thus suggesting a cross between an abattoir and a brothel. We put on masks, were vetted by an expert in a white surgeon's coat (which unnerved me) and were herded into an airtight room where he touched off a small cone which in due course emitted clouds of smoke that turned out to be C.A.P. (a tear gas). I promptly paled, felt convinced that my mask was a misfit and that I could already smell gas and that the gas was Phosgene and nothing less. Phosgene, my sweet creature, is a Lung Irritant, and the symptoms that you turn first blue in the face and then leaden; the only hope is oxygen and even then you're a crock for life if you pull through at all. I feel convinced that when or if we're ever called upon to treat a real casualty, he won't look in the least like what the handbook says he ought to, but will either be no colour at all or some colour which calls for a totally different treatment. By the way: one of the gases is called "B.B.C.". It's also an Eye Irritant. I feel there's a mistake here and it should be listed under Ears. I emerged from the gas chamber shaken but unscathed and was promptly herded back without mask in order to get a confidence-whiff of what we should have got if we'd got it. Left with eyes and nose pouring. So you can tell the family that at least the Civilian respirators do their work. And the end of all my striving is a seat at a table in an ex-committee room with another hag at one defenceless telephone. Our work, to date, has consisted of answering a call from the Town Hall as to whether the load of coke for the stove was delivered, two Yellow Warnings which came to nothing but gave us some idea of the difficulty of recalling Wardens on patrol or of catching them at home if off duty, one practice at telephone in our masks, during which neither party could hear more words than The Ancient Mariner who "stopped one in three", and the staging of an "incident" in the next street, in which volunteers stand in for casualties, get shocking colds while propped in shelters, and informed that their ankle is broken by falling débris, are then removed to a (real) hospital where, in more draughts, a (real) doctor comes along and says the First Aiders' bandages are like nothing under the sun.

'Last week, a collection of haversacks was sent in for the men patrols. Inside one was a bottle of brownish liquid which defied the united intelligence of the Post. I scored heavily by suggesting it was tannic acid, against burns, and Godammy! I wasn't far out, for by dint of telephoning we found it was cold tea which the Post Warden's wife had put in through some misguided maternal instinct. An essential requirement for Wardenship, so far, seems to be an ability to play darts. The game appears to consist of loud cries of "Oh my God", "Hell", "Treble Three" and "Bust" together with long sums in subtraction. We women have no tin hats against raids when going on or from duty, but as against this, we are going to be dished out with entirely unnecessary twill overalls and felt hats at a cost to the ratepayer of fourteen shillings each outfit. But A.R.P. *is* a good idea, and I quite see that these Posts must either be kept on their toes all the time or disbanded altogether. One can't do anything if there's nothing to do any more than the Army can. Incidentally, a lot of our Patrol Wardens *are* retired Army men, of any age you like up to eighty. We used to wonder where all the gentlefolk had vanished to when we were at the seaside, and even in London to see a genuine specimen further east than Knightsbridge is rare and refreshing. But now I know. They man the A.R.P. Posts! Most of them have been half over the world and have held distinguished positions of all kinds, and it seems extraordinary that the War Office can't find something worthier of their steel than mooching about the streets in tin hats and all weathers catching their deaths of exposure. But of course they have "the manner", and their habit of authority and humour in emergency could be quite invaluable. That's one of the things we're told: to try and reassure the public and/or casualty. One of our dear old Colonels came in the other day and, screwing his monocle into his eye, said "There's one direction in First Aid that I feel I should be really good at, 'When in doubt, do nothing'." (He's the one like a mournful bloodhound).'

Crystal Dunston wrote also, seeing in the war a sign of badly needed world regeneration which called for a New Messiah, and probably would not have to call twice.

CHAPTER XX

1

THAT AFTERNOON, as the house seemed quiet, void of so many of its occupants, Angela had visited its top storey, opening the door of that servant's bedroom, mastering her aversion.

She had made an attempt in the morning, but to her surprise, relief and slight shock, another was there before her. Sue, with dustpan and brush 'doing a bit of tidying up', she explained, at an equal loss on seeing the other girl in the doorway.

Alone, Angela stood by the great, unsuitable bed, receiving and sifting impressions, trying in the light of maturity to be fair to the room and its atmosphere. Although they never spoke of it, she could remember as well as her mother and more vividly the sensation of misery with which it had filled her as a child. That feeling must, if possible, give place.

At first distastefully, she gave the room its chance with her, even sat in the one chair — a prosaic, workaday affair — that it now contained.

Very gradually the room responded, like a dog who has nearly knocked you down and clumsily, apologetically tries to make it right with you. Angela would never like the room, would never, she was sure, be at ease there, but it should have fair dealing from her. Sitting there very still she pieced together what she knew of it by hearsay. It had been a servant's bedroom. The huge bed had been moved in at the order of that Frenchwoman, Marguerite Roundelay who was murdered. Would that, perhaps, account for the room's effect upon Angela? Furniture (she had read it often) could be haunted, especially if made of bog-oak . . . or there was the case of the summerhouse whose supports were contrived from the posts of an ancient gibbet round which the spirits of its hanged victims still clung. But Marguerite was killed in France; this tester was of English workmanship: Carolean, father had said so. The fact had once been confirmed by an expert who visited Delaye.

Then?

Heryn I dye. Thomas Picocke.

'Picocke' was a running footman, he was in the accounts books in the cellars, his bed a settle in the kitchen. He ranked lower than house servants. Neither fish, flesh nor fowl, she'd heard.

Why didn't he die on that settle? But perhaps he died at his home in Delaye, or Rohan? Heryn. That meant in this room and no other; hadn't she schoolmarm'd Sue about 'heryn' only yesterday, without taking in the implications of her own tutorship?

But wasn't it unusual for such a servant to be promoted to a room to himself? That point couldn't have escaped Sir Edmund, his daughter knew, then what was his own version of the affair? What answer had he made the curious sightseeing visitors as they rambled over Delaye exclaiming at this thing and that, talking their nonsense about Guy Fawkes and the inscription on the window-pane?

That would be a question difficult to ask. Angela's feeling against the room was, she supposed, traditional in the family, and a last-minute interest in it would inevitably lead to questions which she in her turn wasn't prepared to answer. Angela had over the years intermittently, sadly sensed that she herself was not as others: one for some reason, unable to face up to life as people like Margaret lived it, one with its subcurrents as her sister was not. Margaret's sentiment for Delaye was a clear-cut thing, a direct affection flowing in its straight line back to an accountable past with historic fact, such as it was, to guide her. Yet it must be so or Angela couldn't be here in this room, labouring to find the answer to a puzzle that she shrank from solving. She felt, she supposed, like those women living apparently happy lives who suddenly, as the phrase went, felt the call to leave the world of friends and pleasant things in order to serve an ideal in a convent, half-ecstatic, half abhorring the compulsion which drove them. 'Why must it be me?' they too must have asked as they shouldered the privilege and the burden. It would have been so easy, so obviously more suitable, had the chosen Roundelay been Margaret, fearless, practical, not to be daunted by the devil himself!

This room might once have slept several servants when Delaye was in its heyday, money easier and wages lower. But when 'Picocke' died in it, if he had, what was the state of current accommodation? Had the man died on a pallet among his fellow servants? Or was the great bed already relegated to the top storey and he alone at the end? Was it conceivable (a settle in the kitchen!) that if the bed were already here such a person would have been allowed to go near it, let alone use it? And Angela must start searching at once.

Anything in those cupboards would probably be known; she expected little of them, though it was true that scattered in holes and comers all about the house were presses and chests that even her mother had never got to the bottom of. Anything found by Angela in this bare and secretless room must be of scant interest to the uninitiate; mother herself had merely damned a crossbow when it hit her by falling out of a recess though the thing was probably a museum piece.

It was with little surprise and no excitement at all that Angela, wrenching it from a corner of a built-in cupboard where it had stuck, bore into the light a dusty stave, its metal cap browned and crisp with rust.

Well? . . . They carried them, those running footmen, and there was the container for the hardboiled egg to sustain him on his run. It opened on a hinge, the snap of which was pointed. On impulse, Angela polished it with her handkerchief and took it to the window, carefully inserting it, letter by letter, to the traced inscription. The tip fitted the faint writing.

He won't never eat that, Miss Angela.

Her own wrist bleeding from the dig of an angry beak.

And then she guessed.

A suspicion so monstrous, so insane shot into Angela's mind that she clung to one of the great posts of the bed, a white cheek pressed against the coolness of the wood.

The bird on a moonlit lawn, signalling, hoping for death to the owners of Delaye.

> *One body for a noble,*
> *Run, running runner, run.*

'Oh God, it couldn't be *that*. You wouldn't let it be *that*,' prayed Angela, like a child.

2

Her thoughts scurried like trapped animals. It was some time before she realized that the fact that she hadn't run away from the shock of a dim, groping instinct confirmed might mean a mutual relenting between herself and the room. She felt only that already it was less alien through her own, brief presence there: here was a panel she had touched, there an object she and no other had displaced . . . a species of what in happy, normal circumstances people called 'housewarming', meaning the merging of their personalities, with, the impression of their wills upon, that which is contained within four walls.

And there was Sue. Also contributing her share towards the humanizing of the room. Angela took it for granted that 'tidying up' there was a part of the girl's duties, thought it pathetic, measured by the yardstick of her own sensations, that she should be under a routine compulsion to go in and out. . . .

Was one rather mad? There were degrees of insanity, of course, from those who raved under restraint to people like Nursie, no harm to anyone, still relishing life in their gradual, general loss of grip. 'Perfectly sane on every subject but one,' people said of other types of subnormality. Was Angela of their number? Could anyone in the whole house be sounded about this personal trouble? She thought not. The family knew her too well by now for theories which might enlighten. But to someone she must go.

Sue was ruled out even about the matter-in-chief. She wouldn't understand — small blame to her! and her response to Angela's surmises might be one of many and all unpleasant or inimical to domestic peace. Of that whole household there was no Roundelay with all the necessary qualities to face up to this affair. Evelyn would give love and patience and humour invalidated by maternal anxiety; father would give affection and worried, cautious, kid-gloved incredulity, and Margaret invaluable common sense which shoo'd away your bogeys without glancing at them and seeing them for what they were. You must *know* before you can fight, or heal. And this wasn't a fight.

Like a rap on the knuckles a name clicked into her brain.

Basil Winchcombe.

Of what help he could be Angela had no idea: her impulse to him was as irrational as instinctive. With the name came also a change of mood, and she looked the room over once more as her eyes filled.

'You poor thing. Oh, you *poor* thing!'

There might be time to reach the village and return before tea. Mother and aunt Sapphy would be late, they had thought.

But, running downstairs, the sound of voices in the drive told her that she was later still. Time had gone quickly, in that room. On the second landing she peered from the window; mother and aunt Sapphy were already back from Norminster and there seemed to be a crowd by the front steps: mother was offering tea to a man Angela failed to identify, doing it in her dinnerparty voice that meant she was bored and tired and civil to the last! Her daughter sympathetically hoped he would refuse even one cup, but he wasn't doing anything but gape, and Angela's eyes followed the direction of his own as Joe Dale scudded into view, the peacock in his wake.

Leaning against a long shutter, Angela, unaware of the sound of the tea-gong far below, unhappily pondered the manifestation.

3

The Reverend Basil Winchcombe was in the parlour of his cottage lodgings poring over an album of old theatrical postcards when, the following afternoon, Miss Angela Roundelay was shown in. He closed the book with a smack.

'How very pleasant this is, and *what* a pretty creature Gabrielle Ray was! I was maddened with boredom: too early for tea, too soon to begin my sermon for next Sunday, not due to guard my bridge for another twenty-four hours and all the village obstinately stainless, for the moment, except for the infant evacuees' language. Sit there. The other chair has springs that play Debussy's *Danses Sacrées et Profanes* when you sit in it. D'you remember Maud Allan at the Palace — no, of course you weren't born then.'

But the girl's manner and looks worried him. Unless this visit were a message from her mother?

'Thank you. Mr. Winchcombe, I don't know quite why I've come here. I felt somehow that you were the only person who could help.'

The stage, thought Winchcombe, might be and indeed was going to the dogs but an apprenticeship to it had its uses, one of which was a command of the poker face. This evidently wasn't being a message from Evelyn Roundelay, and if it were a trouble with which *she* couldn't cope . . . and his own appalling habit of downright comment might upset some apple-cart with the best intentions in the world. He temporized. 'One moment. Are you quite certain that I'm the right person?'

'Yes.' She thought a second or two and repeated 'Yes. Quite certain.'

'I want to be sure because I'm not very good at compromise or gilded pills, you know; it's not exactly tactlessness so much as not remembering that the truth unvarnished isn't always the helpful thing. I tell people what in their place I should want to be told myself.'

'That's what I want. People *shelter* one so.' She was, he noted, too loyal to say 'families'.

'Yes, and isn't it curiously difficult to say one's piece to them! I was enormously fond of my father but went to pieces whenever I preached and he was in front. I hated it, for some reason. Had to tell him. He thought it "unkind" of me. Ye gods! how one's nearest and dearest can misunderstand one.' He was secretly watchful of the lessening of tension in the young face opposite him. 'That feeling against preaching before my father was rather in the same class as kissing the one woman in the world in the middle of a sherry party: as far as I'm concerned it just can't be done. A certain degree of lack of intimacy between the parties is essential to any good confidence. That, I take it, is how the confessional came into being, a kind of legalized air-raid shelter for the reserved.' He smiled at Angela. 'You and I know each other quite nice and badly enough to make a go of it, so suppose you begin, if I'd only leave off talking!'

She was going through all the tricks of stage-fright, first night nerves and of what in parishioners he privately called 'confidence tricks' that he knew so thoroughly; twisting her hands, avoiding his eye, muffing her lines, deliberately postponing the business she had come upon. A bad rehearser but could put up a good, sincere performance, given a sympathetic audience and producer.

'Mr. Winchcombe, I suppose that when you worked in a London parish people told you some pretty odd things?'

'They did. Go on.'

'No, but — really kind of rather unbelievable?'

'Yes, I've met that, too. I've even been made a present of the confession of a reasonably celebrated murder by the man who committed it, when the tecs were well on his tracks.'

'And you never gave him away?'

'Oh . . . I see what you're getting at. You're thinking I'll sit here all sympathy, drawing you out, and then go off to Lady Roundelay and spill the beans and have a mutual-anxiety society together over you.'

That roused her and the relief on her face intensified. He spared her the embarrassment of admission by continuing, 'Mind you, if it's anything to do with your health I warn you I may feel bound to pass it on. Sick people aren't always the best judges of what's for their good — ', but at that, her changed expression so disturbed him that he waited for what might be coming. She certainly looked very far from well, white, worn, though his own allusion to her health he had intended merely to rank as one of a number of possible barriers to absolute confidence.

She said with unwilling honesty, 'That's one of the things I want to find out. Supposing it weren't a physical but a mental thing?'

'In that case, don't you suppose your parents would know all about you better than I?' He was thinking that young girls . . . some love affair that even her mother didn't guess? Those constant visits . . . it would be possible, and she's the ferociously reserved type who'd take a disappointment or disillusion hard. Yet — one didn't associate Angela Roundelay with men. Too elusive and fastidious, no good for the dogfight of backchat and pachydermatousness that was the fashion among young men and maidens these days.

She looked at him squarely at last. 'Would you say that I am perfectly sane?'

His smile concealed his sudden pang of anxiety. 'Bernard Shaw says that none of us is, and apart from that being a clever-clever gag for the groundlings there's a lot of truth in it. When he was at his best, which was a quarter of a century ago, I always used to consider that his angle on life and manners and morals was the only normal one in Great Britain because he saw straight through things to their logical and real conclusions, however unflattering to our egos they turned out to be, yet Great Britain which only, at best, saw half-way, content to accept secondhand ideas and morals, thought him a freak and a poseur, and that resulted in such eminents as W. S. Gilbert writing "his topsy-turvy fancies" — the bourgeois, patronizing complacence of it!' He smiled. 'Even Lewis Carroll saw the light occasionally. But what makes you think you're topsy-turvy?'

She thought, hard, looking clean through him to the window that gave on to the pretty, ramshackle little garden.

'You've seen over Delaye, haven't you?'

'Rather.'

'Do you remember a servant's bedroom on the top storey?' He looked at her keenly. '"Heryn I dye". That one?' She flinched but nodded. 'Can you remember if you thought anything particular about it?'

'I remember very well indeed, Angela, and told your mother so. It's rather a lovely place. It moved me. It has beauty.' Her voice was forlorn as she said, 'You felt that and I didn't. You see? . . . Did mother ever tell you I couldn't bear it?'

'Yes.'

'As though she thought I wasn't quite — '

'Not in the least, my dear. She doesn't understand your feeling, but there's no *patronage* about it.'

'But why can't I feel as you do?' Angela asked desperately.

'Oh, my dear child, why isn't an orange an onion? Why aren't I a fishmonger in Fulham, or an atheist? Can't you make any allowances for yourself? A diamond has many facets: hold it with me facing you and you can see one facet, I another, but they're both on the same stone. It's the angle-of-sight question. There may be a third or a fourth angle we know nothing about, meanwhile we both feel *something*, you aversion, I attraction. That's a starting-point. Tell me exactly what's in your mind. If it's a bit beyond me I'll say so, but that needn't mean my disbelief. Come on!'

'I — I don't know where to begin.'

'Start anywhere and we can sort it out later. You can trust me to do the interrupting and being tiresome if I don't follow you.'

CHAPTER XXI

1

'You know we have a kitchenmaid. Sue Privett.'

He nodded. 'Her old Granny's pretty bad, I'm afraid she won't last much longer; I must go and look her up again. There have been Privetts at Delaye for two hundred years, I'm told.'

'Oh yes, one if not the first was a Polly Privett — father, by the way, has just found out that she was sent away at no notice, she was paid a week's money.'

He pricked up his ears. 'Oh? . . . It's too much to hope that Sir Edmund discovered the reason, I suppose?'

'Yes, this — about Polly, I mean — was on a loose piece of paper in one of the accounts books.'

'What date?'

'1792.'

'And then what?'

'Another Privett was engaged almost at once. Susan.'

'She sounds efficient! Why is Sue so much more likeable a name than Susan? Tell me, who was mistress of Delaye at that time?'

'The French one, Marguerite.'

'The poor soul who got done in in one of the Revolutions?'

'Yes.'

'Why did she leave Delaye?'

Angela stared, ever so slightly impatient of side-issues. 'She went on a visit to relations.'

'Seems a rather odd time to choose, with the whole of Paris in a ferment. You'd have thought her husband would have put his foot down . . . but let that pass. Go on about Sue.'

'Where had I got to?'

'Sorry! I warned you I'd interrupt. You were saying that the accounts books — '

'I remember. Well, Sue and I are friends. It began, I think, even before our interest in the peacock. He's really rather awful to everyone but Sue, and for over a year now, to me, though I've done my best to tame him. But in his way he's really fond of Sue, eats out of her hand, comes to her, even the servants notice it. He was all right to me until one morning when I gave him some hardboiled egg, and he bit me rather badly. Sue was upset, quite faint, I'm told. She bound up my wrist. Father tried to get rid of him then, and Sue was miserable, and the peacock wouldn't stay at the Severns and came back until we had to let him have his way. And yet he hates us all but Sue and me.

'One afternoon, I saw Sue and the peacock together in a field. He was walking with her — like a *person*, you know. It wasn't just following, as a pet does.'

'One minute. What did you think when you saw them?'

'I didn't like it, and yet . . . I was somehow glad. I know it sounds ridiculous.'

'And then?'

'Yesterday afternoon — I'm probably getting things in the wrong order but it's so difficult to think *neatly*, you know — Sue went for a walk with Joe Dale; he's the Severns' footman, the one who came three times to try to take the peacock away. He seems to be fond of her.'

'In love?'

'I think so, but she won't marry him.'

'Just an effort on his part at "keeping company"?'

'Yes. Well, when I was leaving that room, I looked out of the window and I saw Joe Dale run across the further drive towards the avenue, and the peacock was after him.'

'In a temper?'

'Yes. And there was blood on Dale's face.'

'He'd gone for the chap?'

'Evidently. Mother tackled Sue about it and she couldn't get much out of her, she just agreed that Dale had better keep away from Delaye.'

'The country girl can be formidably modest, you know. If this Dale had taken liberties or even kissed her that type is quite capable of closing up like a clam as though they'd been disgraced. They have their own code of morality. Please go on.'

'Just before war broke out the peacock got right into the drawing-room. He'd never done it before. He wouldn't go, though mother was there and Musgrave had to drive him out. That night when war had been declared I saw him on the lawn. This is where you've got to try and believe me. I had the impression he knew about the war and was glad. He was parading as though he were hoping to make Delaye a target. There was a moon, you see.'

'In short, you think the peacock has a definite grievance against the house?'

Her voice was apologetic. 'Yes. Could it be possible?'

'Why not? I believe most creatures have the capacity for malice, and all things considered I think they let us down uncommonly lightly! Peacocks are orientals — I fancy they were originally imported from Persia — so a certain element of subtlety could enter into the business! We shall probably never know the extent of the memory of any creature. Peacocks aren't usually pets in the cat and dog sense; we use them as garnishings, so we are hardly entitled to know what goes on in their small brainpans, and the fact that you and Sue have elected to make a pet of this bird isn't enough to counteract generations of the splendid isolation to which we have relegated them. How long have you had him?'

'Ever since I can remember. There were always peacocks at Delaye.'

'And this one is the last descendant of the original muster?'

'Probably, yes.'

'Not one of the Severn Court hatchings?'

'Oh no, he's a Delaye bird.'

'Um . . . well, go on.'

'Have you ever heard The Running Song they sing at Rohan?'

'No, but I've heard of it through your mother. She's very keen on Rohan, isn't she? So am I, though I'm ashamed to say that she started me off. She loves that song, and also hates it and says it's horrible.'

'Yes, it's all that, and there again I can't feel as she does about it. It seems — oh, I can't explain — to have something personal to me in it, as though there were something about it I knew of and can't remember.'

'How does it go?'

'I can only remember odd lines:

> One body for a noble . . .
> Bodies are cheap, . . .

and

> or make south?
> Is there blood on your mouth? . . .

Mother thinks it's a hunting song. I felt it wasn't when she first sang bits of it in the garden. It upset me. And then, just as mother was being worried, about *me*, you know, Sue ran up to us. She had no coat though it was cold. She said she'd heard me calling out to her. I hadn't.'

'Just a second: you mean you thought, then, that Sue sensed you were distressed, and came?'

'Yes. I never said anything, of course.'

'And did you feel you suddenly needed her?'

'I wasn't aware of it.'

'Unconscious telepathy . . . well, that usually means the existence of some bond. Let's assume your bond's the peacock. What happened next?'

'Oh, we went into the kitchen, we were both cold . . . then when war broke out Sue was anxious about the peacock and made him a shelter in the temple. She took things from all over the place. I let her. I only told her I must see them first.'

'Take your time.'

'Thanks . . . One of the things she brought was an old shirt, it had faint stains on it, like ironmould, or the colour old linen goes, only it wasn't that.'

'How d'you know?'

'I don't think I did know for certain, at the time. I didn't want to know.'

'But you're certain now?'

'Yes.'

'And you think the stains are — '

'Blood. Mr. Winchcombe, when father was showing you over the house, did you see the accounts books in the cellars?'

'Yes. Thomas Peacock is among the expenses items, a running footman.'

'Yes. Did father, when he showed you that top room, ever say why he thought Peacock was allowed up there?'

'He said, as far as I can remember, that he didn't really know but supposed the man was bundled up there to be out of the way. Curiously enough, that explanation never satisfied me.'

'Why not?'

'Because of the sensations I myself experienced in that room. They weren't compatible with callousness, I see that now . . . Anything more?'

She thought, and hesitated, and picked at the ball-fringe of the tablecloth. 'Stop fidgeting,' levelly observed Basil Winchcombe. The deliberate rudeness steadied her. 'Yesterday, I was up in that room, I thought I might find out something. I don't know if you will think I did or not. It was jammed in a cupboard. A stave that running footmen carried.'

'Ah . . .'

'It had the metal cap for the hardboiled egg — ' her voice dwindled until his straining ears could barely catch the words, ' — that the peacock wouldn't eat.'

He waited with a supreme effort. 'Something made me go to the window and see if the tip fitted the writing. It did. It was written with that stave.'

'By Thomas Peacock. Well . . . I don't say I wasn't rather expecting something of the sort.'

'Then you see what I'm getting at?'

He seized the opening unsparingly. 'What are you trying to say, Angela?'

'That the peacock *is* the running footman. He's come back, you see.'

2

She was waiting in a pitiable anxiety, relaxed as he remarked, 'You know, I do admire you, that couldn't have been easy to say. Well, I can accept it, too.'

'It is possible, then?'

'Who are we to say what is or isn't possible if we limit everything by our own piffling little experience? That's being smug. *And* impudent. After all, most of us have got round to the idea of transmigration of souls and of reincarnation, even if we can't personally believe either of 'em.'

'It seems to point to that,' she agreed. 'The peacock wants revenge for what our family made him suffer in serving us. That shirt . . . I'm convinced it was the footman's and The Running Song was his — not his alone, of course, but about *any* running servant of those days. Mr. Winchcombe, would he be buried in this churchyard?'

'Possibly, but — a pauper's grave, you know. No headstone.'

'The poor thing . . . and not even at rest.'

He answered, 'Perhaps one day we may find some means of assuring it to him. Evidently this chap is earthbound, half through hate and half by his affection.'

Angela looked absently about the parlour. 'What I can't make out is, does Sue guess?'

'I very much doubt that; not enough education and general reading. Sue is behaving entirely instinctively.'

'How, instinctively?'

'Dear Angela, what a singularly unsatisfactory playwright you would make! Have you never contemplated that curse of the drama and literature, "the love interest?" Here you are, working yourself up, worrying yourself thin over the finale and scamping Act One entirely.'

'You mean Sue Privett and the peacock?'

'I mean, my dear, Polly Privett and Thomas Peacock.'

3

He leant elbows on table. 'This Polly Privett got the sack. Suddenly. In the year Thomas Peacock died. Is it straining coincidence too far to assume a connection between those happenings? Oh, of course he may have pinched things, or she for him, and God knows one wouldn't blame either of 'em. They'd be a bit thrown together, I imagine: kitchenmaid and running footman, the humblest members of the domestic staff. Or they may have been in love, or Polly found to be "in trouble" as the charming phrase goes in describing the results of a natural instinct that the prayer-book says in black and white is "implanted in us". That's point one.

'Point two is Sue's unaccountable predilection for the peacock's society and his even more unaccountable liking for hers. Here, I rather think, we're seeing a working case of inherited memory (Privetts at Delaye for two hundred years in an unbroken line, remember). I think it likely that *as* bird and *as* kitchenmaid in this year of grace 1939 they don't consciously know anything about each other, but their mutual subjective memories of a shared past won't let them escape.'

'But if that's so, why didn't it happen to any one of the Privetts after Polly? Why Sue?'

'Why does red hair skip whole generations and then crop up again in families, to cite a purely physical instance? Why this gap occurred is a thing that we shall never know. I have a friend, a novelist, who has a theory that nothing is ever lost; that in time, every event and scene and set of persons come together again as the pieces of a kaleidoscope fall into the same pattern, and re-enact their particular set of words, movements and so on in the same sequence. I can't say I can quite swallow that, but I *do* believe that memory can be handed down in the way in which Sue Privett in her degree is carrying on for Polly. Perhaps you've got a place in this as well. Your mother tells me you're very like the portrait of Marguerite Roundelay, and a bodily resemblance could carry with it some psychic traits, though that's not to be counted on. It's more some things you've said that make me think it not unlikely. Now, can't you put the whole business out of your mind?'

'I can't do that, but I do thank you.'

He grinned guiltily. 'I can't either, to be quite candid! But the difference between us is that I'm interested and you're obsessed. That's a mistake. There's prayer, don't forget. I'm afraid I'm talking like a clergyman, but you know what I mean. Now, if anything else should happen let me know. I appreciate your having told me more than I can say.'

'I will. I'll go now.'

'We have now lost our reputations in the village' — Basil Winchcombe glanced at his wristwatch — 'for exactly one hour and four minutes; that being the case why not stay to tea?'

CHAPTER XXII

1

CERTAINLY AT Delaye just now it was a matter of all hands to the pump. The helpfulness of Miss Sapphy was only to be equalled in labour-making futility by the uselessness of Miss Amy and the patient dejection of Miss Jessie who was now, thanks to war conditions, unable to get in to the village to attend Evensong at 3.30 p.m., and so finding her lifetime of occupation between tea-time and dinner wiped out indefinitely at one blow, a seemingly trivial deprivation which thousands of other insufficiently occupied women all over England were to overcome in ways strange and unforeseen. Some discovered unsuspected talents, books, cards, their kitchens and even their families, while others discovered that politics actually had a bearing upon their shopping, or entered the world for the first time in all their sheltered years. But Miss Jessie had the strength of ten because her heart was pure and successfully resisted any innovation or substitute for the known and trodden way, and it was, Evelyn Roundelay learned, impossible to pack all three sisters off to the Cloudesleys even if they'd go and one could speed them plausibly, because the Cloudesleys had evacuees who were deriving much stomach upset from the change of air and biliousness from unaccustomed food.

It was Emerald Cloudesley (née Roundelay) who died suddenly in the following January of 1940 of nervous exhaustion and worry when about to celebrate her eighty-second birthday. Of this circumstance, those London newspapers *The Daily Wire* and *The Daily Cable* secured stories woven about the venerable dowager which, beginning as 'human', ended in a fracas that nearly resulted in a libel action. *The Wire* contended stoutly that the thirty billeted children were favourites of the entire household of Cloudesley Hall — with a posed photograph of the most tractable cases who were hustled into the dining-room where a reporter, deputizing for the stricken butler, was smilingly photographed handing one of them a silver salver on which he had laid his note-book that would with luck come out like sandwiches in the print — and for the rest fell back upon the age of the defunct as explanation of her tactless action. No more, wrote the reporter who was later to be fined ten pounds himself for refusing to billet a mother and two children on his wife in the throes of her first confinement in a one-servant villa on the Bakerloo line, would Mrs. Cloudesley's ears be cheered by the sound of childish laughter about the great house, nor her days be enlivened by their quaint, cockney confidences and the small tight posies that they picked for her. The feature article concluded with two quaint cockney confidences that the reporter composed in the train, though his ears still chimed with the infant comments of the thirty, most of which appeared to consist of adjectives beginning with F.B. and S.

The Daily Cable, on the other hand, enjoyed itself thoroughly, pointing out that the end of Mrs. Cloudesley, who on the testimony of her son and of her butler had hitherto enjoyed perfect health, had been hastened and brought about by the arrival of the evacuated, upon which, as was only to be expected, the noise, upset and domestic dissatisfaction had caused her system to succumb. And the paragraph was illustrated by two photographs depicting a broken window and a dresser of smashed Crown Derby, half of which the staff, catching the idea, enthusiastically exhumed from sundry cupboards where it had lain for up to ten years.

After that the fat was comfortably in the fire, with *Wire* chiding *Cable* for fomenting trivial discomforts at this grave time and *Cable* advising *Wire* to check up more conscientiously on its facts in future and to cease to attempt the whitewashing of an unworkable and undesirable scheme that had been foisted, half-baked, upon a helpless public at a time of already sufficient nerve-wrack, grief, anxiety and gravity. And *The Cable* viewed with disquiet the increasingly Socialistic tone of *The Wire*, which in its turn challenged *The Cable* to come forward in the interests of its readers with its reason for its consistent policy of opposition to the safe-guarding of Our Future Citizens.

Which circumstance closed a valuable and familiar door to Evelyn Roundelay, daughter-in-law of the deceased, on behalf of Angela who was, her mother thought, looking extraordinarily worn and frail as she sewed reams of black-out curtains, while Margaret, Edmund and even Maxwell seemed to live in the carpenter's shop constructing shutters for the top-lights in which Delaye was so plenteously found.

The dimming of Nursie's room remained together with its occupant a well-nigh insoluble problem, though Mrs. Hatchett did by no means badly in criticizing the régime of candles which had set in in her own bedroom, while aunt Sapphy's war effort consisted of blocking the bathroom to all comers at unexpected times of day to save electric light, though the required valance had already been supplied to that part of the window containing the vent of the geyser. Lady Roundelay more than suspected at least one of her maids of a desire to obtain factory work in Norminster on the principle, parentally handed down, that where there was war there was big money, and oblivious that one factory was turning off hands already owing to shortage of raw materials and that the other had closed altogether, while the second housemaid might have to leave any day to 'mind' a horde of young brothers and sisters who, displaced at school by the evacuees, were now on half-time education and under their distracted mother's feet for the entire morning. Even Sue had recently joined the procession by intermittent flittings over to Rohan to tend her ailing grandmother. Musgrave alone remained a rock of ages and was invaluable at reproving-parties over the matter of forgotten switches when the house was shut up for the night; but Lady Roundelay, mounting the staircase to her bed, was sometimes moved to ejaculate 'I'd swap the day *I've* had for an old saucepan with a hole in the bottom', before halting to adore the effect of moonlight on foliated balustrade.

2

Basil Winchcombe walked over to Rohan to see the grandmother of Sue Privett. His liking for and interest in the hamlet had grown into a self-supporting pleasure, and now he was interested in the old woman on Lady Roundelay's kitchenmaid's account as well.

Besides, he had an idea . . .

He hoped that the ancient Mrs. Privett might live to help Angela, though Doctor Elmslie had passed him the word that she could not hold out much longer. The autumnal mists usually took toll of Rohan folk.

There was if not a chance a distinct possibility that Sue's grand-mother might throw some light upon the clouded record of Polly Privett. Winchcombe calculated as he walked. Polly had been dismissed less than a hundred and fifty years ago; it sounded a long time when expressed in terms of date, but was actually only the lifetime of two men and not notable ancients, at that. Curious . . . yet the French Revolution epoch was in point of thought well-nigh as remote as that of the Tudors. It was all too far back for the old woman's memory but not remote in terms of possible souvenir . . . the highest and the lowest preserved their relics, it was the classes in between that destroyed them. And the old were hoarders, like that poor dear awful old nurse at Delaye whose room was a brain-less museum.

Angela must have considered Rohan as a possible source of information, but unfortunately that song had made her sheer right off the place, her mother had conveyed, and of course, Winchcombe himself had early sensed, the Rohanites were not to be lightly undertaken by the sensitive. Impersonality alone could survive in your approaches: you must—like Lady Roundelay — *think* these people but never if possible feel them. Knowing that, you were free to appreciate the drama of their being, the essential good theatre that was their self-sufficiency and alien thought, customs and turns of speech. As to the matter of Polly Privett as a bedside topic for a dying woman, it only remained to hope that the old lady would take to it kindly and not elect to close down on him in the Rohan manner.

As he passed the farrier's, Ronsell, apparently oblivious of the fact that he was a singer, was behaving exactly like a farrier; he inclined his head to the Reverend Basil Winchcombe in a motion that was something less than a leisured bow yet considerably more than a nod. There was, the clergyman observed, a lantern in the window of the vast barn that meant an impending Harvest-Festal 'brannel', and Winchcombe petulantly wished for the fiftieth time that he might be of the chosen gathering. He could dance as well as any of 'em, better, through having shaken a period leg in so many carefully documented Shakespearean productions. Dammit, hadn't they all nearly passed out at His Majesty's over the rehearsals of that Cushion Dance that Queen Elizabeth had been reported to dance 'high

and disposedly'? But far be it from him to take the floor in the role
of thin end of the wedge. Let Rohan keep its secrets.

3

Mrs. Privett, that handsome high-nosed veteran, was quite willing to see the Reverend Basil Winchcombe. Sitting by her bed he
hoped that he wasn't trading unfairly upon her state in directing
the virtual monologue into his own channels. A sentence of hers
with reference to her condition ('It displeases me to leave Roon')
gave him his cue. He spoke of her long and he hoped happy life,
of the family association with Delaye, of Miss Angela's affectionate
friendship for Sue.

'She would never presume,' said Mrs. Privett.

Winchcombe was certain of that: Sue was universally liked by
the Roundelays and Miss Angela had told him that she and Sue had
very nearly tamed the peacock, 'Quite a feat', added Mr. Winchcombe brightly, and — curious, wasn't it? — that a former servant
at Delaye had been called Peacock? And sat back with shoulders
mentally hunched as a man does against a downpour.

'He was a lackey,' assented the old woman, 'a current lackey.'
(Current? Did she mean of his time or *courant?*)

Mr. Winchcombe believed that even as far back as that there
was a Privett at Delaye, wasn't her name Polly?

Very surely.

That would be when the French lady was mistress?

(Now, was there or was there not an alteration in the face upon
the pillow at this comment? Or was it that Winchcombe, knowing
the Rohan folk to excel at poker faces, was on the look out for it?)
But she assented, quite normally.

He wondered aloud what the lady had been like to work for,
whether, for instance, her charm stood up to that of Delaye's present mistress.

Mrs. Privett had always understood that it did, refuging, he wondered, in the no-man's-land of hearsay. And then she volunteer'd a
remark. 'She was just.' Mr. Winchcombe was politely glad to hear
that. It was only on his return home that it occurred to him that the
adjective might after all be a Rohan locution for 'right'. *Juste* . . .

Underlying his conversation an interior questioner asked: Can one refer to the sacking of Polly? Still undecided, he blurted provisionally, 'Has your family, by any chance, any souvenir of Mrs. Marguerite Roundelay?'

'The family has made us presents; Lady Roundelay is always generous and gentle and the French lady had in her turn', Mrs. Privett had heard. If Mr. Winchcombe was interested in French knick-knacks (she called them 'brellocks'), she had an object that it would give her great pleasure to present to him for his kindness. A souvenir. It was below in the parlour and — understood — must be suitably wrapped. But if he would call in again?

He would, and left the cottage well pleased.

4

It was during the first of Sue's late absences from Delaye that the screaming began again in the garden at night.

To Angela's ears the peacock's outcries were, this time, of a different quality from those of rage or mockery; there was anger, but here there was also an element of indignation, as when you pick up a flustered hen.

Throwing aside the bedclothes she pulled on a sweater and huddled into a coat. The nights were already beginning to be sharp, the peacock had evidently found that, too, and had sought his temple shelter — the sounds came from there. He missed Sue? Then Angela must take over and quiet him, if he would let her. It would be quite awful if father chose this opportunity to get rid of him, and of course it *was* an atrocious noise and would disturb Nursie and the aunts.

Groping and flashing her torch over the front door she unbolted it, ran down the steps and over the lawn. The outcries ceased as she neared the temple although her feet could have made no sound across the turf.

When she stood in the entrance, the torch's ray training upon the uncouth improvisation of materials lashed to its pillars, focusing at last upon a splodge of green and blue, she understood why. For the great bird, struggling furiously at the linen already slashed by its beak, had caught its head in a larger rent and was, in the brainless way of all creatures in difficulty, half strangling itself in the effort to wrench free.

Angela up-ended her torch upon a ledge, and nervously approached. To herself she was urgently saying, 'Oh, if Sue were here, or Mr. Winchcombe!' Then she set to work.

The peacock stayed his efforts at her voice. 'I'll do it for you: you'll be all right.'

Easing the material backwards over his head — he wonderfully docile — a mark upon it caught her eye. It was the shirt brought from that room by Sue for her to see.

He was quiet, now, leaning against her as she crouched on the floor among the hay and old carpeting, her hands at her eyes, while the time passed.

The beam from a second torch picked out the pair as Basil Winchcombe came into the temple.

'I saw your light,' he remarked, but his attention was for the bird, his absent 'ahh . . .' the intonation of a suspicion confirmed as he set his torch by Angela's and dropped to one knee. Her relief was so enormous that she was able to revert to the saneness of curiosity. 'How did you know?'

'Was over at Sue's grandmother, met Sue there. We were going upstairs and she told me you wanted me as if she'd just remembered to tell me. I took it for a message, at first. She's coming along too. I had my bicycle and she's borrowing one.'

'But — it's *late*.'

'Half past tennish.'

'I was wanting you here.'

'So Sue thought! I helped her out a bit — took her remark about you naturally, even suggested her coming with me. Don't allude to it when she turns up, it may worry her. She evidently doesn't know that you can send out these S.O.S's to her. Fortunately, I think old Mrs. Privett's illness will sidetrack her. She's dying, I'm afraid. She's just given me something which may or may not be helpful, by the way. We'll see later. Now then, my son.' His hands were gently feeling the peacock. 'Accident?'

'No, not really. He caught his neck in that shirt, you know. The stained one.'

He stared at her, muttered pitifully as his fingers cupped the bird's breast, neck and saddle. She asked faintly, 'Is he — all right?'

'Angela, I may be absolutely out, but I'm afraid he's dying. I don't think he's in any bodily pain.' He had sunk his voice as doctors and nurses do before patients. Tears rained down her face suddenly, and, to her, shamefully.

'You mean, it's his mind. His feelings were so hurt about the shirt being used . . . he'd forgotten it, or *never* forgotten it And then, seeing it suddenly . . . as though we thought it was all he was fit for . . .'

He stroked the peacock as he considered. 'I've always wondered if it's literally possible to die of a broken heart. One reads so many stories and newspaper accounts of pet animals which seem to point to it beyond doubt, and yet — '

'What can we *do*?'

He got up. 'Well, I may sound rather crazy, but my instinct is to explain to him. Talk to the Thomas Peacock, running footman, that he once was. If he understands, all right. If he can't, we're none the worse, except for having made blazing fools of ourselves that nobody will ever know about except the two of us. If Sue gets here, stop. She won't understand. I think this is worth trying. After all, one apologizes to a dog if one's trodden on his paw . . .' He thought a second or two. 'Know any French?'

'The usual school stuff: very ungrammatic.'

'Try. It may help him to remember you.'

Uncomprehending but obedient she bent to the peacock.

'*Mon pauvre garçon, vous avez couru si loin aujourd'hui, et il me chagrine tant. Il faut donc se reposer.*'

The peacock leaned doser, listening to the halting words.

'*Prenez garde que les chevaux ne vous attrapent . . .*'

Sadly, fascinated, Winchcombe listened.

'We have been cruel and stupid, but never again, I promise. *Jamais encore.* Sue loves you, she couldn't hurt your feelings. And I never meant to, about the egg I gave you. It was stupidity. I didn't recognize you, Thomas, for the moment. We want to give you the best we have. You're among friends who know you. Do you think you can ever forgive us? *Enfin, dormez bien, mon ami.*'

As once before in the coppice with Sue, the creature lifted his head and brushed her fingers with his crest.

And then Sue ran in, her eyes only for him as she flumped to her knees beside Angela.

'He's ailing,' she stated.

'Yes, my dear,' the clergyman assented. 'Say good-bye to him, Sue. He's not been alone long, Miss Angela came at once.'

'He was calling out?' the servant's voice was accusatory.

'He probably missed you.'

'What's the matter with 'im?'

'The nights are very sharp, you know, and he must have caught a chill,' lied Winchcombe easily, 'you couldn't have done more and he's not a young bird, remember.'

They waited in a silence broken by the kitchenmaid's whimpering. It was Basil Winchcombe whose more experienced eye saw the sudden slackening of the peacock's muscles, though all three watchers stared amazed as languidly the great tail feathers unfolded, spreading their fan over the lap of Angela, and the little jewelled head fell forward into the palm of Sue Privett's hand.

'Lord now lettest Thou Thy servant depart in peace,' murmured Winchcombe.

5

Between them, he and Angela coaxed Sue back to the house, and she went, crying. 'She'll get over it,' he said, 'to her the bird was only a pet. Now look here, Angela, with your sanction, I'm going to send the poor soul to the vet and find out what he *did* die of, and then, have him buried here. Find him a pleasant corner.'

'Here? After what he went through?'

'My dear, in life his poor affections were centred at Delaye, if we've guessed right.'

'Oh, I see. Yes. He shall have a quiet place where there is sun. And I'd like to wrap him in something special. There is that dress of Marguerite's — does that seem ridiculous?' She asked as amateur does to professional, with diffidence and apology, and he smiled as he answered with conviction, 'I think it is the perfect shroud'.

6

Next day, the Reverend Basil Winchcombe examined the Rohan souvenir formally presented him by Mrs. Privett.

Absurdly excited he unwrapped it. To his incredulous gaze there was exposed a china vase of cheerful curlicues and imitation fishing-nets across the front of which was writ in gilt

Souvenir de Boulogne.

'Why — the old faggot!' exploded the man who that very morning had administered to her the Holy Sacrament.

Rohan had scored once more.

But inextinguishable memories of Conan Doyle and The Adventure Of The Five Napoleons stirred him to recollection that Holmes had experienced his usual luck with the fifth plaster bust in which was embedded the great black pearl (whereat even the Inspector had burst into applause that made Holmes's thin cheeks flush with gratification), and taking up the egregious vase Winchcombe rapped it heartily against the fender. It fell into seven clanking pieces of cheap pottery in which there was nothing at all.

'Well, it's bust, that's one thing,' he remarked to himself, 'that's what *I* call A Vawse.' Then he laughed till he cried.

A week later came the verdict of the Norminster veterinary surgeon.

'Dear Sir,

'With reference to the peacock deposited by you on the 17th ult., I beg to inform you that examination has revealed the presence of valvular weakness of long standing, which, however, was not in my opinion other than a contributory factor. The bird was an old one, and death was due to some sudden strain upon the heart which would be consistent with overexertion, or chasing by children, a similar condition being commonly present in the cases of death from excessive running.'

As instructed, he was returning the bird to Delaye, and he was very truly Mr. Winchcombe's.

7

Sue Privett, Angela and Evelyn buried the peacock one fresh October morning in a border near the sunk garden. The gardener, kicking clods of earth from his spade and addressing the defunct with rough comradeship as Hitler, informed the satin-wrapped burden that now perhaps his early peas would have a chance. The Misses Sapphire and Amethyst, ubiquitously appearing from nowhere, pottered round the grave, ignoring each the presence of the other, and remarking (aunt Sapphy) that we should all be quite strange without him and (aunt Amy) what was that they'd put round him?

'Only some old stuff, aunt. I hate putting people's pets into just the ground,' answered Evelyn. Hers not to reason why . . . it was a pity about the dress but Angela had seemed so set on it. The wrecked face of Sue Privett was accepted by everyone as being within the bounds of understanding, and it was with Lady Roundelay's arm round her shoulders that they returned to the house.

CHAPTER XXIII

1

THE AUTUMN TOOK its toll of Mrs. Privett and turned attention to other Rohan prospects. The sight of Vicar and curate in their midst became a commonplace to the inhabitants.

It was on one of his parochial visits that Basil Winchcombe walked into a small crowd gathered about a mound of household effects piled outside the empty cottage of Mrs. Privett. The auctioneer, bowler hat pushed to back of head, was making halfhearted efforts to extol the collection, his harangue interspersed by facetiae received by the Rohan folk with impassive faces of flint.

Winchcombe joined the group, the gesture of greeting of Ronsell the farrier delighting him no less than his own finished response (like Lord Sandys and Buckingham in Henry The Eighth, he gloated), as, salutations completed, his eyes were free to assess the goods displayed in all their defencelessness — sentences without context. Extraordinary how pathetic was a brass fender laid on the ground, no more to know the pressure of its clique of neighbourly feet. The lesser pieces went in lots, a senseless and horrid system by which willy-nilly you became owner of the unwanted in order to secure the thing you did want. Lot 3 consisted of two frying-pans, an ancient mop and a corner cupboard, Lot 4 of a set of crockery, a warming-pan and a clothes-brush, Lot 5 of a large framed picture of a labourer driving a flock of sheep nowhere in particular on an evening of singular depression, a bundle of fusty-looking books and a group of shell silk and bead flowers under a glass dome. Quite good of its kind, he saw: early Victorian stuff. Winchcombe flicked his fingers and acquired it for seven-and-sixpence; the picture and books he tactfully offered to remit, but the auctioneer wanted a clearance, and damning the picture, the clergyman parked it in his first place of call against the umbrella stand, returning home with books and the flower piece, having anti-socially omitted to reclaim the picture on leaving.

The books smelt, the familiar odour like long-closed rooms and rust, and he damned them as well, as, conscientiously, he ran through them in his own living-room that afternoon.

The inevitable Royal Gift Book, a repellent-looking and date-less novel called *Beulah*, a copy of *The Giant-Killer* by A. L. O. E. which he put aside with a reminiscent grin and anticipation of an-other comfortable dose of nineteenth-century bathos ('Sunday! A clergyman's lawn! A pretty sight for all the village!') What a ghastly prig the excellent *Aleck* was: what the sailors would make of him on board baffled imagination.

Before he reached the bottom of the pile Winchcome's interest blunted and his glances at titles became cursory. One book, an al-bum bound in worn leather, hadn't even got a title, and he opened it bored in advance.

'. . . *et je lui disait, "Mon pauvre garçon, vous avez couru si loin, aujourd' hui . . ."*'

Three minutes later he was at the post-office, telephoning to Delaye, being charming and casual with the fluttered Miss Tybon-net (who thought him quite beautiful), even lounging an unnec-essary half-minute in chat while excitement clanged within him, remembering that a village was a village and the postmistress's eye, ear and tongue in excellent condition. There was no call box; when you telephoned at Delaye post-office you did so for all the world to hear with your elbow propped on a chiffonier in her parlour, your eye gazing unwillingly into the enlarged face of her uncle Frederick framed in fumed oak.

'Oh, that you, Musgrave? Mr. Winchcombe speaking. Is Miss Angela in? Thanks . . . Miss Roundelay? This is Winchcombe. Can you come over? . . . well, partly to show you a rather nice piece I picked up at Mrs. Privett's sale, but mainly the usual cadge for pro-duce and flowers for the Harvest Festival. Marguerites aren't still on, are they? I'm no gardener. And about that French dictionary you very kindly offered to lend me — if it isn't burdening you too much . . .'

The faint 'ohh' from the other end of the line told him she had understood and he muttered 'good girl!' as he rang off.

2

It was Angela who held the dictionary, Winchcombe who roughly translated the diary of Marguerite Roundelay, sometimes reading aloud the entire French original if a sentence was obscure or beyond their united knowledge, sometimes breaking in with his own comments and interpretations, colliding as they did with Angela's. The pauses for the hunting of unfamiliar or forgotten words were maddening.

The entries covered a period of ten months, from October 1791 to the following July where they ended abruptly. They were with one exception headed 'Delaye': the exception seemed to indicate a visit to some English country house of which the writer had nothing salient to say.

The temptation to gorge themselves at one sitting upon the whole diary was almost irresistible and had it been written in English they might have succumbed, but their typical education in translation slowed them up to an extent which, Winchcombe decided, called for system, and he suggested that first they run to earth that which might bear upon Thomas Peacock and Polly Privett, and later absorb the general gist of the dead woman's statements. He found what they wanted almost immediately. Translated into colloquial English, the writer said:

"'The cold is already beginning to be abominable and once again I ask myself how I shall survive another English winter. The invitations from mother and my friends in France are equally heartening and depressing: they keep up my spirits and half kill me with longing. And I could go! The house runs itself, as they go their ways whatever I say — in the matter of custom, of course. Even Marcus would dismiss a servant who disobeyed me. He doesn't really need me either now he's got me. I might have known it. He wants me because it is the thing and he won't travel with me because his voyaging is over. Like that. Like a purge for the *grippe*! I'm really a table ornament, rather costly, like my comfit boxes, that he points out to his friends before beginning the real business of the evening, drinking and talk of hunting and dogs. Frenchmen make better husbands. They neglect their wives with charm and politeness. The Englishman is faithful (too much so!) until he's unfaithful and runs amok like a bull in a china shop. Our men conduct their affairs with finesse — you'd hardly know you'd lost their affection, so my married friends tell me.

"'I've got another bed. Marcus will probably break the new one which is delightful, except when he's in it: gilt and adorable lovers' knots. Hah! The old one could only be tolerable for a honeymoon while your attention is being well distracted. An ark! A sarcophagus! It is gone to some attic. I believe the servants sleep upstairs except, of course, the running footman. We have a new one, I hear. Marcus says he has been here two months, but one doesn't notice servants' faces.

"'I wish they'd learn to call me 'Madame'; they say 'Mam' or what sounds like 'Mum'. Terrible! If I can manage their language they ought to mine. I speak English quite nicely now, though I do relapse into French, I'm told — when I'm excited or annoyed, I suppose. One is annoyed, oftener.

"'With evenings dark and cold the garden is largely closed to me and our nightly round of cards and solitaire lies before me. The grounds of Delaye are beautiful — no manner or chic, but open and a little formal, like the English themselves. No fuss.

"'The temple I had built is finished and looks far too new and as out of place as I, and the peacocks and I make a charming effect when I sit there sewing or writing, only there is nobody to admire us. Marcus sets store by the peacocks, the only artistic trait I have observed in him. He won't admit it and when I chaff him says that peacocks are an appurtenance of what he called 'Landed gentlemen. (*Haute Noblesse?*) England is full of landed gentlemen. Here, they aren't quite *Noblesse* or *Haute*, but in good standing. This trick of calling themselves 'Roundelay' I find ridiculous, when they are Rohan de l'Oeux. False modesty, I expect. I won't do it. It annoys Marcus so much, poor man.'"

Winchcombe, his eyes still on the album, said, 'And that was to be her downfall, poor little thing. One can see, now, how that fixed French outlook must have overflowed when she returned to her own country, making her more French than the French, out of pure cussedness and relief, fairly oozing caste at a time when the bottom was being knocked out of privilege . . . Er — what the dickens do "*d'ailleurs*" and "*d'abord*" mean? I never can remember.'

Angela fluttered the dictionary. '"Moreover" and "at first".'

'Oh. Ah . . . "Moreover, it's snobbery, as though to be of French descent had to palliated, though at first it amused me to be 'Missis

Roundelay.' When one's in love one will accept anything, it's nature's way of cheating us: one of them, for the sake of the family,
of course, and I haven't even one child, yet. Extraordinary in the
circumstances!'" (At this point, Basil Winchcombe flicked an eye
of tentative apprehension at Angela Roundelay, but her answering smile was amused and appreciative.) "'I would *love* a daughter. There aren't enough women to talk to, here. She must be just
like *me*, Rohan de l'Oeux looks won't come out so well in women
as they do in men: we St. Lunaires are all dark and small and a
little becomingly pale, that ceruse looks well on. I am glad I am
well stocked with cosmetics, they don't understand these things in
England, certainly not in the country. Marcus will be disappointed
about having a daughter, and his vanity piqued, but he has the estate and his dogs and his foxes to amuse him.

"'Our chief diversion of late has been a round of autumn visits
to big houses in this and other counties, returning late the same
day. I become abominably sleepy and fatigued. Being driven for
hours is always tiring, yet the coach is more comfortable than our
French ones. Even looking out of the window loses its novelty after
a few miles and sometimes there is nothing to see for hours except
hedges and fields and, if the road takes a curve, the footman running in front. I watch him out of sheer boredom and wonder when
the horses will catch him up, as they sometimes do, which makes
Marcus angry and the coachman sulky, and shout at him. Once, he
actually got left behind by the coach and Marcus said if it happened
again he'd have to go. And, of course, it does look bad to arrive in
a village and see your courier whooping for breath in a ditch fifty
yards behind, as if the horses sat down suddenly and refused to stir.
But the harness keeps them in their place and Marcus would never
permit the coachman to overdrive them, they are so valuable, and
Marcus actually knows their names.'"

Winchcombe's hand lay for a second on Angela's wrist as he
made a brief, involuntary pause in the reading.

"'I suppose they get tired? One doesn't think of them in that way
because it's their job, any more than one would go into the kitchen
and ask the cook if she liked stirring soup.'"

'And so on, and so on,' murmured Winchcombe, turning the
pages, 'nothing for us until — oh, here, some weeks later:

'"This evening, when home from a long drive I saw a serv-antmaid loitering at the back-door to one of the kitchens. She was crying."

'And, from entries covering another three weeks:

'"Does this girl spend her time in tears? My curiosity is aroused, and I must make enquiries. Besides, it is depressing to be greeted by this spectacle when getting, tired and stiff, out of the coach. I think it unlikely that the girl ought even to be in sight on our returns.

'"I asked who she was, to-day, and it seems she is a kitch-en-maid here. I gave her a comfit, she was so alarmed at being spoken to! When I gave her the comfit she curtseyed and wept anew. A fountain! I left her to it. My maid was disapproving and hinted that Madame mustn't *trop s'encanailler*."'

Angela here applied herself to the dictionary, but Winchcombe said, 'You won't find it; it's a nice portmanteau verb for which there's no exact English equivalent. Marguerite doesn't tell us if this maid was French or local: if the latter she probably said "You don't want to demean yourself, M'm". It means a lowering, a mild form of touching pitch, or social defilement, like our vicar says I risk doing when I try and play darts at The Coach and Horses here.'

'"The worst of initial good deeds is that you are impelled to follow them up! If I could have stopped at a comfit and a smile all might have been different, but curiosity and boredom together have done their work. Bore a woman enough, deprive her at one blow of modiste, milliner, mantua-maker, *friseur* and light conversation and it's a hundred to one but that she'll start being philanthropic. This, 'Polly', I see now, is quite ruining her looks, for she is pretty, in her way — was, rather, for a face *abreuvée* — "'

('Soaked' supplied Angela)

' — "with tears gives no girl a chance and I suppose she expects to marry one day or where would our future servants come from? though heaven knows where and how they contrive to, in places like Delaye.

'"The girl scuttles whenever she sees me, now. It's an incalculable class. She's probably conceived a humble, squalid little passion for Marcus. What a joke! *Droits de Seigneur*. Do they have that in England, too?"

'And two weeks later:

"'Glancing out of the coach this afternoon I saw we had a new footman, though 'new' as applied to such a sorry object is not at all the right word. Thin as a rake and his face a kind of blue-white and when we returned home the girl 'Polly' was on the main staircase. Even I know she should not be in this part of the house at such a time. It is impertinence and I am outraged after my condescension. Is she then a pilferer? . . .

"'This evening I saw 'Polly' once more and there *was* something in her hand, so I was right. As though one hasn't enough to worry and sadden and enrage one, with the packet delayed and no news out of France for two weeks, and Maman and Clymène in the hands of the rabble for all I know. Has France gone quite mad? Even if the harvest *has* failed there'll be another one next year. And who is this Danton? We seem to know nothing of him until he is the talk of the town and apparently all-powerful and a sort of dictator. *That* system won't last. The Bourbons aren't perfect but they are gentlemen, and if there are injustices, Royalty at least gives the mob something picturesque to look at, and inherited dynastic faults are surely more tolerable than those which you elect and set up yourself to rule you — like the difference between a father and a husband: the former is a providence for good or ill, the latter the outcome of caprice, your own fault if he turns bad on your hands. We haven't even been outside our own gates for three weeks.

"'Still no news.

"'A letter at last! Maman writes that as far as they can see, life in Paris is far more nearly normal than is believed, though those iniquitous executions go on. Even Tussaud carries on with his wax models! Plenty of subjects now, when the knife falls. Ugh! As for life *aux environs*, except that the lower classes are looking sulky there is nothing sensational toward. The Chateau de St. Enogat was visited by some rapscallions with scythes — the *insolence* of it! — but M. le Marquis strolled into their midst and told them some of his best stories and made them rather tipsy and they went, roaring with laughter and very unsteadily. And they want to 'down' men like the Marquis! Blood tells. *They* think so, too, but their solution is to shed it. Tragic foolery! The people aren't fit to govern the country: they can't even govern themselves and their lusts. And the family want me to come over. Oh God, how I'd love to!

"'. . . That girl again. This time, I saw her skirts vanishing up the main staircase above my bedroom. I called her, had her into my room, and at long last she told me that she and this fellow, the running footman, are in love. I said 'Which one?' thinking of the new scarecrow I had observed from the coach window, and she stared, and said he was *the same man* who had been in our service for months.

"'I was shocked. So he is as ill as that? Unrecognizable. And they cannot marry on his wage, I suppose? I asked, and reached for my purse, but it wasn't that, she explained, but he is dying. I said, 'Take me to him', and then she began to be terrified and to cry again. I waited — the only way with these people, and at last she confessed that she had smuggled him upstairs to nurse, using the front staircase to avoid comment in the kitchen. She knew, they both did, the presumption of it, and the danger of dismissal, and it fretted him all the time. The cook was glad to be rid of the sight of him in the kitchens: his home is in the village, too far for him to attempt — now, and he was always too tired to visit it often, with the long runs he must make. He had, of course, never had a place of his own at Delaye, and it was the beautiful bed of 'Ma'am' (that ark!) which had tempted her. He has never lain soft in his life. The whole affair began through pity — that fatal snare of us women! The 'Polly' girl used to admire him when first he came to Delaye; she told me he was young and handsome and a picture when he ran . . . as time went on, he lost looks, weight — everything. She knew it wasn't right, but she used to watch for his returns with the coach to see how he had stood the day, and always he was whiter and more blown, too exhausted to eat. She would help him to wash, when the other servants were scattered, but there was little privacy in the outer kitchen . . .'"

Over the next four lines the compassionate eye of Basil Winchcombe ran swiftly and he deliberately omitted them from the reading. Details of illness, of such an illness, were not for the ears or imagination of Angela when recorded from the stark statement of a servant by the practical realism of a Frenchwoman.

"'She says that now he is living like the gentry, and is so proud of it.

"'I have just come down from that bleak servant's room, writing in my diary to take my mind off.

"'The man (it is 'Peacock', I find, and means *Paon*) is dying, no doubt of that. He has consumption. I saw, and bit back a scream of pity and — I must confess it — disgust. It is terrible. He tried to struggle to his feet when I came in, but the girl said 'She is our friend, Thomas,' and then begged my pardon which I freely gave. He was incredulous, relieved and distressed; he feared he had fouled the fine sheets (they were servants' sheets, coarse cotton: 'Polly' has taken them from her own bed).

"'I sat by his side. I believe I took his hand — who cares? I told him the room was his henceforth. He couldn't speak much. My mind was confused with sorrow so that, the girl told me, I spoke to him in French. I remember, now. I said, 'Poor lad, you've run so far, to-day,' and promised him it should never happen again. He hasn't of course. We haven't made an expedition for weeks. And yet, though he was all lackey's gratitude, I think his wrongs have bitten very deep. Can he really forgive? Who knows? They are never themselves with Us.

"'By the bed I saw pieces of food that the girl had brought him, the best bits from her own meals, she admitted, although I doubt but that it has come too late.

"'I have told Marcus about it: what's a husband for if not to sympathize? And I am going to France. For he was coldly angry with me — no noise or scenes, but the Englishman's edged incisiveness, like a rapier that cuts. I had overstepped my province . . . the menservants were *his* affair . . . I had grossly encouraged the staff to presume . . . run the risk of infection . . . made an awkward situation, and so on and so on. I said I was going out of England on a long visit; he said I should *not*. I said he had lost my heart and if he cared to detain my body he was without pride. That stung him, and he gave permission at once with eyes like chill blue steel. The English have a sense of justice: I salute that, at least. I made him promise that the man shall be allowed to remain up there, and he assented, too proud to argue such an affair. He will keep his word, I know him well enough to know that.'"

('And so he may have,' interpolated Winchcombe, 'but he sacked Polly at no notice afterwards!')

'"The packet sails at sunset to-morrow. I have given 'Polly' two papers written 'He is better' and 'He is dead', and my address and a sum of money. I shall entrust my diary to her — not safe, here! but she can't read my language, or her own? I may come back, or I may not. It will depend on Marcus.'"

Basil Winchcombe closed the book at that final entry.

'And fate disposed of *that* domestic problem. Well, well . . .'

'And Marguerite never had the daughter who was to be "exactly like" her.'

The clergyman's glance rested speculatively upon Angela's face.

'M'm, no . . . no. A pity . . . and no indication of where Peacock is buried. One sees now what made him scrawl those words on the pane: the proud sense of possession and dignity that Marguerite was perceptive enough to give him . . . *his* room . . . *his* grand bed (that ark!). I think I should have liked Marguerite.'

'Oh *yes!*'

He smote the table with his fist. 'What I'd give something to know is: did old Granny Privett know about this diary?'

'She couldn't read French, I think, even if she did know *of* it.'

He grinned. 'Perhaps not; but as Marguerite would say, I am now sufficiently "*Enrohané*" to suspect her!'

'Of what?'

'I don't know. That, my dear, is the essence of being *enrohané*.'

Through the second little window which overlooked the street a small procession filed into the village. It consisted of Dickon wheeling a barrow full of cut flowers and Miss Jessie Roundelay bearing a basket of potatoes and onions. With her other hand she mirthlessly clasped a giant marrow to her bosom.

They turned into the churchyard.

TAILPIECE

1

QUITE OFTEN, when shopping in Norminster, the residents and those from surrounding estates and villages remember to throw into their temporary farewells a little something about the war, though, by now, all have omitted to bring in their gas-masks.

Dolly's goes on and on: her cakes are wonderfully as before, her prices slightly more so, her prestige unassailed. No less than three of the Archbishop's evacuated boys are now, to their helpless consternation, actually in the cathedral choir. They do not know how it happened. One, still feeling his upheaval and realizing that in this epoch anything may happen, is even experimenting with the hobby of good behaviour. Everything once.

Mrs. Galbraith's cats are all reprieved, as their owner now believes that as there was no air-raid over the village on that fatal Sunday or even upon the following Monday, there will now be none at all, the Germans having obviously overlooked the county of Normanshire.

There is already talk of re-opening Guild Hall and City walls to the public, while innumerable shops have removed from across their windows those zig-zags of buff paper designed for protection against non-arriving splinters, so that the goods are now seen to full advantage. Occasionally a British bomber, outward bound, zooms over the ancient city, to the singular non-disturbance of its soul. Indeed, a far more significant sign of upheaval lies in the homely fact that owing to present restrictions upon meat, the confection of Norminster's celebrated 'puddings' can now no longer be undertaken. An army marches on its stomach, but the evanishment from their lives of an institution as stable as and far more warming than the Church of England goes deeper than creature comfort, and trenches perilously upon the realms of sentiment, and to tamper with the feelings of a citizen is a dangerous thing, from which, blindly, instinctively, evolves the heartier bayonet thrust, the grimmer determination.

2

At Delaye, the staff is at present up to strength, the housemaids' impulse to profit and patriotism having been flung back in their teeth by a government which, inconsiderately, was more prepared for war than they had bargained for.

Miss Jessie has founded a working party in the village, and having done so, is finding an extreme difficulty in getting herself to the meetings which cannot be timed to suit everybody, a circumstance which she bears without complaint.

Nursie is one year older. But the Roundelays' intermittent, secret impulses to strangle her are tempered by recollections of the unconscious part she played in keeping their home free of evacuees.

Stacey Roundelay, like the housemaids of Delaye, is finding his intention of assisting the war very politely obstructed in all directions, and the army a thought more difficult of membership than the Athenaeum; he is too old, and, simultaneously, not old enough to fight. Relieved, puzzled, incredulous, he is, in this waning spring of 1940, resentfully and happily working with his father the land that, if all goes well, will one day be his.

Major Dunston's concern for his railway dividends and a possible and unthinkable necessity to reduce his weekly payments to his cousin was after all unnecessary: but the mental torment he went through has resulted in a canvas of the coach-house-studio itself (for the execution of which he actually moved outside), which, such was his worry and anxiety, is easily the best bit of work he has ever done.

And that's not saying much.

Contrary to local expectation, the Reverend Basil Winchcombe has not yet proposed to Miss Angela Roundelay. They are warm and trusted allies, their affection a glowing thing, but Winchcombe still considers that her mother is the pick of that basket, as, still waiting to go out to France, he patrols his Norminster bridge at night. Sometimes he hopes he is glad, in the Christian manner, that Evelyn Roundelay loves her husband.

The family misses the peacock but little, though the face of Sue Privett is overcast as, even now, she runs to door and window, forgetting he is gone. The flowers upon his little grave are bright and gaudy: Miss Angela, as they plant and water them, has told the kitchenmaid that he would like that kind the best. It is as far as she permits herself to go with Sue Privett . . . Angela and Winchcombe have agreed that Evelyn must be told the whole story. Her relief and interest were enormous, and she senses a new serenity in her younger daughter, to-day. The diary of Marguerite Roundelay is in The Lacquer Room under a glass case.

On a certain morning, the war news has not been so good, and Musgrave ponders it as he polishes his silver.

Upon the steps of Delaye, three hours later, stood a solitary figure scanning the avenue with nervous, restless glances. Some bad tidings, the observer might diagnose, that she alone is singled out to bear or break.

But the observer would be wrong. For the hired cab from Jamieson arrives, after all, to time, and Miss Sapphire Roundelay descends the flight, card-case in hand, to make her calls and keep in touch with the County.

THE END

FURROWED MIDDLEBROW

Lightning Source UK Ltd.
Milton Keynes UK
UKOW05f1332071116
287054UK00001BA/127/P